Book One - Fire

Michael Jay Steen

© 2020 Michael Jay Steen, All Rights Reserved.

Editing, Layout, and Cover Design by Sheila R. Muñoz, EdD, sheila.r.munoz@gmail.com.

No part of this publication may be reproduced, stored in a retrieval system, or transmitted in any form by any means electronic, mechanical, photocopying, recording, or otherwise, except brief extracts for the purpose of review, without written permission from the copyright owner.

Dedication

To all first responders:
all those who rush into a burning building
when everyone else is running out;
all those who run toward the sound of gunfire
when everyone else is running away;
and all those medical professionals who work to save lives
in all the above situations—
I dedicate this book to you!

Table of Contents

Dedication...3
Chapter 1 Captain Ike: Living the Dream 7
Chapter 2 Captain Ike: The Phone Call That Changed My World...11
Chapter 3 Captain Ike: The Investigation Begins...............21
Chapter 4 Captain Ike: Diving the Fire Scene....................29
Chapter 5 Captain Ike: Gina and I Reconnect 51
Chapter 6 Captain Ike: A Bad Feeling................................73
Chapter 7 Tony Morgan: My Back Story............................79
Chapter 8 Captain Ike: Dope on the Rocks........................85
Chapter 9 Tony Morgan: My Three Worst Days................99
Chapter 10 Captain Ike: A Ping in the Night 107
Chapter 11 Tony Morgan: A Cop's Worst Nightmare 117
Chapter 12 Captain Ike: Finding Morgan 125
Chapter 13 Hillsborough County Sheriff Department: Office Reports 133
Chapter 14 Captain Ike: Hospital Recovery.....................137
Chapter 15 Tony Morgan: An Introduction to the Cartel 149
Chapter 16 Captain Ike: Going Home 155
Chapter 17 Tony Morgan: Going to the Dark Side............163
Chapter 18 Captain Ike: Opening Up to Gina 175
Chapter 19 Tony Morgan: The Drug Deal........................189
Chapter 20 Felix Cardona: No Witnesses 195
Chapter 21 Captain Ike: A Text from Morgan...................201
Chapter 22 Tony Morgan: Pay Day..................................209
Chapter 23 Captain Ike: A Meeting with Morgan............ 219
Chapter 24 Captain Ike: Just When Things Were Looking Up 227

Chapter 25 Tony Morgan: Bring in the DEA 239
Chapter 26 Captain Ike: Face-To-Face with
    Cartel Thugs... 245
Chapter 27 Tony Morgan: A Meeting with the
    DEA Top Brass 253
Chapter 28 Captain Ike: Sleeping with a Pistol 259
Chapter 29 The DEA: The Bust 273
Chapter 30 Captain Ike: Hiding at Beer Can Island 283
Chapter 31 Tony Morgan: The Largest Fentanyl
    Bust in U.S. History.. 291
Chapter 32 Captain Ike: Felix Cardona Wants
    Me Dead! 295
Acknowledgements... 304
Learn More About the Author.. 305

Chapter 1
Captain Ike: Living the Dream

February 23, 2018
Fort Desoto, Tampa Bay, Florida

As I sat at anchor reminiscing on my 32-foot Carver aft cabin cruiser named *Good Times*, a smile crossed my face: I thought about how I got paid to be on the water, my truly happy place. Little did I know that a few minutes later I would receive a phone call from an old supervisor and be plunged back into the fiery world of arson and homicide again!

A few years ago I was employed with the city as a fire investigator. I had previously held the titles of firefighter, engineer, lieutenant, and fire inspector with the last few years being a fire investigator. In order to have powers of arrest as a fire investigator, I attended the police academy and became a police officer with the same city. After early retirement from the city, I became a private fire investigator (PFI).

Unknown to many, there are both public and private fire investigators. Public fire investigators work for a government agency, whether it be federal, state, county, or city. Private fire investigators usually work for insurance companies, private businesses, individual people, etc. Quite a few public fire investigators carry their work over into retirement as a PFI because it is something they know. It is much more lucrative than working for the city . . . but more on that later. Me? I finally decided to become a boat captain. This job had been one of my bucket list items.

I am Captain Ike Smith. I was certified through the United States Coast Guard. As jobs go, it is the best one I have ever had. I get to meet people, take them out on the water, and introduce them to my backyard. Unlike many jobs, my clients are usually very happy to be aboard; and their excitement makes for fun times. Of course, I do get the occasional butthole for whom nothing makes them happy; but they are few.

Good Times was perfectly set up for this type of business. She has two cabins, one forward and one aft.

Here, I should probably explain some common nautical terms. To be "aboard" is to be on a vessel/boat. "Forward"/"Bow" is the front section of the boat. "Stern"/"Aft" refers to the back of the boat. "Starboard" is the right side of the boat, and "port" is the left. The "salon" is what most would call the living area. The "galley" is the kitchen, and the "head" is the bathroom. The uppermost portion of the boat is the "flybridge" and is usually midship, "midship" being the middle part of the boat. The flybridge often has a "helm" or steering wheel.

The day before a fishing trip I would pull up to four kayaks out to the location where we were going to fish. Having the two cabins sleeping four adults plus myself, we would stay the night on the hook (anchored) so we could be on the water as soon as the sun broke the horizon. This allowed the kayakers to be ready to fish at the best possible time: as a general rule here on the flats, fish mostly feed early in the morning and again later in the afternoon.

I usually had some type of food ready as the fishermen returned for lunch, and I would sit and listen to their excitement and the stories of how the experience had been so far. In our area due to the beautiful weather, a kayaker can often see dolphins and manatees almost year around. Even during the occasional times when the fish weren't biting, the kayakers were usually still very excited about something they had seen or about the experience of the trip overall.

After the morning fishing and depending on how well the fish were biting, we sometimes deployed kayakers again from the same spot or pulled the anchor and tried a different spot. This was easy on the kayakers as they could eat and rest until the next location.

Chapter 2
Captain Ike: The Phone Call That Changed My World

It was sunny and 75 degrees on Tampa Bay on a beautiful, Florida spring day. I had three kayak customers out in the area fishing. As I watched my kayakers working the edge of the red mangroves for the elusive snook, I decided to go down below to the galley for something to drink. My cell phone vibrated; and I looked, only to see I had several missed calls from my ex-supervisor, June. Now that I was "retired," I had the ability to not answer my phone except when I wanted, so I left it on vibrate most of the time.

June, like me, retired from the city as a fire marshal and lead investigator. After getting bored with that, she started working as a PFI for a large and well-known insurance company. She convinced me to work as a PFI for several years before I got my captain's license. Once I got my captain's license and took the plunge as a business owner and a boat captain, however, I gave up my job as PFI and never looked back . . . that is, until today.

I dialed June's number. A firm, professional voice answered, "This is June."

"Hey, this is Ike. I see I've missed seven calls from you today. What's got you so fired up?"

Even though I had not talked to her in a while, we had grown close over the years. She was always fair—but stern when she needed to be; and I enjoyed my time working with her.

June laughed, "Well, Ike, I have an assignment that I believe only you can do. Want to hear more?"

June knew that I had certifications in diving with deep water and recovery training, and I knew she held the "certification" in smooth ability to butter up a person before placing them in the oven, so to speak!

"*Only me?*" I responded skeptically.

"I just *knew* you would want to hear more!" she laughed. "We have an insurance company that is very eager to find the cause of a boat fire that occurred in Tampa Bay recently. They are paying *double* the usual pay, plus expenses. They really want to know what happened because of some unusual circumstances surrounding the claim."

"Where did this happen?" I inquired.

"The boat burned and sank near the shipping channel at the manmade Bahia Reef."

June was quite aware that I had been boating in those waters for 20-plus years. I had fished that very spot many times and even dove in it to retrieve my lost anchor while on a fishing trip. (By the way, I didn't find my anchor, but I did find eight other anchors—one of which hangs off the front of *Good Times* presently.)

Normally I wouldn't be interested in such an assignment, but *Good Times* was in need of a bottom job (new paint), and I had a few upgrades that I wanted to do. So, since the assignment was technically *on* the water, weeeellllll, maybe I would just have to take a look at that file!

"No promises, yet, June; but I am willing to at least take a look at the file. If I like what I see, I'll put a plan together. When do you think you can get the file to me?"

"Check your email, Ike. I've already sent it to you," June chuckled.

"Well, how did you know I would take the job?" I asked.

June snickered, "After 20-plus years of knowing you, I kind of just know what you will do."

I went topside to check on my kayakers. I could see Kris, one of the kayakers, had a fish on! He had slowly worked around the edges of the mangrove, always casting ahead of his kayak. He knew snook liked to lay up in those edges, looking for food.

When he returned to *Good Times* a few moments later and pulled up alongside the swim platform, he had a big smile on his face.

"How did you do?" I asked.

"Amazing!" he answered before excitedly continuing, "I caught a trout, a catfish, and I believe I even hooked up a snook. I cast up near the shore as I circled the island, and the rod made that forward bend. So, I am sure it was a snook! Whatever I hooked, it jumped and tugged against me, trying to gain its freedom. Eventually, it did escape . . . but the fight was still awesome!"

I looked down at his fish stringer trailing behind the kayak.

"Trout is one of my favorite fish to eat," I said as I eyed the good-sized fish on the stringer. "Hand me the stringer along with your kayak line. Then come on aboard," I instructed him.

Kris handed me his kayak line, and I tied it off to the cleat on the swim platform. He then passed me his stringer holding the trout. I took it topside as Kris gathered his gear and hopped aboard.

When one kayaker heads back to the mothership, others typically follow, thinking it's time to go; or they just realized that they were getting hungry. Ty was the next to return. Enthusiastically he shared his experience.

"Hey guys, listen to this! I was crossing a small channel to another island. The water was only about four feet deep. I saw a large swirl in the water about ten feet from my kayak. I looked down to see a large manatee crossing right under me! Of course, I've often seen them on tv, but I had no idea of how big they really are! At first I was really nervous, but the manatee seemed intent on getting away from me as soon as possible."

Amid the other fishermen's exclamations, I responded lightheartedly, "You just got the bonus of the trip!" After a short pause, I added, "But I won't be charging any extra."

"Oh, good!" Ty laughingly replied.

This was one part of the job I really loved: listening to people and seeing them light up as they recalled what they had just experienced.

Mark was the next to come back aboard as the others were partaking of some meat and crackers and drinks that I had laid out in the galley. He had caught the fighting crevalle jack or jack for short.

"The fish pulled out about half of my line before I could get the drag set right!" he exclaimed. "The jack pulled at right angles across in front of me . . . even pulling my kayak at times! I brought the jack back, but I've heard they weren't good to eat."

"That is nonsense!" I responded. "Just give it to me, and later this evening I will dispel that myth."

After each fisherman had some lunch, we pulled the anchor and moved around the island of Fort Desoto to the northern pass. I knew the tide would be turning out, and the water would begin its powerful flushing out of the bay. I again assisted the kayakers with getting back on the water and pointing out the little channels leading to the pass that they should try. The predator fish would set up at those places, waiting on the smaller fish to be pulled out past them for an easy meal.

Once they were off, I settled down in my captain's chair on the flybridge as it afforded the best 360-degree view to watch them while taking the occasional picture . . . pictures I would send to them after their trip. As I felt the sea breeze ruffle through my hair, it crossed my mind about the conversation I had earlier with June.

"Why did the boat burn and sink near the reef?" I thought.

I thought about the big, dark column of smoke it must have released as it burned, which is usually visible for miles around. I have seen them. I wondered how a fire could start and get out of control with people aboard and not be noticed by them. I also pondered what would be necessary to get down to the area and start the investigation. As June rightly figured, this fire had caught my interest.

As the evening approached and the sun lowered to the horizon, I motioned for the kayakers to return to *Good Times*. They did, one by one, with their stories of what they caught and what got away. Once I had them all aboard and the kayaks secured, we headed to the pass for an unobstructed view of the sunset. The best thing about the west coast of Florida is its sunsets! Many of the best bar and restaurant names start with "sunset" for this reason. We sat there talking about the day's adventures while the sun continued to set on another great day.

Once we could no longer see the sun, we headed for our anchorage for the night. After sunset, there is still actually about 20 minutes or so of light. I drove over to a nearby cove just inside the pass. I dropped the anchor while backing down to confirm a good set, and by then it was dark . . . though dark, there still was enough manmade light that one could see well enough to move around.

I went below and started the generator. The Onan 5kw generator provided plenty of power for *Good Times* when needed.

I took the fish that were caught earlier and cleaned them on the aft deck, tossing the carcasses overboard to return the unused portion to the sea. It would be a welcome find to the catfish surely swimming below the boat.

I went down to the galley as the guys lounged around, taking in the city lights of south St. Petersburg. I filled two pots with oil and brought them up to temperature. While I waited, I grabbed the hushpuppy mix from the cabinet and began coating the fish. The dinner would be complete simply by adding some cold macaroni salad. In minutes we were popping the top on a cold beer and sitting down to a freshly caught fish dinner! As the comment goes, we couldn't do better than this!

After dinner we sat on the back of *Good Times* taking in the sights and sounds of nature. Due to the fact we were a couple hundred yards from shore, we had no mosquitoes to bother us. We talked about our love of fishing, saltwater, and nature in general. All seemed right with the world that night.

Later that evening, each man went to his assigned bunk. I lay in my bunk that night thinking how lucky I was to have this job. It wasn't long before the case about which June had called crept into my thinking. Why was this case so important to the insurance company to pay double the normal rate? A few more thoughts tossed in my mind as I fell asleep.

The next morning before daylight I rose to the smell of coffee. It was unusual as I am normally the one to turn on the coffee pot. When I went into the galley, Kris stood there enjoying a fresh cup of coffee, smiling like a cat who caught the rat.

"I hope you don't mind," he offered, "but my excitement for today kept me from sleeping in. So, I got up and found the coffee maker."

He raised his cup to me as he finished his explanation. I smiled and walked over to the pot to get myself a cup. We walked out together onto the aft deck and chatted about what to expect for the coming day and what a great day it should be. A few more minutes and the smell of coffee floating throughout *Good Times* pleasantly awoke the other two fishermen, and they came topside.

Once everyone was up, I went back to the galley and cooked a breakfast of eggs, sausage, and toast. We all sat on the deck watching the sunrise as we ate. In these settings people often say very similar things, like "What a great job you have," or "This sure is a tough job you got, Captain." I usually just smile and cast my gaze out across the water, nodding in agreement.

Day two was similar to day one. I deployed the kayakers out near St. Antoine Key. This little island is covered with mangroves and is surrounded by the flats (shallow water). It is the closest refuge for sport fish to hide and is often a very productive spot.

Mark and Ty fished close to the island. Kris floated over the flats, trailing out shrimp as he floated with the wind. It wasn't very windy but enough to gently push him along. As Mark and Ty went out-of-sight around the back side of the island, I saw Kris get hooked up. I was sure that while floating over the grassy flats he had found some trout. This time of the year was good for that. Mark continued working the grass flats and ended the day also catching several nice, keeper-size trout.

As I sat in my captain's chair on the flybridge, I saw Ty come into view. Ty's rod was bent over, facing the bow of his kayak; and I could see the smile on his face from the *Good Times*. I sat watching him for several minutes as the fish pulled his kayak around the area of the island. The fish pulled Ty toward deeper water and to the channel where I had *Good Times* anchored.

"Whatcha got, Ty?" I yelled with my hands cupped around my mouth.

"Looks like a tarpon to me," he yelled back, keeping his focus on the fish out in front of him.

I laughingly responded, "Looks like you are on the tarpon sleigh ride, for sure! Just let the fish tire itself out, and you should be able to pull it alongside for a photo before releasing it."

Thirty minutes later the fish had tired enough that Ty was able to pull it out of the water and alongside the kayak for a well-deserved picture.

As the sun rose higher in the sky and warmed the air, the guys continued to fish the area. I sat aboard *Good Times*, watching their activities. My mind once again drifted back to my conversation with June and the sunken boat. I thought that I would need to call my buddy and dive partner, Shane, to assist with the dive and the investigation.

By early afternoon I had all the kayakers aboard and secured for the trip back to port. I provided some snacks, and we chatted about the trip all the way back. Once we arrived at the marina, we got the kayaks off *Good Times*; and I helped each guy with securing his kayak onto his respective vehicle.

We sat on the dock awhile, once more recalling the trip and the experiences. Each guy thanked me for an adventure they would never forget. I thanked them for the opportunity to share it with them, hoping to see them back for another quest. They all assured me they would be back.

Once the guys left, I went aboard *Good Times* to tidy up. As I was storing things away, the upcoming case crept into my thoughts. The investigator in me was beginning to awaken, and my mind returned to the familiar thoughts of years gone by. I completed cleaning *Good Times* and figured it was time for me to look at the file and begin an investigation.

Chapter 3
Captain Ike: The Investigation Begins

February 24, 2018
St. Petersburg Florida

After throwing some chicken on the grill on the deck of the *Good Times* to slow cook, I opened my computer to review the file. A file characteristically contains all the reports from PFIs and law enforcement agencies; in this case there were reports from Tampa Police and Fire Departments, as well as the U.S. Coast Guard. The typical file also contains all the information about the insured, the vessel, pictures of the case, and all other related information. However, since the vessel was sitting on the bottom of Tampa Bay, there were no pictures in the file.

I first reviewed the report from the Tampa Fire Department as I knew from my experience they would have been first on the scene of the fire. The report stated that they had responded in their fire boat to the location of Bahia Reef. They reported seeing a large column of smoke while enroute to the scene. Upon their arrival they saw an approximately 25-foot cuddy cabin boat on fire, and it was taking on water. They specified that by the time they deployed water from their fire boat, the vessel on fire slipped below the waterline out-of-sight. According to the report, there were other boats in the area at the time of the fire; and the Tampa fire boat had retrieved the operator of the boat that was on fire.

The Tampa Police Department also arrived with their boat. The boats tied up together so they could cooperatively get information from the operator about the fire.

The Tampa Fire Department's report listed the boat operator as Tony Morgan, a white male, with a date of birth (DOB) of 3-7-68. The burned boat's name was *Escape*.

I was surprised when I read the boat operator's name because I knew someone from my hometown with the same name; but I also knew it was a common name, so I didn't think much more about it. The report narrative stated that Morgan had been out fishing on the reef. He stated he noticed smoke coming from inside the cabin and jumped down from the bow to investigate. When he looked in through the hatchway, he saw fire everywhere. Morgan said he grabbed a fire extinguisher and tried to extinguish it, but the fire was too large. He also stated he had no idea what started the fire. According to Morgan, people on a boat fishing on the reef nearby came over and assisted. Morgan said the other boat captain helped him aboard and called 9-1-1.

As I read the account of what happened, something just didn't sound right. Most fire investigators start out as firefighters and, therefore, probably would have seen thousands of fires over their career. So, from my experience, while reading Morgan's statement, my first thought was why did Morgan see fire coming from the cabin and not the engine compartment if that's where the fire started? It also sounded like there had been a large amount of fire very quickly! How did the fire go unnoticed and grow so fast? The report further stated that Morgan was the only one aboard the boat. Usually more than one person goes out fishing. These were just some of the questions I had and for which I would need answers during the investigation.

The smell of chicken cooking on the grill brought me back to the present, and I went up on the back deck to check on it. It was about half done, so I went down to the galley and put some green beans on low to cook. I grabbed a cold beer from the fridge and went back up on the back deck to watch the chicken and relax a bit. By now the moon was rising over the water. It was in the high-60s with little humidity. We Floridians always notice and give thanks for low humidity because we know it will soon return to swamp-like conditions.

I sat thinking about how nice it was living on the boat this time of the year. Usually I would be thinking about my next charter trip and where I would be taking the customers, but tonight I was thinking about my next case. I thought about some of the things I would need to do to get started.

One was to contact my dive partner, Shane. Shane was a firefighter friend, as well as a dive master. We worked several recovery cases together. I decided that he needed to be the first contact I made to get eyes on the wreck and see what we had. I went downstairs and sent Shane a text to contact me when he could and that I had a case with which I needed his help.

By now the chicken was fully cooked, and the aroma of my soon-to-be dinner filled the air. I grabbed another beer and my dinner and went back up on the deck to enjoy a nice meal in perfect, Florida weather.

The next morning I arose at daylight. It was a little cool outside, and I decided to drive over to St. Pete Beach for some breakfast—a short three miles from the marina. I went to my usual place, the Waffle House. I ordered steak and eggs over light and upgraded to the T-bone for one dollar extra. I had buttered white toast and grits. Now, I know unless one is from the south, they may not know what grits are; but for southerners, it is a staple over which we put our eggs. I sat there and enjoyed my breakfast with just a few other customers. As with typical beach towns, on a Monday morning I could go to most restaurants and not have to deal with the crowds.

As I was finishing breakfast, I got a text from Shane that he was getting off duty and would call me shortly so we could chat. I finished my breakfast, paid my bill, tipped my waitress my normal 15%, and headed back to the *Good Times*. I pulled in to the marina behind *Good Times* and parked. Just then, Shane called.

"What's up, Brother Man?" Shane lightheartedly inquired.

"Oh, nothing," I said, "but living the dream."

"So, what is this case all about?" Shane prodded.

I filled Shane in with the details of the boat fire and where it was located. He knew the spot immediately as he and I were the ones who dove that spot to retrieve those eight anchors. I explained to Shane that the pay was double and that the insurance company really wanted to know how the fire occurred.

Shane responded, "I will be working my shift again on Wednesday, but I should be available Thursday and Friday."

"Great!" I answered. "I will check the tides and find out what day is best to dive. I will get back with you, but let's shoot for Thursday."

Later that day after I checked Thursday's tides, I texted

Shane, "If you can make it by 10 a.m. Thursday, we should be able to beat the tide; it starts out around noon."

We knew we didn't want to be diving when the tide was in full swing: it is hard to see and hard to hang on.

"Text me when you are enroute Thursday morning," I said in a second text.

I knew he would be getting off shift that morning.

A response text popped up on my phone, "Sounds good! Will text when enroute. Remember, I can't promise anything if I get a late call."

I remembered back when I used to be on shift. It seemed like every morning that I had something planned, I would get a late "BS call" and get off late. I must admit now that what we called a "BS call" might actually be an emergency to the person who called. However, we lived for the *true* emergency call. There is nothing more fulfilling than helping someone who really needs help . . . someone whose life is based on one's doing their job well! These are the calls why most people get into public safety and stay.

I went back aboard *Good Times* and opened my computer to get some information on the owner of the burned boat. I found that section and copied down Tony Morgan's contact information. I called the number, and it went straight to voicemail. As I listened to the voice that prompted me to "leave a message at the tone," my jaw dropped. I recognized the voice to be that of my old friend, Tony Morgan.

Morgan and I had attended the police academy together. He was going into law enforcement, and I was going to work as a reserve police officer with the city where I was employed as a fire investigator.

Morgan also came to work for our city and got promoted up through the ranks. His forte was working drugs. He had a natural ability to make drug dealers believe he was just the average drug addict. This allowed him to set up drug buys and make a lot of arrests for selling drugs. Morgan did so well, he was accepted into the Drug Task Force of Hillsborough County Sheriff's Office (HCSO) and the surrounding agencies. When he was later hired by the HCSO, he had to work on street patrol for a while; but he soon got back into the narcotics unit.

I didn't see much of Morgan during that time because he worked odd hours undercover; he worked during the time when most people are off or asleep. I was friends with him on Facebook; but like a lot of law enforcement officers, he changed his real name on his profile and made only a very few generic posts. He realized that a lot of drug dealers use counter intelligence to try and identify who might be law enforcement.

I had also heard that Morgan had gone through a divorce and was having a tough time dealing with it. He was paying a lot of child support and not able to see his daughter very often due to the shifts he worked. These specialty units work crazy hours, which is not good for families. Oftentimes the spouses can't deal with it, and the families break apart. There was also the rumor that there may have been some infidelity involved, but that was just gossip.

Then a few years ago I heard about an officer-involved shooting in which the suspect was killed during a drug search warrant. It ended up that Morgan was the officer who shot the suspect, and he was placed on normal administrative leave pending the investigation.

The news outlets reported that the victim was a black male suspect and that the victim's family said he was a model citizen and a great dad—that "he never done nothing to nobody." The media reports, however, showcased the victim's long rap sheet with multiple arrests for dealing drugs in addition to a myriad of other offenses.

During that time there were several other cases of officer-involved shootings happening around the country. Every time Morgan's case was updated by the local media, they reported as if the case was predetermined to be a bad shoot. Soon we heard that the victim apparently was unarmed during the shooting. This created a media firestorm around the case, and soon the state attorney came forth with charges of manslaughter. It was a devastating blow to the police community once details of how the shooting actually occurred were leaked because police officers were well aware that something like this could have happened to any one of them.

The actual happenings, as it turned out, was that one of the other officers had accidentally fired his weapon as he was clearing out the house at the exact, same time Morgan entered the suspect's bedroom. The suspect was in bed and rolled over with what Morgan thought was a gun. Hearing the accidental gunfire, Morgan thought the suspect was shooting at him. Morgan fired one lethal round into the suspect's chest, killing him instantly. In the police world a mistake that could happen to anyone may end up costing someone their life and the officer his freedom. In this case, that is precisely what happened.

Later on as I sat scrolling through Facebook, I noticed that Morgan had changed the name on his profile from his alias back to his real name . . . and that his profile photo held a sad expression.

Chapter 4
Captain Ike: Diving the Fire Scene

March 1, 2018
Pasadena Marina, St. Petersburg, Florida

About 8:05 a.m. Thursday morning, my cell phone received a text message notification. It was Shane.

"I am leaving work and should be there around 10 a.m."

"Ok," I replied and got up.

Shane pulled in behind *Good Times* at the dock just after 10 a.m. I smiled as I walked out of the cabin and onto the back deck.

"How's it hanging, Captain?" Shane asked jovially.

"Do you *really* want to know?" I laughed.

"Not really," Shane smilingly replied. "Permission to come aboard, Captain?"

"Well, if you don't, we won't be diving that wreck today."

Shane always used proper seamanship as he had been around boats most of his life. I offered him a cup of coffee, and he accepted. We sat on the back deck of *Good Times* and talked about the upcoming dive and what would be involved.

"The Fire Department placed a buoy marker on the spot where they believe the boat went down. Of course, it's just approximate—the tides could have ripped through there, and it could possibly have moved some," I explained.

"Oh, I remember," Shane responded.

After our coffee and briefing I helped Shane load the scuba tanks onto the back of *Good Times*. We had a metal tank holder on which we would strap the scuba tanks to the dive platform when going diving.

That is why I typically called Shane when diving. He is a dive instructor, and he has all the gear we would ever need and then some. Since I was an advanced diver, I had all my own personal gear, including my mask, snorkel, fins, buoyancy compensator (BC), regulator, flashlight, etc.

Moreover, because Shane was a firefighter, he also was a very safe diver. I deferred most of the logistics of dive trips to him. I knew that he would do it in a safe manner. Hey, I didn't want to die out there—I just wanted to make some extra cash!

While Shane prepped his gear, I went below and checked the engine oils and fluid levels. I always did this before starting the engines. *Good Times* had twin Mercruiser 350 hp inboards, mounted midship. I always stood below in the salon as I cranked the engine and listened for any abnormal engine sounds and watched for anything out of the ordinary—a good practice as any issues can hopefully be found before they become catastrophic. Any morning the engines fired up easily was a good morning, and a good morning it was.

While the engines warmed up, I went back topside and started pulling out my personal gear and getting it all squared away.

Once everything was in order, I asked Shane, "Are you good?"

"I'm ready, Captain," he replied with confidence.

I went up on the flybridge to the helm, and Shane untied the lines.

"Cast off," I said, and Shane stepped aboard with the final line.

I put both engine shifters forward and slowing pulled out of my slip. Directly in front of *Good Times* across the channel were more slips with other boats. This is where an unseasoned captain could run into trouble. There was only about 65 feet between boats from one side to the other. *Good Times* was 32 feet. That is not a lot of room, taking into account the wind and tide. But I had done this many times.

I pulled the port engine back to reverse, leaving the starboard engine forward. This caused *Good Times* to spin to port. Once we headed up the channel, I pushed the port shifter forward; and *Good Times* responded and started down the middle of the channel.

We cleared the last dock and made a slight adjustment port to follow the channel. This section of the Boca Ciega Bay is mostly shallow outside of the channel. *Good Times* can float in three feet of water, but I always stopped if I found myself in less than four feet. The channel is consistently around six to seven feet. I continued on around the islands of Pasadena, staying well clear of Jack Island. The water around that island can get very shallow and wouldn't be good for *Good Times*!

Once I came around the other side of the islands of Pasadena, I turned south into the Intracoastal Waterway. I followed it for a while and turned back through the Boca Ciega Bay Aquatic Preserve and then through the channel at Bayway Isles. At this point we entered the waters of Tampa Bay. I followed the Skyway channel down to the channel at the twin bridges, again turning port. From there it was a straight shot past the tip of St. Petersburg out into the main shipping channel of Tampa Bay.

By then it was around 11 a.m. As we headed to Bahia Reef, I noticed and commented on how nice a day it was. It was sunny with occasional, puffy clouds with a temperature around 79 degrees. With most of the country still cold this time of year, here in Florida we were reminded of how lucky we were! We had a little less than an eight-mile run to reach Bahia Reef. We found ourselves surrounded by land on three sides with the south end dumping into the Gulf of Mexico.

The bay was about eight miles wide in most spots with an average depth of around 12 feet. If a prudent mariner left the channel, he would pay close attention to the charts: the bottom came up quickly in these parts!

Around noon we reached the Bahia Reef. Looking west from that spot was the St. Petersburg skyline to include Tropicana Field, where the Tampa Bay Rays baseball team played, as a landmark. On the other side of the bay is Little Harbor Motel and Marina. It is probably the best-kept little secret of places to stay on Tampa Bay. Looking north we could also see the Tampa skyline and Beer Can Island.

Bahia Reef was a manmade reef of concrete pilings, slabs, and culvert pipes. The depth ranged from 18 to 24 feet in an area of around 300 square yards. Ten to 15 boats could fish the reef with no problem. However, it was a Thursday; there were no boats.

"Better for us," I thought to myself.

I quickly saw the buoy marking the spot of the *Escape*. I watched the flow of the water, and it was starting to move outward.

Just north of the buoy marker, I called to Shane, "Drop the plow anchor!"

We began paying out line to move us over the exact spot. I paid special attention to my chart plotter's sonar feature: it showed bottom contour. Knowing this area of the reef was concrete rubble and the fact I didn't want to lose my anchor again, I dropped it where there appeared to be no rubble. I backed down on the anchor, confirming a good set.

Shane and I began moving our gear to the dive platform. In the time it took to get the anchor set and get ready to dive, the tide was moving pretty hard . . . not the worst I had seen, but floating items could be seen zipping by in the water. We put out our normal safety tagline, a line drifting out behind the boat, as well as hoisted the divers down flag. We discussed our plan of dropping down directly under the boat to the bottom to see if we would get lucky and find the *Escape*. We also used a buddy line between us to maintain contact. Since both of us had dived this reef before, we knew that the visibility could be near zero. As we got into the water, I was reminded that we were coming off winter; and the water was still pretty cool: a temperature in the high-60s.

Once we both were in the water, we gave a simple hand signal to each other, confirming that all was good; and we were ready to descend. When we dipped under, it was apparent the visibility was going to be very poor. Using our buddy line, we each deflated the air from our BC and drifted down toward the bottom, clearing our ears as we went.

Most divers can do this easily; but I have always had a rough time clearing, and it usually takes me longer to get down. Today was no different, and my buddy line was straight down to the bottom.

Shane was already sitting on the bottom, waiting as I came into view. He was hanging onto a rock. The tide was ripping a lot harder than was apparent from topside. Visibility was at a maximum of 4 feet—less at times. We moved slowly along the bottom until we started to see the reef. At the edge was the line going up to the buoy marker that the fire department had dropped. It had moved but fortunately was tucked under a rock or it probably would have moved further away. We started a search pattern using the bottom as a reference and our compasses to confirm direction. Visibility became increasingly harder as time went on because of the tide.

"An earlier start would have been better," I thought, "but here we are."

We had been searching for around 40 minutes when I looked down to check my air gauge. It indicated there was still around 1500 psi. A dive is typically ended at 500 psi, and a diver starts ascending. That way, in the event there is any issue, there is enough air to get topside. Just about the time I checked my gauge, I felt a tug on the buddy line and looked to see Shane pointing toward something. From where I was, I couldn't see to what he was pointing; so, I swam in his direction. The object at which he was pointing slowly began to materialize, and as soon as I saw *Escape*," I knew we had located the vessel. I powered on my head-mounted GoPro camera and began documentation. I took the lead and started circling the boat to get an idea of its size and position on the bottom.

The *Escape* was lying on its side with the bow to the east and stern to the west. As I rounded the bow, I saw the anchor line coming from the bow then out-of-sight into the murky water. I was thinking that the anchor line was the only reason the boat was still here given the strength of the current in this area. The boat appeared to be around 23 feet long and white in color—just what the report had detailed. As I came around the south side of the boat, it was evident it had burned in the area of the cuddy cabin (forward compartment). I continued around the *Escape* until I reached the point where I had started.

One of the first things a fire investigator learns in school is the 360-degree inspection. If I was conducting a fire investigation on a house fire, I would do the same thing. When a fire investigator arrives on the scene and before going interior—or, if possible, *before* talking with anyone—the prudent investigator will walk around the scene taking pictures as he goes to document and look at the total scene before trying to determine the cause of the fire. By doing this he can see and document things that may change, and it also gives a general impression of with what he is dealing. The fire investigator would also be looking for any obvious safety concerns. Once the 360-degree inspection was completed, he would start working from the unburned section and move into the burned section, documenting with pictures what he is seeing. The investigation consists of the same process whether done on land or in water—admittedly a little harder under water!

I double checked my GoPro to confirm it was on and started documenting again, moving to the topside of the sunken boat. Since the boat was lying on her starboard side, I could see the bottom of the boat and that most of the outside was intact rather than burned. I was having a difficult time not swimming into the boat as the current was now very strong. What was already low visibility to begin with was now worsening.

I approached the boat this time from the stern (back). As I came over the engine compartment, I only had about a foot of visibility. I knew Shane was right behind me because I would often tug on the buddy line confirming his presence. I noticed the doors to the engine compartment were closed, and I saw no evidence of fire.

As I moved forward trying to pull myself against the current, I saw that the floor of the boat just past the engine compartment had a large hole measuring about 3 feet by 4 feet. I pulled myself down close to the floor for a better look and saw what appeared to be jagged edges around the hole. I stopped and studied it for several minutes. I pulled Shane up closer to take a look. After he looked for a minute, he gave me a puzzled look, and I responded with the "I don't have a clue" gesture!

I slowly moved around the hole, trying to be sure to document it all on the GoPro. I looked down at my air gauge and saw I was at 800 psi. I pulled myself toward the cuddy cabin where I started to see fire damage.

As I got close enough to look inside the cabin, I saw a large goliath grouper about the same time it saw me. I apparently scared it as it made a very loud noise and vibration in the water. If one has never seen one of these majestic fish, it is hard for them to understand why it almost scared the crap out of me.

Goliath groupers are an endangered species of grouper. Due to their endangered status they have made a great comeback in numbers and can be found on most reefs around Florida. This particular one was at least 500 pounds and roughly 6 feet long, but I couldn't see all of him. He was backed into the cuddy cabin like a guard at the castle gate. They often seek out holes like this so they can ambush any unsuspecting fish.

I backed away slowly as Shane came up on my left side. I could tell he got a glimpse of the grouper, as well. Goliath groupers are not known to attack divers, but the sheer size of their mouths gives a diver pause that one bite and he could swallow an arm or leg very easily.

Shane, the ever-present safety man, pointed to my gauge. and it was already below 500 psi. He motioned upward, and we started ascending to the surface. Since we were only in about 20 feet of water, safety stops were not necessary.

Once at the surface I excitedly asked, "Did you see the size of that thing?"

Shane was all smiles as he said, "I could hear it before I saw it."

"Yup, I heard it about the same time I saw it, and I think we both scared each other!"

I looked around for my boat. The *Good Times* was at least 100 yards away.

"Dang it," I said about the same time Shane noticed it."

"Let's get to it," he prompted.

The *Escape* was down tide to the *Good Times*; and with the speed of the water, we had moved a considerable distance from the *Good Times*.

"Do you have a buoy marker?" I asked Shane.

Shane pulled one from his BC and inflated it using the air from his tank.

"Give me a second," he stated.

Dropping below the surface, he swam back down and attached it to the boat. He resurfaced.

"That should do it," he announced.

We inflated our BCs and started swimming.

We both put on our mask and snorkel so we wouldn't suck in any water. We would look up every so often to confirm we were on the right path. At times I would turn over and swim on my back, which is helpful since different muscles are used to swim this way.

It took what seemed like forever, but we finally made it back to the boat. We got aboard and squared away our gear.

"Dang, that goliath grouper scared the crap out of me!" I exclaimed. "That thing is guarding that boat," I laughed.

"Well, what now, Captain?" Shane asked.

"Hmmm, I'm not sure," I responded. "Let's get something to eat and figure out our next step. I need to check the tide tables."

We dried off and went to the galley. I had some sandwich meat and bread, so we each made a sandwich. We went out on the back deck to soak up some sun as we ate. The water had me a bit chilled.

"That tide was ridiculous!" I remarked.

I got a nod from Shane in the affirmative.

I grabbed my cell phone and opened the Navionics app to check the tide.

"Dude, it looks like we have several hours of this tide left. There is not going to be enough daylight when the tide slows down to re-dive today."

Shane agreed and asked, "So, what is the plan?"

I pointed back toward Cockroach Bay east of where we were.

Fire Aboard

"Since the wind is out of the east, we can anchor up there for tonight up close to Sand Key. We can get an earlier start in the morning and dive during the slack tide," I suggested.

"Sounds like a plan," Shane replied.

"Pull the anchor, and I will get us underway."

Shane went up on the bow. I fired up the engines and slowly moved forward as Shane pulled in the line. Once we were over the anchor, one hard pull from Shane and the anchor was free. He pulled in the rest of the line and stowed the anchor in the bowsprit.

I turned *Good Times*, then pushed the throttles forward, heading east. Sand Key was only about two miles away; so in short order, we came around to the west side of it. We anchored up about 100 yards south of the approach light to the Little Manatee River. This entrance to the Little Manatee River is not often used by bigger boats because it is too shallow, running three to six feet deep, depending on the tide. I knew the only thing coming by tonight would be the occasional fishing boat not more than 23 feet long.

"My buddy, Marty, lives just up the river from here on his boat," I said to Shane. He knew Marty from when we dove the Bahia Reef for the anchors.

"How's he doing?" Shane asked.

"Great," I answered. "He has started a land-based, kayak rental business. He has all types of kayaks, including one- and two-man kayaks . . . heck, he even has a round boat he rents."

"What is that?"

"Hard to explain," I said. "Pull up his website on your phone, and check one out."

Shane reached into the cabin and grabbed his phone.

"What's the web address?" he asked.

"It's Zoffinger.com . . . easy to remember since that's his last name. Marty also has a YouTube channel. He has the biggest kayak fishing channel on YouTube! Besides renting and sailing kayaks, he does all kinds of DIY stuff. He doesn't think twice about cutting a hole in a kayak," I said laughingly. "That's where I get my kayaks from that I use."

As we talked, Shane pulled up the site and scrolled through, checking out his website. "Check out his YouTube channel, also, when you get a chance."

Shane nodded as he looked at his phone.

The spot where we were anchored had been pretty productive for me for fishing in the past. Since we had a few hours to kill, I decided to throw the net to see if I could get some bait. There was a large sandbar about 30 yards behind the boat, so I grabbed my bucket containing the cast net and jumped off the back.

"Whoa! That's cold!" I yelled.

Within a minute I was in knee-deep water. The sandbar had a grassy flat. A few throws of the cast net typically produced all different types of bait fish, including threadfin, herring, pinfish, pilchard, and even shrimp at night during certain times of the year.

After only a few casts, I had several pinfish. In my opinion they were one of the all-around best baits. I would only keep around four or five fish as I don't want to kill them unnecessarily. If the fish were biting and I was trying to catch dinner, one nice-sized fish would do it.

Once I had my bait, I headed back to the boat. When I arrived, I found Shane sitting, watching some of Zoffinger's YouTube videos.

"You starting a binge watch?" I asked, nodding at his phone.

"Oh, it's pretty cool!" Shane replied without looking up.

I grabbed a rod out of the cabin with a one-ounce sinker and a circle hook. I hooked a pinfish through the nose and tossed him off the back of the boat. I placed the rod in the rod holder and sat down to wait.

"If we don't catch some dinner, I have some landfish in the freezer."

Shane looked up at me. "Landfish?" he quizzed.

"Yeah, you probably know them as chicken," I said with a smile.

"Hey, either one sounds good to me, Brother Man."

After a few minutes I got a good hit on the rod. The fish didn't take the bait, but at least I got a hit. A little while later I reeled in the line and discovered I had a bare hook.

"Stole my bait!" I lamented.

I rigged another pinfish and threw it back out behind the boat in the same place as before. This time I kept the rod in my hand, and I could tell by how the bait was twitching from side to side that something was about to eat him.

I imagined being hooked and some large animal was about to eat me. I was sure I would twitch, too!

In just a few seconds the rod bent over, and the fish pulled against me. I let him run until he tired himself out and was rewarded with a nice snapper. I smiled and held up the fish as Shane took a quick picture.

Freshly-caught fish grilled in minutes is about the best way to get it! I fired up the Magma gas grill to let it warm up and went down below to put some canned green beans and corn on the stove. A little seasoning on the snapper and back to the grill I went. In a short time we had fresh fish and sides while sitting on the back deck of *Good Times*.

It was getting late, and the sun was starting to go down. We were looking out across Tampa Bay toward the west. The sunsets from there were always super nice, and this one was no exception.

Once we finished with dinner and got everything cleaned up, it was time to settle in for a night's rest aboard *Good Times*. I found that I sleep so well when I was onboard . . . as long as the weather was decent. The gentle rocking of the boat and the sounds of the water lapping against it are very relaxing. It's times like these that I feel blessed to do what I do.

The next morning we arose with the sun. I got breakfast going, and we had eggs and sausage on the back deck as we contemplated the upcoming day. I pulled up the tide chart and saw that the tide would be slack around 9:42 a.m. Slack tide is just what it sounds to be: the time the water has quit moving in or out; the water is completely non-stressed. It is the best time for diving to stay in one position. Most of the time a moving tide is good for fishing, drift diving, etc. However, to complete an investigation on a sunken boat, a slack tide would be best.

After breakfast I did my morning checks on *Good Times* and fired up the engines. We headed back out to the reef. Since we had a better idea of where the *Escape* lay on the bottom, I headed right to the spot. I had saved it on my GPS. We dropped anchor and floated right back over the top of her. Checking the time, I saw that we were a bit early, so we took our time checking our gear. The hardest thing we would do that day was go into that chilly water. Early in the morning is usually the toughest because the water temp is usually at its coldest. Today it was 68—pretty chilly!

Around 9:30 a.m. Shane and I both slipped into the water and started our descent downward. This was challenging in the cold water. The visibility was much better today, and the tide was perfect. I wondered if the big goliath grouper would be guarding his spot today. The visibility was running around 15 feet. That made it much easier to find the target, and we were on the *Escape* within minutes.

I checked my GoPro and confirmed it was turned on. We came up on the port side of the *Escape* and swam up over the top of her to get an overall video of her lying on the bottom. We could see the hole in the deck of the boat and the burned remains of the forward section leading into the cuddy cabin. The top of the cuddy cabin was burned away.

I swam down for a closer look. I first looked at the hole in the deck. It appeared that someone had cut open the deck with some type of tool. This puzzled me. I knew it was cut before the fire because some of the hole forward had some burn on it. This indicated that the hole had been cut pre-fire; and when the boat burned, the fire extended in that direction.

I moved forward down the centerline of the boat getting as much video as possible. Mr. Grouper was not home this morning, and that suited me just fine. He must be out for breakfast.

I moved into the cuddy cabin for a better look, and Shane was right behind me. I saw that the fire damage was low, down inside of the hull. Basic fire dynamics dictates that fire burns upward. With the effect of wind and other factors, it can sometimes burn sideways.

I envisioned the fire happening in my mind as I do during any investigation. Very low burn in most cases would raise the investigator's suspicion because electrical, mechanical, and other items that may start a fire are not usually at floor level. In the case of boat fires, they almost always start in the engine compartment. This was the forward cabin. Moving down closer to the floor I saw where silt and sand had covered the deck of the cuddy cabin. I used my hand in a side-to-side motion to try to move the debris away from the deck so I could see the lowest point of burn, taking into account that fire burns upward. After the side-to-side motion of my hand, the visibility was bad for a moment; however, when the sand and silt moved out of the cabin, the visibility returned. Just like smoke clearing from an area, I started to see what I was searching for: possibly a pour pattern!

Let's talk Fire Investigation 101. In every fire there is the origin of the fire and the cause of the fire. I located the origin of the fire on my first dive. It was in the cuddy cabin.

Now, to determine the cause of the fire: the lowest point of burn was on the deck of the cuddy cabin. In this area there was nothing apparent that could have caused a fire, such as electrical wiring or something mechanical, such as an engine, etc.

That led me to the pour pattern. Imagine for a moment that someone took a cup of water and poured it onto the floor. What would it do? It would spread out in different directions, making a clear, pour pattern. In most cases the water would simply dry up. Now imagine you poured Kool-Aid on the carpet. What would happen? It would leave a stain, allowing the remaining pour pattern to be seen.

In the case of a pour pattern using an ignitable liquid, just like the Kool-Aid the ignitable liquid would spread out and presumably be set on fire. This would first burn into the surface on which it was poured, then upward and outward, leaving a clear pour pattern!

My hypothesis in this case was that some type of ignitable liquid was poured onto the deck floor in the cuddy cabin and set on fire. The fire followed normal fire behavior, extending upward and outward, burning the inside walls and roof off the cuddy cabin, and eventually burning through the roof. As the fire burned through the fiberglass, it ultimately would have burned low enough to the water line so that water would begin pouring in from the front. The *Escape* would fill with water and finally sink to the bottom.

"Bam!" I yelled in my mask and got the attention of Shane who was on guard for our resident goliath grouper.

Shane swam closer for a better look. I pointed down into the bottom of the cabin and Shane smiled and nodded. Shane is a lieutenant at his fire job, and one of his duties is to try and determine the cause of a fire at sites to which he is called. If the fire is a normal pot on the stove, he would have no need to call for a fire investigator. If he saw something similar to this pour pattern, his training would immediately tell him to call for a fire investigator.

I made sure my GoPro was still on and working for documentary purposes. I took it off and recorded different areas and angles of the damage. I contemplated what else I may need from the scene. In normal investigations at a structure fire, an investigator could return for any additional pictures, samples, etc. In this case it wouldn't be so easy to return because the water was constantly changing the evidence.

I went back aft and again looked at the opening cut into the deck of the boat. I needed to take into consideration how a boat is built: in the factory the hull (bottom) and boat deck (top) are made in different pieces and put together; therefore, there is a space between the deck and hull. I hovered there for a minute, trying to figure out how the hole in the deck could have gotten there.

I turned to Shane and motioned for us to return to the surface. Once at the surface we swam over to *Good Times* and went aboard. It took a few minutes to get our gear squared away. Once complete, we dried ourselves off on the back deck and sat there for a few minutes to dry.

Thinking out loud, I said, "Why is there a hole in the deck?"

Shane did not answer immediately, but then spoke up, "Maybe there was something in there."

"Hmmm," I said out loud as I sat, thinking some more.

At that point I knew that the boat was intentionally burned, and that meant someone committed arson.

Why *burn* the boat, though? I am guessing the payoff on it would be only around $10,000 at most. In other cases I have worked—fires on boats that were valued much higher—boat owners would have reason to burn for the insurance proceeds. I would need to determine if the boat was financed and if possibly they were getting behind in payments or something along those lines. It just seemed strange, though.

"Well, we got what we came here for so let's head back," I told Shane.

Shane agreed, and he got up and headed to the bow while I fired the engines up and motioned for him to pull the anchor. I pulled forward, and within a few seconds Shane had the anchor safely stored aboard.

I turned *Good Times* and headed south, backtracking, following the GPS in the exact route we came. The Garmin

GPS on *Good Times* has a breadcrumbs feature, meaning it will show little dots on the screen, marking the route taken. The safest method to return is to simply follow the same track back. The water depths are known to be safe since it is the same route previously taken.

We had a decent ride back to the marina. On our way back we talked about our dive; however, we continued to be baffled about why a hole had been cut into the deck.

As we came around Pasadena Island, the marina came into view. It was later on Friday afternoon so there wasn't much boat traffic in the marina. I eased back in between the boats down to my slip. Using the engines, I rotated *Good Times* and slowly backed into the slip. Shane jumped off and started tying the boat up, and I got down off the bridge and helped. In a few minutes we had her all tied up. I plugged into shore power and hooked up the water. A nice shower to wash off the salt water would feel good soon.

"Shane, I sure do appreciate your help."

"No problem, Brother," he responded. "So, what are you going to do now?"

"Well, now the *real* investigation begins," I replied. "I need to get some more info on the boat value and see if it was paid off or financed."

"Sounds like you will have your hands full."

"Yup, that I will."

I helped Shane get his gear together and loaded all the dive equipment back into his truck.

"How about a cold beer before you take off?" I asked.

"Nah," Shane answered, shaking his head. "I got to be heading back. Momma already has called a couple of times," he added, referring to his wife.

"Well you better get to it. Get me an invoice, and I will get it turned in to June."

"Will do," he said as he jumped into his truck and turned the ignition. He soon pulled out of the marina.

"Time to go get some dinner. Pasta sounds good," I said to myself.

I went back aboard and jumped into the shower. In a few minutes I was ready to go. People always kid me about how fast I take showers. What can I say? I get it done. "No sense in wasting time," I say!

I got into my truck and drove over to St. Pete Beach. From the marina it's only about three miles across a bridge. I drove down Gulf Boulevard to Gigi's Italian Restaurant.

Gigi's is a small spot, but they serve the best pasta of any style; their lasagna is to die for. I was feeling hungry so I ordered the trio: a sample of lasagna, chicken alfredo, and stuffed shells. It is served with bread and is amazing! I also ordered a cold Michelob Ultra.

I sat outside on the patio by the road. On a Friday night, this was a good place to sit and people watch. I sipped my beer and thought about the dive and the hole in the boat, and I kept questioning why it would be there.

I decided to give June a call and update her on what I had determined so far. I dialed her number, and she picked up on the third ring.

"What's happening? I asked.

"Nothing," she replied. "Just sitting here at the house."

"Well, I dove the boat wreck today."

"What do we have?" she inquired.

"It appears to be arson," I replied. "I found an obvious pour pattern in the cuddy cabin of the boat."

June, not being boat savvy, asked, "What is the cuddy cabin?"

I explained. Then I told her about the hole in the deck. I described how I could tell it obviously had been cut pre-fire. Some of the fire had burned into the area of the hole, and the edges were clearly burned. I further explained how it was a pretty decent-sized area that was exposed.

"It seemed like something was in there, and they took it out," I described.

"So, someone cuts a hole in the boat and burns it . . ." she said, thinking out loud. "Maybe they had something of high value . . . drugs, maybe?"

"Well, that is a possibility . . . but did I tell you I know the owner of the boat?"

"No!" she gasped.

"Yeah, do you remember Tony Morgan? He worked for us years ago and then went to the sheriff's office."

"Yeah, I kinda remember something about him."

I told June the story how Morgan had been fired and charged with manslaughter. I also told her that I tried calling him several times but his number was going straight to voicemail.

"That really sounds strange," June said slowly. "You know, the insurance company agent also told me that they couldn't get in touch with him to pay off the claim."

"Do you know if the boat was paid off or financed?" I asked her.

"I'm not sure," she answered thoughtfully, "but I will contact them and let you know. "Well, it's Friday so I guess you won't be able to contact them till Monday. I am going to ponder it over the weekend, and I will talk to you Monday then."

I finished with dinner and headed back to *Good Times* for an early bedtime. The day of diving had worn me out! I lay in my bunk, thinking and playing out the scenarios in my head of what could have happened in this case.

What I *knew* was that Morgan had called 9-1-1 from his phone and reported the fire. I *knew* the Tampa Fire Department would have had about a 10- to 15-minute response time. I *knew* the statements Morgan told the Fire Department. I also *knew* that the boat had been intentionally burned. I was saddened to think that Morgan was a part in what was looking to be an arson to a vessel.

I knew Morgan pretty well; we had hung out back in the day quite a bit. We had been to police functions with our families together; and this was definitely out-of-character for him, I thought! I started thinking of how this must have played out.

Where did he and the boat come from? Who was the person in the other boat, and what did he see? Knowing the area, I figured he must have come from either the St. Petersburg area or the Cockroach Bay area. I quickly ruled out the St. Pete side as it is a large city with lots of boat traffic on the water. The Cockroach Bay side, however, has very limited boat entry points, one being the EG Simmons State Park. This park has a guard shack with an on-duty guard and camera system. It seemed unlikely that Morgan would have chosen this spot, knowing the security involved. I also thought how the Little Manatee River comes out there. I decided that if I had done something like this, I would have chosen the river . . . that would be what I investigated first.

Chapter 5
Captain Ike: Gina and I Reconnect

The morning sun peeked in through the aft cabin window, and I woke up feeling rested. Last night I had come up with a plan of action, and today I would execute that plan. I made a short list of things to do on my investigative report outline. I decided I would attempt to get any camera footage from the area of the fire, and I needed to contact the other boat captain who helped Morgan during the fire and find out what he saw.

I logged on my computer and looked at the incident report. The fire report said nothing about the other boat owner's information. They wouldn't have any reason or training to ask for that.

I pulled up the Tampa Police Department's (TPD) report. It had most of the same info; however, it listed the other boat info and gave the occupant as a witness. A short statement from the witness confirmed Morgan's account of the incident. The report listed Witness #1 as a Hispanic male, Juan Espinoza, DOB 6-22-75. His cell number was listed, as well as the hull number.

"That's something," I thought.

The day of the fire TPD would have no reason to believe anything illegal was afoot. The vast majority of boat fires are accidental; however, most start in the engine compartment. They would not have known where the fire started since the boat had sunk.

A trip to the Ruskin area was in order since that is where Cockroach Bay is located. So, I jumped into my GMC Sierra and headed in that direction. The fastest way is over the Sunshine Skyway Bridge. I turned onto Pasadena Avenue and then onto Gulf Port Boulevard and headed to I-275 S. This road goes over the Sunshine Skyway Bridge, the tallest bridge in the Tampa Bay area.

Each time I cross the Skyway, I can't help but think about the time in 1980 when the bridge was hit by a barge. Several cars, a truck, and a Greyhound bus were on the bridge at the time; and they all plunged into the bay, killing 35 people! The bridge was later rebuilt and now stands strong as the gateway to Tampa Bay.

I crossed the bridge safely and continued on my way. I turned north onto Highway 41, and I passed the Port Manatee Federal Terminal. I recalled that is where I got my Transportation Worker Identification Credential (TWIC) ID card, which documents one of the federal background checks one must go through to become a licensed boat captain.

I continued north on Highway 41 into Ruskin. I was getting hungry and was nearing College Avenue. If I'm ever in the area of College Avenue and Highway 41, I stop for lunch at Marian's Sub Shop. When I used to keep my boat at the private dock close to here, I would always take my clients there when we were finished fishing. To my consternation, I actually think some of them remembered more about Marian's Sub Shop than our fishing adventure!

I pulled into the parking lot and went in. I didn't know the girl's name who works there, but she always remembers me when I order my sub. I'm sure that one of the reasons she remembers me so easily, of course, is how good looking I am . . . seriously, though, we had gotten into a conversation one day about what I did for a living. I explained how I used to work as a police officer, and she told me she was currently getting the required classes to go into law enforcement. She shared that it was her dream, and I encouraged her to not give up, that it was a long process. Since then, we have been as though we were long-lost co-workers.

I ordered my usual sub, and within just a few minutes I was outside at the picnic table enjoying it . . . my mouth is watering now just thinking about it!

When I finished lunch, I turned back out onto Highway 41 and once again headed north a short distance where I turned onto Shell Point Road. I followed it almost to the end to the entry of Little Harbor. This is the place where I kept boats for years. In addition, I had also kept *Good Times* around the corner at a private dock at Shell Point Marina.

I knew this area well. I also knew that Little Harbor had cameras which face out toward the bay. This is also one of the entrances to the Little Manatee River that I knew most boats used because the channel is deeper and safer to navigate.

I pulled into the parking lot and jumped out. I went into the office, hoping to see my friend, Gina, a manager at Little Harbor. We became friends back when I used to keep my boat there, and I always had a crush on her. She was a cute, little blonde with a banging, little body; and she knew it. She had a great personality and was always smiling. I would flirt with her each time I was there, but she always had a boyfriend . . .

one of those situations of bad timing. When she was single, I would have a girlfriend; and it just never seemed to work out.

The girl behind the desk said Gina wasn't working today but thought she was at the tiki bar, hanging out. The place was one of the best tiki bars to which I have ever been. It sits within feet of the water with no obstruction to the nightly sunsets. It was always packed, and today was no exception. I walked into the outdoor sitting area. When the weather is good, this is the best place for dinner. The attached restaurant is appropriately called Sunset Grill.

I saw Gina sitting at the bar, and I sneaked up behind her and whispered in her ear, "I have a complaint!"

Laughing as she turned, she retorted, "Well, then get in line!"

When she saw who it was, she smiled even bigger and jumped up to give me a hug. "Where have you been?" she asked.

"I have *Good Times* across the bay over in Pasadena," I answered.

"No wonder I haven't seen you lately."

"Can I buy you a beer?" I offered.

"Sure!" she responded.

I stood behind her rather than sit down as there were no seats available.

"What are you drinking these days?" I asked.

"That depends on the day," she said while continuing to smile.

I ordered two Ultras in the bottle. As we caught up, I noticed the band playing on the patio. They always had some type of live music, and tonight was the Fifth Gear Band. They were playing some classic rock. All the patrons seemed to be enjoying it, evidenced by their clapping loudly after each song.

"Good band," I said to Gina.

"Yes!" she replied. "They have been playing a good bit lately, and the crowd loves them, as you can tell."

Just about that time, the band took a break, and the bar put on some dance music. Since there is a decent-sized dance floor, many of the ladies quickly jump up to dance when a good song for dancing comes on. Their dancing abilities, however, will vary . . . usually based on how much they had to drink!

The first song came on, and the music started with "Oh, oh, oh, oh, all the shorties in the club." This brought the girls up out of their seats, yelling. I grabbed Gina by the hand and pulled her toward the dance floor. This is one of the songs often played at weddings and one of the few I like and to which I can dance.

Gina knew it well, so I was sure they played it there every night. It is a line dance that is fun and very popular to which to dance. The song usually goes on for several minutes, so it gives shy people time to get up and dance.

I followed in behind Gina as I knew she would know it well. I watched as she moved her hips and swayed to the motion of the music. She was wearing white shorts and a polo work shirt. I was mesmerized as she danced, and I cursed the song when I had to turn from her. Before the song ended and as the dance floor became too crowded, Gina grabbed my hand and pulled me back to our seats. I sat down beside her, smiling.

"Well what brings you here? I doubt it was to dance with me!" she playfully quizzed.

"Girl, I could dance with you all night," I said, ". . . especially with those beautiful, tan legs!"

She smiled, turning shyly away for a second.

"I *do* need to ask you for a favor . . . but let's catch up first."

We talked and laughed for a good while. I was getting a warm feeling about her just about the time a tall, fit guy walked up behind her and leaned over to kiss her on the neck. She turned around quickly and leaned in to give him a quick kiss on the lips.

"Oh, no!" I thought.

She turned back toward me and introduced me to the guy.

"Tim, this is a friend of mine, Captain Ike."

Tim extended his hand with a friendly smile and a nice-to-meet-you greeting.

"Likewise," I replied.

"What type of a boat captain are you?" he inquired.

I take kayakers out to fish," I explained.

Tim nodded, seeming to know just what I was talking about. Gina went on to tell him how I had retired as a firefighter/police officer.

He seemed genuinely impressed as he said with gratitude, "Thank you for your service!" "Oh, my pleasure," I responded.

Tim was very pleasant and had an outgoing personality.

"I can see why she likes him," I thought to myself.

Apparently, the plan between Tim and Gina was for her to meet him here when they got off work.

Gina explained to Tim, "Ike here needs something and has come to see me about it. But let's go inside," she continued, "where we can talk." The crowd was certainly getting louder, and it was ever getting harder to hear.

"Sure," I replied.

All three of us went in and got a table.

Turning to Tim, I asked, "What are you drinking?"

"Oh, I'll just have what you two are having."

I ordered us all a round of beers and began explaining to Gina the reason for my visit . . . leaving out, of course, the part that I was hoping she would be single. No such luck!

I explained how I had come out of retirement to help on a case. I told her about the fire and where it occurred. From where we were sitting, the Bahia Reef was only about three nautical miles northwest. On most clear days one could just about count the boats sitting at the reef. Since the fire had recently occurred, she had heard about it but wasn't working the day it happened.

"Well, the reason I am here is to ask about your cameras. I know that you guys installed cameras after the boat incident where it ran into the building."

I was aware that about a year before, a boat failed to turn at the channel curve that ran in front of the Little Harbor. The boat was running at a high rate of speed and ran all the way up on the beach and into the building. The picture in the paper showed the boat mostly sitting up in the building. The day had been very foggy, and the captain of the boat explained he hadn't seen the channel marker to turn. What was so amazing to us was how the captain ran his boat so fast in such foggy conditions. How could he see all the other channel makers previous to the one he was supposed to turn on and not run into them? After that incident Little Harbor installed video cameras to have proof in the event it ever happened again.

I explained to Gina how I thought the boat I was now investigating may have passed by Little Harbor going out; and, therefore, I was trying to get more information.

Gina answered, "I am off the rest of the weekend, but

I will be happy to check the cameras as soon as I return on Monday."

I described the boat color and style to her and gave her the hull ID numbers. She quickly jotted the information down on a napkin before she turned and gave me a hug. I shook Tim's hand before walking out.

I drove up Shell Point Road and thought about my buddy, Marty. I thought I should stop and see him, but it was getting late so I decided to give him a call instead. I drove back out to Highway 41 and turned south to Highway 275, then turned north back across the Skyway Bridge. I always love going over this bridge in the afternoon because the sunsets are completely unobstructed!

Driving is a good time for me to think about things when I am in the middle of an investigation. I reminisced back to when I was still working as a fire investigator. I thought about how a lot of the solutions to problems which I faced in an investigation would come to me during travel.

I realized I would need to get more information from the witness, Espinoza. Since I had already determined this to be arson, Espinoza must have been in the area when the boat was burned or Morgan would have been picked up out in the water since, according to most experts, fire doubles in size every minute. In most cases of a boat of this size burning, the boat would have been significantly involved with fire within four to five minutes.

Suddenly, a thought hit me: was Espinoza involved? If he had seen the fire being set, surely he would have said something to the fire department. What if Espinoza was Morgan's getaway vehicle? If Morgan set the fire, he needed a way back.

"That's it!" I thought . . . or at least that was the most reasonable assumption I could come up with right then.

I can say that sometimes when something seems like it *must* be fact, but talking to the person of interest exposes a perfectly reasonable answer, it pushes the investigator in a different direction. I secretly hoped that was the case this time, because I didn't want to believe that Morgan was an arsonist; however, I also would not deny the truth if that is to what the facts of the case lead me.

"I must get in contact with Espinoza," I whispered to myself.

I got back to *Good Times* and went down to check the fridge to see what I could have for dinner. I had some chicken breast and some salad. I decided I would grill the chicken and make a hot chicken salad.

"Sounds yummy!" I thought, and my stomach growled its agreement.

I fired up the grill and seasoned the chicken and let it sit while the grill warmed up. I grabbed a beer and went out on the back deck—a great place to think.

The back deck was open, but *Good Times* was moored under a large roof, so it felt very homey there. Directly behind her was the concrete dock, and three feet from there was the parking lot. I could park my truck and be steps from the boat, making this very convenient for getting supplies and such.

I could tell the grill was heated up, so I went below and got the chicken and put it on the grill. Often when I am cooking, someone will walk past on the dock and smile and comment about how good it smells. I usually agree, and some small talk ensues about what's been going on around the marina. It is what makes marina life so appealing—getting to know one's neighbors and depending on each other when help is needed. The boating motto is "Help any fellow boater because one day you will need help yourself." Trust me, I have found that to be very true!

After a little bit, the chicken was done; and I took it off the grill and went down below. I cut it into small, bite-sized chunks. I made my salad and poured the chicken across the top and topped it with some ranch dressing for a great meal.

After dinner I sat around thinking about the day's events and how I wished Gina was single. I wondered how the day might have turned out differently. I sat there for a while, daydreaming about her for several minutes before I finally realized what I was doing.

"Not a bad way to spend ten minutes," I laughed.

While I sat in the salon relaxing and thinking, I heard a familiar voice yell outside, "Big Daddy, what the hell are you doing?"

Okay, pause the story for a moment . . . two points: first point, the person doing the yelling was my longtime friend and a fellow marina compadre, Jack. Jack, a retired firefighter, was one of the reasons I came to this marina since he had his boat here. He was what is known as a "blow boater" because he owns a sailboat.

Power boaters and sail boaters always have a friendly rivalry going when talking about boating. The rules that govern boating always favor sail boaters when the sailboat is under sail . . . meaning the sailboat always has the right of way if her sails are up; but as soon as she turns on her engine, she becomes a power boat and must follow all the rules of the road for power boats.

The second point is that my nickname was Big Daddy. I got it back when I was working as a firefighter in the early days. I always called *others* Big Daddy, but somehow it became *my* nickname. I even had people say they didn't even know my real name for a while.

Now, back to the story: I got up and went up on the back deck.

"What the heck is going on?" I asked Jack.

"Oh, just chilling," Jack replied.

Since he wasn't doing anything, I offered him a cold beer, so he came aboard. We sat while I told him about the investigation on which I was working.

"Big Daddy," he gigged me, "I thought you said you were done with that stuff."

"Yeah, yeah," I answered, "but in my defense, it is *on* the water or *below* the water . . . besides *Good Times* needs some new toys. The pay is double, and June talked me into it. It's her fault!"

I shared with him the story and what I had found out so far.

"Sounds like they were bringing something in and trying to dispose of the evidence," he offered.

"Yup, that *is* what it's looking like," I agreed. "The thing that bothers me, though, is that I know the suspect. What are the chances of that?"

"How do you know him?" Jack quizzed.

I told him the story. One good thing about being a private fire investigator is that one is not bound under the same rules to not discuss a case with someone. A *government* investigator may not discuss a case with others who are not involved with that case, but the rule does not apply to private fire investigators.

While we sat there, I got a text from Gina. Apparently, she was back at work early because she had already checked the cameras from the morning in question.

The message read, "The boats didn't pass in front of Little Harbor, but I can see the entrance to the Little Manatee River. I saw two boats come out from the river and head in the direction of Bahia Reef. The boats then both went out-of-sight of the camera. I hope that helps."

I texted her back, "I thought you weren't working until Monday."

"Long story," she responded. "My boyfriend and I got into an argument after you left. He is very jealous and doesn't trust me."

"Sorry," I texted back.

"No, not your problem," she said. "It's HIS," she texted with multiple exclamation points.

"I owe you one," I responded.

She texted back, "Maybe you will need to pay that off sooner than later."

I texted back a smiley face and left it at that. I told Jack whom I was texting. He knew about Gina because I had mentioned her several times before.

"Maybe she is soon to-be-free," he suggested.

"Well, maaaaaybeeee," I said, somewhat hopefully.

Jack and I finished off a few more beers and talked about our boats: some issues we were experiencing with the boats on which we were working and some upgrades I was thinking about adding.

Jack suddenly asked, "Have you heard about the old guy who got flipped by a boater's wake and drowned?"

"No. What happened?"

"A fast boat was coming into Tampa Bay. There was an old guy fishing near the Skyway Bridge. The fast boat flew by the old guy's boat, and the wake from it flipped it. There was a Florida Wildlife Commission (FWC) officer boat nearby who gave chase; but the boat was so fast, it quickly went out-of-sight. They went back to check on the old guy, but he was missing. His boat was capsized. They found his body the next day floating in the water."

"What the hell is wrong with people?" I asked out loud to no one in particular.

"I don't know, Bro," he said. "Sad how some people are."

I finished another beer before Jack said he needed to get back to his boat. Best thing about having a few beers in the marina is that no one has to drive to get back home.

I lay in bed that night thinking about what Gina had said about the boats. I thought I would need to try and check upriver and see if anyone had cameras up that way. I also remembered what she said about paying her back sooner than later.

"Now, that is a debt I *want* to pay!" I thought.

I drifted off to sleep. Gina was a big part of my dreams that night!

The next morning I awoke to the sound of rain. The roof over *Good Times* was metal, so I always knew when it was raining. I lay there just enjoying the sound for a while. Then I thought about my buddy, Marty, who ran a kayak rental business up the Little Manatee.

"Wonder if he has any cameras . . ." I thought, "or maybe he would know where to look for some on other buildings in the area."

I got up and cooked myself some breakfast, just killing time. I figured Marty would be working, because weekends are his best days for business . . . but with this rain I wondered if he would be busy.

I took my time with breakfast; but afterwards, I texted Marty, "Call me when you have time."

He replied, "Will do in a few minutes."

I was sitting on the back deck when my phone rang. The caller ID showed it was Marty.

"What's happening there, Captain?" Marty inquired.

"Oh, just sitting here on *Good Times* enjoying the morning," I responded.

Marty and I attended captain's school together and have been friends for a long time. I told Marty I was investigating a case.

I continued, "I was hoping you have some cameras up at your place . . . or do you know of any other camera locations in your area?"

"Are you not working as a boat captain?" he asked.

"Just taking a short break for this case," I said. "It is technically *on* the water."

Marty agreed that was little better.

"In fact, I *do* have cameras on my building," he said. "They point up and down the river, as well as across the river. It was one of the requirements for me when I got insurance on the place."

I went ahead and told Marty the full story of what I knew so far and asked if he could take a look in his free time to see if he saw boats matching the descriptions in my case. I knew the time frame was between 0600 and 0740, which was the time of the 9-1-1 call.

"No problem," he said, "In fact, I just sent out some customers and currently don't have any waiting."

Marty put me on speaker phone and walked inside. He talked aloud, indicating he was looking at his computer.

"Okay, let's see," he started as I sat listening to him typing on his computer. "Okay, okay. No, that's too early," he said, speaking about a boat heading down the river. "Okay, let's see now . . . this may be something. Okay, I see a center console headed out at 0614. Looks like a charter boat. I have seen him pass here several times. Okay, maybe this is something: at 0720 two boats are up on plane headed down the river. One is a cuddy cabin, and it looks like a single operator; and the other is a center console which had one operator. That guy kinda looks Hispanic. From this angle he looks like he has longer hair."

"Brother, I think you just found what I was looking for!" I said excitedly. "Okay, now can you scan forward to around 0800 hours? Tell me what you see."

Marty scanned through the video, mumbling. "Heading out," he said repeatedly as if he was seeing boats running down river, heading out.

"That is what you would expect this time of the morning . . . wait! Here is something at 0819. Here is a boat heading in or up river. Okay let's see," he drawled out as he slowed down the video, talking out loud. "Well, well," he said.

"What?" I impatiently asked.

"It looks to me like the same boat in which I saw the

Hispanic dude heading up river with the guy that was in the other boat."

"Wow!" I said out loud. "Which way are they headed?"

"Let's see," Marty said slowly as he continued to watch the video. "Looks like they are heading up river and just about to go out-of-sight . . . wait!" he all but shouted. "Now they are slowing down at the Highway 41 bridge. It looks like they are pulling up to the pilings at the bridge. Dang, they went out-of-sight just past the mangrove at the end of the bridge."

"What is up there?" I asked Marty.

"I have been there on the kayaks a few times fishing," he said, "but there's not a lot there. People park their cars on the side of the road just before the bridge and walk down to fish—"

"Easy access to the river," I thought.

"I need to call you back; I got a customer walking in."

"Thanks, Buddy; I owe you a beer."

I sat back in my chair and pondered for a few minutes. So far I knew both boats had headed out together. One burned, and it appeared both occupants were on the other boat when it returned. That was the moment a sickening feeling came over me. My buddy, Morgan, had committed arson and may be involved in some type of drug transportation. Morgan used to be so passionate as a police officer against drug dealers. He excelled in that area of policing due to that passion. I found it saddening to think what must have happened to him.

I grabbed my cell phone and called his number again. I wasn't sure if I really wanted him to answer, but I had a job to do. It again went directly to voicemail and was apparently full of messages.

I texted June, "We need to talk."

"Give me a few minutes," she answered.

While I was waiting to call her, I wondered if Morgan had a new cell phone number. "Maybe that's why he doesn't answer," I thought to myself.

I decided that I would try and call his ex-wife to see if she had any information. However, I was interrupted with my phone ringing.

"I know I said I would call on Monday," I started, "but you will want to know about this!"

I explained to June about Little Harbor and how a friend of mine had checked their camera and what it showed. Then I told her about my buddy, Marty.

"Marty said the boats both went out together; and when the witness's boat returned back up river, Morgan was on the witness's boat. It appeared the boat stopped at the Highway 41 bridge. I believe now they had something in the boat, they took it out, and then burned the boat . . . you know, maybe drugs or something."

"Yes, it sounds like it," June agreed.

"I am going to try and find Morgan. I know his ex-wife, so I will try to contact her. Also, it's strange . . . every time I call Morgan, his phone appears to be off. Maybe he got a new phone number . . . maybe he is hiding . . . I just don't know. You'd think he would contact the insurance company for the payoff money."

"If he brought in drugs, though, he is probably laying low," June speculated.

"Very true," I replied. "I am going to continue trying to find him for an interview. I will update you when I have something new. Oh . . . and June . . . can you contact the insurance company and get a background done on the witness, Juan

Espinoza? I need to start looking at him and see how he ties into all of this."

We both hung up.

I never had Morgan's wife's phone number, so I called a few friends to see if anyone knew it. Each person I talked to asked how Morgan was doing and gave their opinion of how he got shafted for the shooting. Not wanting to gossip about something I wasn't sure, I just agreed with them.

Morgan's ex-wife's name was Cyndi. After a few calls around I found someone who would give me her number. I called her. Cyndi answered the phone.

"Cyndi, this is Ike Smith . . . you remember, Morgan's friend?"

"Oh, yes!" she said. "Hi! How are you, Ike?"

"Fine . . . just fine," I said.

We made small talk for a few minutes. I told her how I had retired and now was a boat captain most of the time. I didn't want to tell her right away that her ex was suspected of arson and maybe drug transportation, so I eased in to it.

"Hey, I am looking for Morgan."

In the public safety field many of us refer to each other by our last names. It's much like the military; and since many who join public safety are prior military, the habit seems to have carried over.

"Ike, I haven't heard from him," she said, "and, truthfully, I am concerned." Her voice cracked. "Tony was supposed to pick up our daughter this weekend but never showed up or called.

"After he got fired and charged, he went downhill. He started drinking a lot and couldn't find a job. He was acquitted of the charges," she said, "but no one will hire him now. He got behind on his child support, so he is going through a really tough time. I tried to help him as much as I could, but my new boyfriend gets angry if I say much to him. He had been getting better with the child support . . . paying a little here and there. He kept telling me he had something he was working on and would catch it all up soon.

"Then, if that wasn't enough, our daughter, Mia, got sick. She has a benign tumor in her brain. It is growing very quickly, and we must have it removed. Since we don't have the county insurance anymore, I don't know what we are going to do. Tony just keeps saying he will have the money soon, but I just don't know how he is going to come up with it if he can't even pay child support.

"He was supposed to keep Mia this weekend so I could work," she repeated, "but he never showed up. Ike, even in the tough times he always showed up for her. I have called his cell number like a hundred times, and it just goes directly to voicemail. I am very concerned," she explained. "I even called his brother, and they haven't heard from him, either."

"Okay, Cyndi. I am sure he will come around soon," I spoke, trying to sound positive. "When I talk with him, I will tell him to call you."

"Ike, we had our problems; but I always respected him and cared for him," she said in a trembling voice.

Knowing she was about to cry, I wished her and the baby well and hung up. I sat back in my chair in the salon on *Good Times*.

"This doesn't sound good," I mulled. "Why would he just disappear like that? If he did move some dope and got paid, I would think spending time and money on his daughter would be the first thing he would do."

Subconsciously people who commit crimes often do good things to help them feel better about themselves . . . except hardened criminals—they couldn't care less. Morgan was not a hardened criminal.

I needed to figure this out. The hair on the back of my neck stood up, and I was getting a bad feeling about Morgan. The drug world is a very dangerous place. Drug dealers get killed all the time by other drug dealers. There is no code, no character, no feelings—just the pursuit of money!

My head started to hurt. I hadn't done this much intense thinking in quite a while. As an investigator, one of the things I knew I must do was to put myself in the mindset of the bad guy. It was often the only way I could figure out what the truth was . . . but it was also draining. When a good person delves into the world of crime and depraved thinking, it can take a toll on them. I realized I hadn't had to do that in a long time since becoming a boat captain . . . and I also realized I didn't miss it!

It was afternoon at the marina.

"I need a beer," I mumbled half out loud.

I went down and got a beer from the fridge and went back up on deck. I sat down and started taking in the sights and sounds that were around me. It was beautiful outside I realized for the first time that day. That was why I always said the boat was my happy place. When I just sit back and take it all in, I always feel better.

Living on a boat, there are never two days that are the same. There was always something different happening. For instance, as I walked out on deck, a duck was under the edge of the dock; and I scared it. Thinking it was a fish, I leaned over to look; but there it went swimming away as quickly as it could.

One beer turned into two, then three; and before I knew it, I was having a party of one sitting right there on the back deck of *Good Times*. Thoughts of the investigation sneaked into my mind; and I would drink another beer, not wanting to think about it anymore that day. When I started pondering what could have happened, I would grab another beer. I pondered a lot that evening and drank a lot of beer.

The next thing I knew, I was walking down the side of the road, looking over into the ditch. Mangroves were just behind the ditch, and I could see the water through the branches. There were trash and junk everywhere, as well as an old couch, a chair, bags—apparently this is where people dumped unwanted trash. I walked forever it seemed.

Something drew me to the ditch. As I looked up ahead, I saw something out of the ordinary. It was clothing; and as I got closer, I caught a whiff of a foul odor. That smell I knew because many times I had smelled it when I was a firefighter, walking up to a house of an older person who hadn't been seen in a while.

I walked closer to the thing; and the closer I got, the more it started to take on the shape of a body! I got up closer and realized I was looking at someone's back. I walked around it to see the face, knowing that once I saw it, I could never unsee it! I looked around the body first and then up to the face. I gasped as I saw the face of my friend, Tony Morgan!

Suddenly, I felt queasy to my stomach, and my head hurt badly! I started rocking back and forth. I could feel the sweat pop out on my forehead. I must have passed out. As I came to, I found myself lying on some carpet . . .

"Wait a minute!" I thought. "I know this carpet. I put this carpet down . . . every piece of it!"

The rocking continued, and I heard yelling. I slowly raised my head up and looked around.

"Slow down!" someone yelled.

As all my senses returned, I was aware of where I was. I was lying on the floor of the salon on *Good Times*. The boat was rocking but slowly settling down. I pulled myself to my feet as I heard people talking outside. I looked to see a boat moving way too fast through the marina and throwing off a rather large wake. I became aware that the yelling came from other boat owners who had come out on their decks to yell at the captain of the fast-moving vessel.

Ugh, my head hurt. That is what happens when one wakes from a nightmare. The feeling of relief came over me when I realized I had been dreaming and obviously drinking too much the night before.

"What was I thinking? Maybe I was just trying *not* to think," I rationalized in my mind.

I sat down in the salon, looking outside trying to get my bearings.

"Dang, I am hungry!" I thought as I tried to remember when was the last time I had eaten. I guessed it to be some time yesterday.

Looking at the clock it read 0930. Normally I wake feeling rested when I am able to sleep in that late, but this morning I was feeling a hangover.

Chapter 6
Captain Ike: A Bad Feeling

My first mission for the day was to get some food. I jumped into my truck and pulled out onto Pasadena Boulevard and headed west. In about a half mile I pulled into the parking lot of a great little breakfast spot named the Comfort Cafe. I walked in and found several waiting for a table. There was a free seat at the bar, so I sat down.

"Coffee?" Madison asked,

"Yes, please; and make it strong."

"Looks like you had a late night," Madison suggested.

"Yes, I guess you could say that."

Madison was a waitress at the Comfort Cafe. Right then she looked to be 10 months pregnant, but she had the hustle of someone who was in their first week as a waitress on a trial period. She was always smiling and friendly, and I considered myself lucky that she was my waitress. She served up the coffee quickly.

As she jotted down my order of two eggs over light, grits, and a double side of sausage with one pancake, she laughingly probed, "Hungry this morning, Captain?"

"Yeah, I didn't eat last night . . . long story," I mumbled.

She served my breakfast, and I took to it like a fish

to a shrimp. As I was eating, I started thinking about the investigation and that dang dream.

"Where did that come from?" I asked myself. "It was the last thing I was thinking before apparently passing out on the floor the night before," I surmised.

Funny how a person dreams about things they are worried about. I hoped the dream was not some kind of premonition. I wondered that if the dream became reality, how would I contact Cyndi? Surely when I walked up to her door, the look on my face would say it all. She would burst into tears . . . I stopped that thought right there.

My cell phone chirped, and I looked down to see a text from June.

"Check your email for the background on Espinoza. Looks like you are on the right path."

I finished my breakfast and drove back to *Good Times*. It was Monday. I always worked out on Monday, Wednesday, and Friday. I quickly changed and headed up to the gym. Today's workout was chest, shoulders, and triceps. Getting the blood pumping is the best medicine for a hangover in my opinion . . . and lots of coffee, of course. Feeling better and strong after a long, hard workout, I jumped back in my truck and returned to *Good Times*.

Thinking a shower was in order, I went to the forward head. I showered and took care of my morning duties.

Feeling refreshed, I opened my laptop and pulled up the email from June. I opened the attached file and sat down in the salon to take a look. Espinoza had a lengthy criminal history, including charges of possession and distribution of drugs, possession of firearms, and many other charges.

"Yup, yup," I thought in my mind.

When things like that start to line up, I begin seeing the facts: Morgan and Espinoza apparently committed arson, and they moved some type of drugs up the river and then to who knows where?

At this point in a private investigation, I usually would be nearing completion. I had determined that an arson had occurred. I had evidence that some other type of drug crime had occurred but no proof . . . just suspicion. I sat back in my chair, pondering what I should do next.

After my conversation with Cyndi, I was becoming suspicious that something *had* happened to Morgan. I decided I must notify the Tampa Police Department (TPD) of my findings since it was in their jurisdiction. I had proof that an arson occurred and the possibility of a missing person. I decided to contact my buddy, Chris Thompson. I used to work with him at the city police department. He now worked at TPD.

Typically, when a crime is reported, one normally calls 9-1-1 or the regular TPD line. The crime is reported to a call taker, and that call taker dispatches a street officer (mostly new officers). They write up a report; and if there is no immediate evidence of a crime or an arrest to be made, they forward that report to a detective. Based on case load the detective then contacts the person who reported the possible crime for a follow-up. This can take hours or days, again depending on the case load of the detective and how the crime is rated . . . meaning did it just occur and is there evidence to obtain, or has it been a while? If it has been a while, it mostly likely will be some time before the reporting person is contacted.

Knowing something may have happened to Morgan, I wanted to skip those steps. Since I didn't have Chris's number in my phone, I went on Facebook and sent him a message. He responded right away.

"What's up?" he wrote.

"Hey, I need to talk to you. Can you send me your number? It is important."

"Sure," he said, followed by his number.

I asked, "When would be a good time to call?"

"Now is good. I am just sitting here at my desk doing reports."

I called him immediately.

"Hey, Bro. How you doing?"

"Good," Chris replied.

"What are you doing there at TPD now?" I asked. "Last time we talked you were working that task force for a serial killer."

"I am now a detective," he said.

"Oh, perfect! That's just what I need. I have information on an arson and probably some dope transportation in your jurisdiction."

"I'm all ears. What do you have?"

"Okay, do you remember Tony Morgan? He used to work for the city and then went to work for the Hillsborough County Sheriff's Office (HCSO)."

"No, I don't really remember him," Chris answered.

I went on to tell the story of Morgan's getting involved in the shooting, getting fired, and the aftermath.

That must have jogged his memory because Chris spoke up, "Yeah . . . I remember reading about it now. We even talked a lot about it over here. The guy is out there trying to do a job, he makes a mistake, and then is brought up on charges. I have always worried the same thing could happen to me."

"I sure do remember having those fears myself when I was working. It is a crazy time," I said. "Anyway, back to the case: I was contracted privately to do an investigation on a boat fire."

I went on to tell Chris about the fire and how I believed it occurred, the info I had on the boats, and what the video showed. I told him why I feared something may be wrong with Morgan. I gave him the TPD and TFD case numbers from the reports.

"Okay, I am working on some reports that I am behind on now; but as soon as the boss gets back in the office, I will talk with him about this case. I will call you when I know something."

"Okay, that sounds great. I appreciate it."

After we hung up, I began thinking about Morgan. He was weighing heavily on my mind. I thought about how he must have felt after the accidental shooting of the unarmed subject.

Every officer I have ever talked to about this scenario has always been very afraid of this possibility happening to them. They all worry that if in a split-second decision they decide to pull the trigger, they will be critiqued for days, months, or even years about that decision. Too many times like this the decision turns political, and the officer and their family are often destroyed.

"Was that the case here?" I pondered.

I believed it was as I continued to contemplate the subject. I thought about how it must have gone down the day he was told that charges were being filed against him . . . how he was looked at as a criminal and how abandoned he must have felt: after giving so many years of service to be turned against as if *he* was the criminal . . . how that most likely led to his divorce and family break-up . . . how, when meeting someone new, he would have to tell again what happened, knowing he would again be judged based on that one, split-second decision!

My phone chirped, and I looked down to see a new message. It was my business line, and someone left a message about interest in a charter. It seemed they were referred from a previous client. He wanted me to return the call and set up a date for this coming weekend, if possible.

I pondered the thought for a minute. There was so much happening with the case right now, and I may be the only person who was aware that something had possibly happened to Morgan. I owed it to Morgan to stay on this case until we had some kind of resolution. I decided I would call the guy back and put him on ice for a few days—tell him I was unavailable and would contact him as soon as I could give him a date.

"I would much rather be booking this charter right now instead of dealing with this case," I thought. "However, priorities are priorities; and a life may be hanging in the balance here."

I returned the call to the prospective client and told him I would get back with him soon with some concrete dates.

Chapter 7
Tony Morgan: My Back Story

Mid-February 2018

"Morgan, Tony Morgan," the lady called out.

I got up slowly, looked around, and walked up to the counter.

"Have you completed the application?" the lady asked.

"Yes, Ma'am, the best I know how," I said. "I have never applied for food stamps before, Ma'am."

The lady held out her hand, and I passed her the application. She perused the paperwork, her eyes scanning down to the bottom.

"You understand it's a felony to knowingly apply for and receive food stamps under false pretenses?" she quizzed.

"Yes, Ma'am," I replied. "I am unable to get a job right now, but I hope to soon. I just need help for a little bit until I get back on my feet."

"Okay," she replied, "just have a seat, and someone will be with you in a minute."

I walked back over and sat down in the seat and looked around the noisy room. Moms with their kids, senior citizens, and some really rough-looking people filled the waiting area.

I felt like the biggest loser ever. How could I be doing so well just a few years ago and now I am sitting in the food stamp line?

"I know why," I answered myself.

A few years ago I was on top of the world. I worked my way up through the city police department and then was hired on at the sheriff's department. My forte was working narcotics . . . or dope as we more commonly called it. When I was a kid, I lost my only brother to a drug overdose. As I got older and got into law enforcement, I swore that I would do everything I could to stop the flow of illegal drugs. I worked hard and became very well known for my narcotic seizures.

I was promoted to sergeant in the narcotics unit. I was so motivated I ended up writing and being the case agent on most search warrants issued out of our unit. My goal was to execute at least one warrant a week, and we often made that goal and more.

One time we were working a known dope area. We looked for and found known dealers by conducting lawful traffic stops, looking for dope.

This particular night we stopped a vehicle, and I walked up to the passenger side of the car; my partner went to the driver's side. There was a black male sitting in the passenger seat. I had my light in one hand and was looking down through the windshield toward the floorboard. I saw a gun sticking out from under the seat right below the black male's legs.

I yelled, "Gun!" and told the guy not to move.

I pulled my weapon and had it pointed right at the guy. He was sweating profusely.

I yelled again, "Do not move toward that gun, or I *will* shoot you!"

Just about the time I said that, the guy reached down toward the gun. Just as he touched it, I fired once, striking him in the abdomen. We secured the weapon and called an ambulance. Additional officers arrived along with fire department and ambulance personnel. The guy was taken to the hospital and survived his injuries.

I was placed on administrative leave for a few days and later was removed from the narcotics unit until the state attorney's office finally cleared me of the shooting . . . after four, long months.

It became clear to me that most people have no clue how stressful it is to be under that type of investigation. The first thing they tell an officer under investigation is not to discuss the case with anyone . . . not a co-worker, a boss, or *anyone*! Imagine how it would feel to not be able to speak with anyone about the case . . . about the mind's doubts or the reassurance that any human would crave at a time like this. It's natural to question if something could have been done differently. However, every time I thought about it, I came back to the same conclusion: if the bad guy had not reached for the gun, I would have never shot; and both of us would be better off today.

After that shooting, I would often think about getting out of law enforcement. I worried that if I had to shoot someone again that I may react slowly and be killed myself . . . or I could shoot and kill a person and be brought up on charges. I found myself not wanting to get into situations that could go badly. I realized after that shooting that I lost the drive to work dope cases. I knew that each case I worked I may be one step closer to being involved in a shooting.

Early one Friday morning I, along with my team, had obtained a search warrant for a known dope house. We had confidential informants (CIs) buying dope from the house. We knew who the occupants were because we had been working the case for several months. This case was what we called high risk. During the dope buy a CI gave detailed intelligence (intel) about guns that were seen in the house. He stated there was a shotgun at the door, and each of the subjects inside always carried a handgun.

Dope houses are extremely dangerous places. The dopers have to worry about law enforcement, as well as dope robbers, people who rob dope houses of the drugs and cash. Background checks on the subjects showed violence toward law enforcement and violence charges against the public in general.

Due to the extreme threat in this case we were given a "no knock" search warrant. This meant when we executed the warrant, we didn't have to knock and yell "Police!" which would possibly give the bad guys time to get their guns.

This particular house had been hit before by our unit. In these areas when one bad guy gets caught and goes to jail, another simply opens up shop behind him. During briefing we were given detailed information on the layout of the house. The layout showed that when we entered the front door, we would be in the living room/kitchen. Immediately to our left was a bedroom door, and looking forward down the hall would be a bedroom with a bathroom on the right.

I was placed as fifth person in the stack, meaning I was the fifth person in line to enter the house. The first two guys were the entry guys; they had forcible entry tools. Their job was to force the door open quickly. Then the rest of the guys on the team would flow in behind them, searching the house as they went.

We all lined up early that morning for our safety gear check. The commander of the team would go man-by-man, confirming all their gear was on and squared away. Starting at the head he would touch the helmet, looking for safety goggles. Working down he would check the gun strap and long gun, checking the magazine. He checked the vest and then checked the sidearm and magazine. The commander then turned the officer around to confirm their radio was on and at the proper channel. A slap on the back meant they were good to go, and the approved officer would then load into the van.

Once we were all loaded up in the van, we headed to the search warrant location. Enroute to the target we began a mental checklist of our equipment again, knowing this would be the last possible chance to be sure we were ready. In our mind we each went through what our duties were and go over all the training we had leading up to this point. A quick prayer would be in order here, praying that every man would enter and exit the building safely. A thought of my wife and child would always go through my mind at this time. I would suppress it because I had a job to do, and others were counting on me just as I was counting on them to get it right!

We would do this early in the morning because most bad guys would be sleeping at that time.

"Two blocks," the commander barked, and we were all quiet, intensely thinking about the job ahead.

"One block," the commander announced a little quieter.

Holding onto the overhead grab bar, we each felt the van slow and then stop. Everyone was quiet now. We pulled up one house shy of the intended target house. In single file the team slowly and quietly headed from the van to the house. The only sound heard was from a few dogs barking in the neighborhood and the sounds of men and boots moving slowly—but deliberately—across the ground.

We stacked up on the front porch—ten men in all—standing inches from each other. Each man had one hand on his brother's shoulder standing in front of him. The first two entry guys readied their tools and nodded to the commander standing last in the stack. He quietly and gently squeezed the shoulder of the man standing in front of him. Then that man would do the same shoulder-squeeze to the man in front of him. This would continue like dominos falling until the shoulder-squeeze reached the first person in the stack. That meant all were ready.

The commander's final nod to the forcible entry tool guys would start the entry. Using a large battering ram, they would swing it, hitting the knob of the door until it broke open. Once the door was broken open, the next man would throw a flash bang or distraction device into the house.

The flash bang is a small, can-like device with a handle mechanism. Once released, it makes a very loud bang and concussion. Any person standing near the flash bang would be distracted for a few seconds. After the device was thrown into the house, we would wait for a couple of seconds until we heard the loud boom. The team would then start flowing through the doorway like water, one-by-one.

Chapter 8
Captain Ike: Dope on the Rocks

My phone chirped again, and I looked down to see a message from Chris Thompson.

"Call me," it read, so I quickly called him back.

"What's up, Bud?"

"I talked to the captain," Chris said, "and he wants to meet with you and see what all you've got."

"No problem; how about in the morning first thing?"

Chris must have been standing near his captain because I heard him ask if the early morning worked.

"Good," I heard Chris say. Then turning back to me over the phone, he continued, "Can you make 9 a.m.?"

"No problem," I replied. "Downtown on Franklin Street?"

"Yes," Chris replied. "I will meet you in the lobby at 9."

"I will be there."

I spent the rest of the afternoon and evening thinking about some of the things I needed to do. I needed to find Morgan and was working mentally on that. Okay, his cell wouldn't help because it appeared to be turned off. What was the last known place he was seen? Marty's video put him on the river at the Highway 41 bridge. I needed to check that spot out; I needed to put eyes on it and see what was there.

I also needed to find Espinoza. I looked in the report under the witness section and found his cell number. I wrote it down in my case notes and thought about calling it, but I figured I better get a burner phone and call from that phone. The last thing I wanted was a bad guy with my cell number. I hadn't had the need for a burner phone in a long time. I decided to run up to Walmart and purchase one. This was an expense that I would be able to add to my expense account.

A burner phone is a cell phone from which a person can make a phone call to someone whom they don't want calling them back. Once the call is made, they can get rid of it. A rookie mistake would be to call the bad guy from one's own cell number and have them call the officer back in order to figure out who they are.

The good thing about Walmart is that they are everywhere. There was one about a mile away. I needed some beer, anyway, so I thought I would kill two birds with one stone. It didn't take me 30 minutes, and I was back.

I sat down and contemplated the phone call. I really wasn't sure that it would be his actual number, but I had to try anyway. I got the burner phone and dialed the number. After three rings a Spanish voice answered the phone.

"Bob, how are you doing, Man?"

"You got the wrong number," the other person said.

Acting as if I was drinking and a little intoxicated, I kept saying, "Bob, come on, Man. Quit playing."

The other voice finally said, "Listen, you drunk, old man. I don't know no Bob. This is Juan."

Okay, okay, I am sorry, Man. Just trying to reach Bob," I played it off.

Click, and the call ended.

"Hmmm, well, what were the chances that Juan gave a fake number and someone by the name of Juan answered? That's slim to none. Not such a smart guy," I figured.

I decided when Juan was asked for his number for the report, he didn't think quickly enough to come up with a different number. I added the date and time of the call into the case notes.

The next morning I awoke around 7 and got going. Tampa is only about 45 minutes to an hour away, depending on traffic. I fired up the coffee pot and made myself some eggs and sausage for breakfast. I sat on the back deck, enjoying the early morning hours as I ate my breakfast and drank coffee. Speaking to the occasional passerby on the docks, time quickly slipped by, and it was almost 8. I needed to get going. I grabbed my best Guy Harvey shirt; I already had shorts on. I thought about changing but figured who am I trying to impress? I slipped on my crocs and jumped in the truck.

This time of the morning is a crap shoot as to which way to go: I-275 N through St. Pete or over the Skyway Bridge? I decided on the I-275 N route, hoping the traffic wouldn't be too bad. I must have been living right because, other than the occasional slow-down at the inevitable wreck, I made it to Tampa in 50 minutes. It took another five minutes to find parking.

Inside the lobby I found Chris waiting, talking with another officer.

"Hey, Bro, how's it going?" I asked.

"Good, good," he said. "I see you put on your best clothes," he gigged me.

"See, now, I thought about that for a minute but realized I

don't have to impress anyone . . . so here I am." I held out my arms as I spoke.

"Well, come on in," Chris laughed. "The captain is waiting. Have you got any weapons on you?"

"Nah, I knew better than to bring that in."

"Good!" he said. "One less thing we have to check."

Up the elevator we went, chatting about what he had been up to lately. We stepped out of the elevator and strolled down a short hall of offices.

Chris stopped at one and leaned into it as he said, "We are here, Cap."

The captain was on the phone and nodded toward the conference room. We walked in and sat down. Chris and I sat there for a minute as he told me about his new detective gig and how much he enjoyed it there.

The captain walked in. I stood and extended my hand.

"Captain Henry," he introduced himself.

"Captain Ike," I replied with a smirk.

Looking at my attire he asked, "*Boat* captain?"

"Yes, Sir," I replied. "The best rank I have ever held . . . and a lot less stressful," I added. "Detective Thompson tells me you were a fire investigator."

"Yes, Sir. I worked in the public sector for 23 years, then several years as a private fire investigator."

"So, tell me about this case," he prompted.

I told the captain that I was contacted and then contracted to work the case. I told him about my diving training and why June reached out to me. I told him about the arson and about the hole in the boat. I also informed him of the camera footage I got and where the boat was last seen at the Highway 41 bridge. More importantly, I told him about knowing Tony Morgan and a little about him. I told him about the conversations with Morgan's ex-wife. I also told him about Espinoza and how I had confirmed his phone number.

At this point Chris broke in, "We have already looked at the file about him, and he's a real winner looks like."

"Yes," I said, "that's why I am concerned. I mean, why hasn't Morgan contacted his ex? Based on my conversation with her, he would have contacted her by now."

Captain Henry spoke up, "Okay, based on the info about the boat I will put in a work order to have it raised and brought in for evidence. Do we know the whereabouts of Espinoza?" he asked.

Chris answered, "His last known address is in Polk County."

"We need to reach out to the sheriff's office there and see if we can get them to do a ride by to see if Espinoza is still living there."

"I will take care of that," Chris said.

I spoke up, "I am planning to ride by the Highway 41 bridge to see if any evidence might be found there."

Chris interjected, "Captain, should I go with him?"

"It's out of our jurisdiction," he replied, "but it should be okay." As an afterthought, the captain added, "Also reach out to the HCSO and let them know what we are working on since it is in their district. One more thing: we should find out if they brought some dope in at the Highway 41 bridge."

The captain stood as if to end the meeting.

"Captain, I have Espinoza's cell number," I offered. "Can you guys ping it and see where it shows up? I think he is actually still using it."

"Okay, good idea," he said, looking and nodding at Chris.

"I am on it, Sir," Chris responded.

"Is there anything else?" the Captain asked, looking at the two of us.

I shook my head no; and Chris did, as well.

"Let me grab my bag," Chris said, "and I will meet you downstairs."

I nodded okay. I went down to the lobby.

They have old police cars and police memorabilia in the lobby at TPD. They even have an old helicopter there. I was looking inside of it when Chris made a slight whistle and nodded toward the door. I caught up with him; and we discussed that he would need to drive his car, and I would drive mine.

"Of course. I don't want to drive back through all this traffic," I laughed.

"I need to fuel up," Chris said, "so how about we meet at the bridge?"

"Sounds good," I said. "I will see ya there."

I made my way east on Highway 60 to South 22nd Street. This section runs by the docks of Tampa. It has a taller bridge, and one can see all of the boats in dock, as well as cruise ships in port. It is one of my favorite drives in Tampa . . . but the wise driver won't go through there early in the morning or later in the afternoon: the traffic will make a non-cursing man curse! I have even made up a few new words. I turned on Highway 41 S and didn't stop until I reached the bridge at Highway 41 and the Little Manatee River, the spot where I believed the dope came ashore.

I pulled over on the side of the road and parked. I didn't see Chris, yet, so I got out to have a look around. I walked up on the bridge to look down near the water's edge. I saw areas that looked like fishermen had walked down to the bank.

About that time I heard a siren chirp and looked up to see Chris pulling in. He walked up on the bridge where I was. It didn't feel really safe because cars were whizzing by us at 60 mph. I told Chris this was the spot that my buddy, Marty, had seen on his camera where the boat turned. However, with all of this traffic it seemed to be visible only to passersby to me.

I then looked down river and realized I couldn't see Marty's place from the bridge. At that moment, I noticed that the bridge where Marty said he saw the boat turn in was the fixed rail bridge about 50 yards down river. I pointed this out to Chris, so we walked back down off the bridge and looked for a way to get through the red mangroves to some railroad tracks. With some searching we found a spot and walked up on the tracks and toward the river. Once we reached the river, we could tell the path down to the water was much less used ... probably due to how hard it was to get to.

We walked out on the bridge. Now, from there, we could see Marty's place. Marty had said the boat turned just before the bridge. Looking down off the edge of the bridge I could see the water was deep right up to the bank.

About that time I heard the familiar sound of a loud horn. Looking north I saw a large train headed toward us. We were about a quarter of the way on the bridge, so we turned and started to move quickly toward the end of the bridge. It's pretty hard to move fast on these types of bridges because there is no good solid surface to walk on. The train gave several more, quick bursts as if to say "Get off the bridge, you idiots!" We both made it to the end just as the train started to come onto the bridge from the other side. Stumbling down the rocks I went down one side and Chris the other. As the train came barreling by us, I became aware of just how big they are. The thought crossed my mind of what would have been the result if we hadn't made it.

I pushed myself back into the branches of the mangrove trees, getting as much distance between me and the train. It was a long train, and it took about three minutes to pass. While it was passing and I became more confident I wasn't going to die, I started looking down the edge of the bridge toward the water. Noticing how secluded it was I thought how they might feel comfortable bringing in the dope here.

I looked at the ground down the path toward the bridge. I noticed some small, colorful things lying on the ground. It looked like it spread mostly down the bank toward the water. As soon as the train had completely passed, I hollered over to Chris.

He yelled back, "You good?"

"Yup," I said, "but I must admit that this is not my favorite place to hang out."

As we talked, I got a closer look at what I saw on the ground. It looked like little pills. I yelled for Chris to come over and take a look.

Chris walked up, and I pointed to the pills. I reached down and picked up a couple of them. They looked very weathered as if they had been here for a while. I passed one to Chris; he bounced it around in his palm. I asked him what he thought. He shrugged as he examined them more closely.

"Some kind of drugs," he finally said.

"Oh, you think?" I laughed.

"Well, damn, Man. You don't expect me to know every drug, do you? I have been working in detectives, you know.

This stuff changes so fast out there on the street, you can't keep up with it."

"Looking at them, they look like they were dropped somehow as they were carried up the bank," I observed.

"Let me take a picture for evidence before you go any closer," Chris said.

I stepped back, and he took several pictures from different angles.

"I need to get an evidence bag from my car," Chris said.

I responded, "I am going to take a closer look down by the water."

"Okay, but can you at least stay out of the evidence?"

"Okay, I will try," I retorted as I smiled and started down the bank.

I eased down the edge, trying to stay clear of the pills. I wondered what could have happened for the pills to be scattered here. I got down to the bottom and had to squeeze past the bridge edge and the mangrove trees that were sticking out. After clearing the trees, it opened to a sandy area under the bridge. It looked like a typical tidal area where water had moved in and out over the sand. Looking around I could see the pill trail stopped at the bridge area and the mangroves; however, in the dirt were around 50 of the little pills piled together.

Chris came walking down the path.

"They stop there," I said, pointing.

"Well, come on. You got me in this mess; you can help pick them all up."

He handed me a bag, and we both started collecting the pills. Once we picked them all up, we walked back down to the water.

"So, it looks like they brought whatever this is," Chris started, holding up a plastic bag of pills, "and took them up the bank. I guess they had a car parked up there." Chris projected. "I'm thinking that they didn't bring the boat in here because the bank is way too steep and not wide enough."

"Very true," I said as I looked around and pondered his statement.

Looking down the river at Marty's place I didn't see anyone outside . . . but then again, it was a Monday, so I wouldn't expect to see anyone.

"I need to call Marty back," I told Chris.

"Why is that?"

"Well, he said he saw the boat pull in here behind these mangroves and then go out-of-sight; but if they didn't get out here, where did they get the boat out?"

We stood there for a minute, both thinking and looking around.

"Okay, check this out," I said. "If they brought drugs in at this spot, there must have been a reason. They didn't want to bring them in the boat—to either a dock or a boat ramp—so there must be a boat ramp close to here."

Chris nodded in agreement while still thinking about it.

"Well, there's nothing else here," Chris said, "so let's head back up."

"Okay," I said as I nodded.

We worked our way back up the bank across the tracks and through the mangroves out to our vehicles.

"Okay, let's get off the side of the road. Pull down to the next road and let's talk," Chris suggested.

We got into our cars and drove just a few hundred feet down to Gulf City Road. We pulled in and parked driver side to driver side so we could easily talk without getting out of our vehicles.

"I am going to call Marty back to see if he can see anything else from the cameras."

"Okay," Chris answered. "I will get the lab to tell us what this is."

"Chris, did you have time to contact anyone from the sheriff's office yet about the case?"

"Yes, I put in a call to a counterpart there on my way down here but haven't gotten a call back yet. I will keep trying," he said.

"Here is the problem I see, Ike. Based on what we know so far, a boat was burned in the bay; so, we have an arson that occurred within the city limits. These drugs appeared to have been brought ashore in the county. Both Espinoza and Morgan last resided in Polk County. So, we are dealing with three different jurisdictions. I don't have to tell you what a cluster that is, right?"

"No," I agreed, "but I had a bad dream about finding Morgan dead the other night. Based on my conversation with Morgan's wife, Cyndi, the other day, I think something has happened to Morgan; and we have to do something."

"I feel your pain, Buddy. I know he was a friend to you, but now it just looks like a bad cop gone even more badly."

"I know," I answered quietly, shaking my head, "but can you do me a big favor?"

"That question doesn't sound good," Chris answered with a smile.

"You got Espinoza's number, right?"

He nodded.

"Will you ping it for me, get me a last known location . . . and do it in the middle of the night?"

"Why in the middle of the night?"

"If he still has it on and you can ping it, then wherever it hits in the night will be where he is staying."

Grinning, Chris nodded.

"Okay, Old Guy. Seems like you still got it."

I laughed, "'Old guy'? You are quickly catching up to me!"

"Okay, expect a text tonight," he said.

"Thanks, Buddy."

I started my truck and pulled away, turning south back onto Highway 41. It was getting close to noon, and I was getting hungry. Little Harbor was just a few minutes away, so I decided to go by there for lunch.

"Maybe Gina is working," I thought as I pulled into the parking lot and went to the beach side tiki bar.

Walking in I saw Gina standing near the entrance, talking to some guests. As soon as she saw me, a big smile crossed her face. I sat down at the tiki bar as she quickly ended the conversation with the couple and headed straight over to me. She walked up smiling and gave me a very nice hug. If felt like she held it much longer than ever before.

"How are you doing, My Captain?" she asked.

"'My Captain' . . ." I repeated. "Well, I sure would love to be *your* captain," I added as I smiled and winked at her.

As she pulled back from me and looked up in my eyes, I noticed what looked like a faded, black eye. I softly reached out and caressed her chin and asked her what happened.

"It's a long story," she said as her smile turned into a look of sadness.

I was processing in my mind what could be going on.

"Did someone hit you, Gina?"

"I can't go into it right now, Ike; it makes me cry, and I have done too much of that at work lately. Can we talk about it at another time?"

I patted and rubbed her shoulders as I answered, "Yes, we can . . . no problem."

"I want to hear about this case you are working on," she said, shifting the subject.

"Pull up a seat . . . do you have time to chat for a bit?"

"Yes, just for a few minutes, though. Then I have to get back to work."

"Okay. Well, since we talked, I have met with TPD. We talked about the arson and all that has occurred up to this point. Chris, a buddy of mine who works at TPD, and I went down to the Highway 41 bridge at the train trestle. Another buddy of mine has video cameras on the river, and he saw the boat pass his place and stop near the bridge. Chris and I went down to see if anything was there. We found some drugs scattered around, but we don't yet know what it is."

"Wow!" she said. "So, I helped solve a crime?"

"Yup, you were a vital aspect of this investigation, Ma'am," I laughed. "I will have to put you in for a commendation with the chief of police!"

Gina smiled and asked, "So, what's next?"

"Well, I hope to get a text tonight from Chris with information on where a cell phone is located. The owner of the cell phone is a suspect in the case; and hopefully, he is still using it so we can get his location. Then maybe I can find my friend, Morgan. He has a young daughter who is sick, and I am worried something has happened to him."

"I hope not," Gina replied.

"Yeah, me, too."

Gina got up and said she needed to get back to work. She leaned over and lightly kissed me on the cheek.

"We need to talk, Gina."

"Okay," she answered. "Can I text you later?"

"Sure. I am headed back to the *Good Times* now, so I will wait on your text."

She smiled and walked away.

Chapter 9
Tony Morgan: My Three Worst Days

As soon as we heard the boom, the team flowed into the house. The first two guys in the door turned and went into the first door on the left while yelling, "Police, search warrant . . . police, search warrant." This was always constantly yelled during any entry to warn the occupants of who was incoming.

During an entry, a doorway is never passed until the room is cleared. A bad guy could be standing there with a gun and shoot an officer in the back. Within seconds of entering the room, a familiar "all clear" was heard. The next two guys in the stack ahead of me moved right into the living room/kitchen area.

I was next in line. I moved toward the door of the bedroom left.

"Door left," I yelled.

This message informed the other team members to stack up behind me so we could enter that room. I felt the squeeze on my shoulder and the familiar "I am with you" behind me. I kicked the door open and started to enter the room. It was still dark outside, and no lights were on in the house.

My MP5 has a light attached to the end of the barrel, and that was how we would see to clear rooms. I stepped into the room hollering, "Police, search warrant . . . police, search warrant." Just as I cleared the doorway and turned right, I saw a black male subject lean up from a bed and point at me what I thought was a gun. At that split second, I heard one loud shot. I fired my MP5 twice into the center mass of the suspect's chest. The suspect fell back into the bed and didn't move again.

"What happened?" the commander barked from the other room.

"Suspect down," I yelled. In a quieter tone, I repeated, "Suspect down."

I quickly keyed the mike on the radio and called dispatch.

"Respond, EMS and fire," I said into my ear piece. "One suspect down with two gunshots to the chest."

The information regarding the suspect's condition is intended to be passed along to EMS so they know ahead of time with what they are dealing. After telling this story many times, I'm often questioned about why I called EMS. Under the law we don't shoot to kill; we shoot to stop the threat. Once the threat is stopped, we must try and save the suspect's life.

I stood covering the suspect with my gun, waiting for the commander to move up. I heard someone talking behind me. One of the officers mentioned "AD" (accidental discharge). I wasn't sure what they were talking about as I was focused on the guy I had just shot. He was not moving, and I could tell his breathing was slowing. The commander moved into the room behind me.

"What happened?" he repeated as he looked at the downed suspect.

"The suspect shot at me," I said, "and I returned fire two times."

Someone behind me flipped the light on in the room. The commander moved up, slowly looking over the scene.

"Where is his gun?" he asked.

"Up under him, I guess."

The commander reached into his pocket and pulled out some rubber gloves and put them on. The first thing we are trained to do after a shooting is to secure the suspect's gun. I heard the sirens of the ambulance pulling up outside. The commander moved the blanket around under which the suspect was lying, looking for the gun.

"I don't see it," he said.

Lying beside the suspect was a cell phone. The commander reached down and picked it up. About that time, the ambulance crew bustled into the room with their medical equipment.

"Is the scene secure?" they asked.

"Not sure," the commander answered. "Anyway, can we get this guy out of the room?" he asked.

"Sure," one of the EMS workers responded.

The room filled with EMS workers and fire personnel. They got a sheet from the stretcher and laid it beside the suspect. They rolled him over onto the sheet and lifted him up. This left the scene intact. After moving him into the living room, they started working on him.

I stayed in the room with the commander and other team members. We started moving stuff around, looking for the gun.

"Where did he drop it?" the commander quizzed.

"Not sure," I replied. "When I fired the two shots, he fell right back onto the bed. It should be there."

I stood watching as the commander and team members moved the entire bed, piece by piece. The search went on for several minutes. I watched the search and listened to the EMS workers talking in the living room. Suddenly, I heard one of them say the suspect was dead! A sinking feeling started in my gut.

"What just happened?" I thought.

In just a few minutes the team and commander had moved just about everything around in the room, and there was no gun. The commander looked up and walked over to me.

"Let's walk outside," he said.

At the time there were at least 15 people moving around inside the house. As I walked past the suspect lying on the floor, I noticed he was hooked up to a monitor that had a flat line on the screen. This was usually the definitive confirmation that the person was dead.

"So, tell me what happened," the commander said.

"I moved into the room. The suspect sat up and pointed what I thought was a gun. I heard a gunshot, and I fired," I said.

"He didn't shoot," the commander said. "That was an AD from Frans behind you."

That feeling came back in my stomach, and I felt like I was going to puke. The commander stepped back and keyed up his mike and requested the chief be notified of a suspect shooting and crime scene be dispatched.

The commander stood talking to a lieutenant and a sergeant who came by the scene.

Within moments the commander walked back over to me and said, "I am going to need your weapons."

Those words to this day run chills down my spine each time I think of them. I wake up with nightmares about that moment because I knew that an investigation would now be done on me.

The next few days and weeks were a blur. An internal investigation was initiated by the sheriff's department per the request of the chief. This is common in an officer-involved shooting.

During that time as the news spread throughout our agency that I had apparently mistakenly shot an unarmed man, I was placed on administrative leave pending the outcome of the investigation. Though I had been through this before, this time was different. I found myself sitting around at home, thinking about the case . . . thinking about what I could have done differently and why it had happened to me. In a situation like this, one's mind can turn to the worse outcomes; and that is what one ponders. I wished many times I had never become a cop!

I was going crazy sitting around at home. My wife, Cyndi, tried to console me, but she didn't understand the gravity of the situation. I would find reasons to stop by the sheriff's office, trying to find out any information. However, per the rules, no one would talk to me about the case except for those simply saying "it will all work out" or "it could happen to anyone." None of those gave me any solace. Funny thing about a situation like this is people quit talking and simply hurry past . . . whether out of protocol or that they just don't know what else to say, the silence and furtive glances only isolate all the more.

Time went by very slowly, and I was losing my mind!

Waiting to hear my fate was the worst part. Watching tv only made it worse. There were stories every couple of days about the shooting. Soon the story painted me as a racist cop who ran around shooting black people. The black community started having marches on city hall calling for charges against me. The media interviewed some family member of the suspect who described how he was a "good boy who has never done anything wrong" or "he just did what he had to do" or "he wasn't hurtin' nobody." The voices got louder and louder.

Administration wouldn't speak up for me. They would just say it was "under investigation" or "no comment."

I logged into Facebook and read the stories of the shooting and then read the comments. People called me every name in the book and threatened me and my family. My wife also read these stories and started getting scared that something would happen to herself or our daughter.

Then someone somehow got my address and posted it on Facebook. People started spreading it, and I started getting threats on other social media outlets. One night someone drove by the house and shot a paintball at the front door. Though no one was hurt, it was enough to spook my wife. Our daughter's bedroom was on the front of the house, and Cyndi just kept worrying that someone might use an actual gun the next time.

About a week and a half later, Cyndi came home from work. She had a look on her face like something was wrong.

"What's wrong?" I asked.

"We need to talk," she said.

Another sinking feeling grew in my gut. She went on about how her parents thought it would be best if she moved in there for a while . . . just until the situation all blew over.

"It is only temporary," she said. "It's for our safety. As soon as it's all over, we will come home."

I protested but could tell her mind was made up. I helped her pack some stuff . . . mostly clothing. I looked into her eyes occasionally and saw tears collecting in the corners. It took only about 30 minutes, and she said she had what she needed.

"It will only be a little while," she repeated.

I helped her load the stuff into the car. I held my daughter and felt tears rolling down my face. Trying to stay tough, I used my shirt sleeve to wipe them away.

That was the second worst day of my entire life . . . that Wednesday when she put my daughter in the car and drove out the driveway.

The third worst day happened only a couple of days later on Friday morning. I had been moping around the house on Thursday and started drinking heavily that night, trying to kill the pain, I think. That next morning on Friday around 10 a.m. I heard a knock on the door. Reaching for my pistol I walked over to the door and looked out the peephole. My captain, along with the commander, were standing there. I put down the pistol and opened the door. When I saw the look on their faces, it said it all.

"Can we come in, Morgan?"

"Sure," I said. "What's up?"

"Morgan, I hate to tell you this but the State Attorney has decided to file charges against you for manslaughter."

"What?" I exclaimed.

"I am sorry, Morgan, but we are here to take you down to the county jail for booking."

It felt like someone punched me in the gut! I couldn't believe it.

"Why?" I asked.

"They just kept saying they couldn't do anything about it, and it had become political. People are marching on city hall," the captain tried unsuccessfully to explain. "You can secure your weapons here, Morgan. You don't need to bring anything."

I locked my gun in the safe. They put handcuffs on me and transported me to the county jail.

Chapter 10
Captain Ike: A Ping in the Night

I thought about Gina the entire trip back to the boat. I tried to figure out what had happened... how she felt different when she hugged and kissed me on the cheek. The more I thought about her injury, I realized it had to be her boyfriend.

"Who else would have done that?" I wondered.

I also realized how strong my feelings were for her because I wanted to break the neck of whoever did that!

I stopped by and got some chicken breast on the way back to the *Good Times*. Once I got onto the boat, I fired the grill up and let it heat. I also picked up a bowl of salad. I grilled up the chicken breast, chopped it into chunks, and put it atop the salad. It made for a good and healthy dinner.

I sat in the salon just thinking when my cell phone chirped. Gina sent a message.

"If you want to talk, I can chat on my way home," she texted.

"Sure," I answered.

In about two minutes she called.

"How was work?" I opened the conversation.

"Tiring," she replied. "I have been running back and forth between the restaurant and the hotel all day."

"Yeah, well, that's why you have such pretty legs," I said.

I could tell she was smiling through the phone.

"Okay, Gina, there is a huge elephant in the room; and I want to know what's up."

There was a long pause, and I waited until she sorted out what she was going to say.

"It's my boyfriend," she said. "The other day when you stopped by, he got mad at me. We argued, and he just wouldn't let it go. He kept going on and on about how I acted differently around you. Later in the evening he started drinking, and he got worse and worse. I was outside beside the pool on my phone, and he thought I was texting you, I guess; but I was texting my mom. He came out and snatched the cell phone from my hands and threw it in the pool. I stood up and started yelling at him. He grabbed my wrist, and when I tried to push back on him, he hit me."

"Son of a bitch!" I said. "I thought it had to be him. Did you call the police?" I asked.

"I wanted to," she said, "but he threw my phone in the water. Of course, it was dead when I fished it out. After that I locked myself in the bedroom and didn't talk to him the rest of the night, although he came to the door a few times and tried to talk to me."

"So, what now, Gina? Are you going to leave him?"

"It's very complicated, Ike," she said.

"What do you mean?" I asked. "He hit you, Gina; and if he did it once, he will do it again."

"I know," she said quietly. "He begged me all the next day to forgive him and even went down and got me a new cell phone. My eye was black and blue, so I just stayed home."

"Well, are you going to leave him?" I pushed.

"It's not so easy, Ike," she said.

I could hear her voice starting to tremble.

"Why, Gina? Do you own the house together or something?"

"No, no, nothing like that," she replied. "I own this house. I had it before he moved in." "Well, what then?"

Gina was quiet for a little while. I sat listening.

"I am pregnant, Ike," she said, ". . . or at least I *think* I am. I have been having morning sickness, and I took a pregnancy test. It was positive."

I was shocked; I stumbled over my words.

"Well . . . well . . . how far along are you?"

"I don't know," she said.

I could tell she was getting more emotional the more we talked about it.

"It's okay, Gina. I didn't mean to push you. I just don't like someone hitting you. Is there anything I can do?"

"No . . . I don't know . . ." she trailed off. "I am trying to figure it all out. Sometimes I think I should try and fix things, and other times I just want him gone."

"Gina, this is no way to start a family . . . this I know for sure."

Gina was quiet for a little longer.

"I guess I need to go," she said.

"Can we talk some other time, Gina? I am worried about you."

"Yes, I would like that."

"Gina, you call me anytime if you need anything . . . and I *do* mean *anything*."

"Thanks, Ike. You are sweet. Take care."

She hung up.

I sat back in my chair. I couldn't believe it. I had all kinds of thoughts rumbling in my head. Most of the time when I heard someone was pregnant, I congratulated them; but this time I didn't know what to think. I wondered if she would stay with him for the baby. I even thought about what would happen if they split up. What if we started dating? How would all that work out?

"DAMN!" I thought.

I was lost in my thoughts about Gina when my cell chirped. Chris texted me.

"Expect a number to text you around 3 a.m.," it said. "It won't be mine. I have a buddy who will ping the number and text you the coordinates. Let me know tomorrow how it turns out."

"Okay, Buddy," I replied. "And thanks! I owe you one."

I figured I needed to get to bed early. I would be up before sunrise it looked like.

I decided to get a shower before bed. I jumped in and took my usual two-minute shower from start to finish. Every time someone is onboard when I take a shower, there is a comment about how quick they are. On a boat one must always think about water consumption, and over the years I have just gotten used to it. I jump in, wash what needs to be washed, and get out. I can't imagine what people must be doing in there when they take a 30-minute shower. I just don't have that much body!

Once cleaned, I went to the back bunk. I thought about what I would need the next morning. I opened the drawer and pulled out my Springfield XD .45-caliber handgun. I kept it in the same paddle holster I used when I worked as a fire investigator. This was one of the few things I kept when I

Fire Aboard

left the city. It felt a lot like the Glock .37 the city issued as a service weapon. It is so close that I can use the same holster. Never knowing what I may get into and knowing the type of people with whom I was dealing, I felt it necessary to put it in my go-bag backpack.

I climbed in the bunk and lay back. I contemplated what the next morning may bring. It wasn't long before my thoughts turned back to Gina. I wondered what she was thinking and feeling . . . confusion, I was sure. I felt like I needed to protect her and wished I was there. I soon drifted off to sleep.

I fell into a deep sleep, waking up only a couple of times throughout the night. Right at 3 a.m. my cell chirped. I reached up to the end of the bunk and took it off the charger. I let my eyes adjust and saw the words "Good luck" and a series of numbers, recognizing right away they were GPS coordinates. I felt a bit of excitement as I rolled out of the bunk . . . kind of like how I used to feel when I worked as a firefighter and got a call for a structure fire in the middle of the night.

I opened GPS Coordinates on my phone. I needed simply to punch in the numbers, and it would give me an exact location. It showed a location in Polk County, the county next to where I and my boat were located. I punched the coordinates into Google Maps and got the exact address. It showed a drive time of one hour and 20 minutes. Looking at my watch, I figured that was just about right. Calculating the time, I should be there before 5 a.m. Just like in the old SWAT days, it was the perfect time to look at a house because most people are sleeping at that time.

I quickly grabbed my go-bag and jumped into the truck. I turned out on Pasadena Avenue and headed for I-275 S going over the Skyway Bridge and north on I-75. I turned east on

Highway 62 and took it to Highway 37 N. I made great time because there weren't many vehicles on the roadway at this time.

As I was driving, I thought about what I may be getting into. I thought about how no one would really know where I was headed except for the person sending me the text. I decided I should text June and send a quick message, giving her the address of where I was headed just in case I got into some bad stuff.

I texted, "Headed to check on a lead. Could be dangerous. This is the address."

After typing in the address, I told her I would call tomorrow and let her know what was going on.

Within a minute I got a reply, "Okay. Be safe."

As I drove, I wondered if I should contact the local law enforcement . . . but what would I tell them? I had a hunch that some bad cop was at this address and maybe something was wrong. Then I thought that if a rookie got the call, he might just roll up on the scene, tipping someone off. I figured I would wait and take a look at it myself first and then determine what to do.

I pulled the location back up on the map and looked at the satellite view. It appeared to be some type of commercial building that sat off in the back of a wooded area. It seemed pretty concealed as it had woods around two sides.

"What was I looking for?" I wondered. "Maybe some sign of Morgan. Maybe Espinoza . . . or anything that would tell me more than I knew now," I answered myself.

The map took me up Highway 37 just south of a town called Mulberry. The area was mostly old phosphate mines.

Some houses were being constructed in the area on reclaimed phosphate pits.

When I got about a mile out, I pulled over and studied the map for a bit. The road leading up to the destination, Doc Durrance Road, looked to be a dead end.

"That's not good," I whispered to myself.

I slowed down and looked down the road as far as I could see. It was dark, but I didn't see any lights on anything. I went further up and turned around. Since it was about half a mile down to the end of the road, I reckoned I wouldn't get burned if I drove in.

I figured I would do a slow drive down the road, looking for any sign of people. I turned onto the road and, as I got to where the map showed the destination address, I saw a building sitting back off the road.

"Strange," I thought. "Certainly, he wouldn't live here."

I could see a dim light from the back of the building but no lights in the front. I decided to go to the end of the road and park. The road turned 90 degrees left and ended. I slowed to a quiet stop and parked.

Getting out of the truck, I noticed how nice the weather was. The moon was almost full and cast a good amount of light. I quietly got my bag and stood for a bit, letting my eyes adjust to the lower light levels. I confirmed my cell was turned down. The difference between now and previously when I did investigations was back then I would tell the dispatch on the radio in what general area I would be; and I knew that if I needed help, I could call via the radio.

"No help here tonight," I thought.

I took my .45 out of my pack and put it on my hip. I started cautiously up to the curve of the road. Staying in the shadows of the trees that lined the road, I moved slowly so I wouldn't make any noise. Once I got to the curve, I stood in the shadows and watched and listened for a few minutes. Not hearing anything other than the occasional dog barking in the distance, I quietly walked further up the road. I got within a half block of the building and decided to move into the wood line along the road. I eased up to the clearing of the lot on which the building sat. There was a car sitting near the side of the building, and I watched it for several minutes to be sure no one was inside.

Standing there I could hear a faint voice coming from the building. I tried to understand what the voice was saying but realized I was just too far away. I eased along the wood line toward the car, approaching it on an angle. I understood it was the best approach to sneak up on a vehicle undetected. From this angle, the closer I got I could tell no one was in it. I looked inside and couldn't see much. I could hear the voice better now, and occasionally I would hear the voice yell. I reached up and touched the hood of the car. It was cold.

"It's been here awhile," I figured.

Studying the building I could see the door was closed on this side, and I could see light coming from the back of the building from a window. It was my best chance to see something.

I moved around the back of the car. It was about 20 feet from where the car was parked to the door. The corner of the building was about 10 feet from the door. I figured this would be the most dangerous position for me if I was spotted. I quickly but quietly moved across the lot to the corner of the building and went around the corner.

The window was now about 10 feet away, and I could

hear the talking much better from here. The voice sounded Spanglish—mostly English with some Spanish mixed in.

"Maybe that is Espinoza," I told myself.

The man was yelling about something having to do with pissing someone off. I slowly eased up to the window, crouching as I moved. I pulled my weapon from the holster and held it in the low-ready position . . . straight in front of me, aiming slightly downward. I moved up to the window very slowly, listening to what was being said. The guy went on about not pissing the boss off and something about someone bringing it on themselves.

I would "cut the pie" on the window (that is what we call moving slowly past a window or door). When done properly, a person can be seen through a window or door without their seeing the officer first.

I moved slowly and quietly up to the window. As I got towards the edge of the window, a man's body came into view. It was the back of a long-haired guy. He was facing the opposite wall as if he was yelling at someone out-of-sight. The light shone on his back, so I couldn't see his face. I stayed at that angle, trying to look around the room. I could see a couple of chairs and a table and a lot of junk. Whomever he was talking to was on the other side of him, but I couldn't see them.

I stayed there, listening and watching. The guy made all kinds of hand gestures as if he was mad; and now that I could hear him better, it also sounded like he was drunk. As he threw up his right hand in the light, I saw a gun in his hand. I got that chill knowing this situation was not good.

He kept saying something about "This is your fault" and "You should have kept your mouth shut!"

I kept watching, trying to see to whom he was talking.

The guy's cell phone rang, and he answered, "Yes, Boss, he is here." After a pause, he said, "Sorry, Boss," followed by "Boss, are we good?"

Apparently not liking what he heard, he simply hung up.

"You are fucked!" he said, talking to the other person.

I still couldn't see the other person because he was in the shadow of the Spanish guy doing the speaking. The Spanish guy stepped closer to the other person. He cursed him half in Spanish and half in English.

In a rage, the Spanish guy hit the other person with the gun. I heard the person hit the floor.

The Spanish guy kneeled down and spoke to the man lying on the floor, "It will be a whole lot worse when the boss gets here."

The Spanish guy finally moved a little to his left, and I could see he had the gun pressed up to the guy's head.

He pushed the gun deeper into the side of the guy's head as he spoke, "What a fucking idiot you are!"

He stepped a little more to the side, and I could finally see the other guy's face: it was Morgan!

Chapter 11
Tony Morgan: A Cop's Worst Nightmare

This was the first time I had been in the back of a police car under arrest, and I was in shock. Everything I had worked for in the past several years had just come to an end. A cop who has been arrested will never get another job in law enforcement.

I had so many emotional thoughts running through my mind. How could this have happened? How can a man be prosecuted for a mistake? I never intended to kill the guy, and I would do anything if I could take that moment back.

Not much was said on the ride to the jail. I recalled how I had made this trip so many times, but I was the one transporting someone to jail.

The captain finally spoke up as we neared the jail, "Morgan, I made a few calls. They will keep you out of the general population. I don't have to tell you to watch your back, right?"

"No," I said quietly.

I felt defeated. That started a whole new thought process. I hadn't even thought about the possibility that I would be arrested. Now that that threat was real, I began contemplating on what would come next.

We pulled into the sally port at the county jail. It was the area where arrestees were brought. It looked like a big garage with big gates on each end. The cruiser pulled in, and they closed the gates behind them so no one could escape. The officer doing the transport got out and secured his weapon in the trunk of his vehicle before letting the arrestee out. I had done this a hundred times.

The car door opened, and I stepped out. Knowing where to go, I went to the glass doors and waited for them to open. They soon opened, and I stepped in. In this area I would be patted down for weapons, and a metal detector would be used to ensure I didn't have any hidden contraband. I would then be fingerprinted, photographed, and led back to change out of my street clothes into an orange jumpsuit. For a cop, this was the most humiliating thing that could happen.

Once inside that area, they would begin processing me. It would then be determined, based on many factors, if I could get a bond. Persons committing a minor offense can bond out at that time. If a bond is granted and the arrested person has the ability to pay, they will soon be let out.

However, I had not made any preparation for this because I didn't know it was coming. Due to the circumstances in my case, I had to wait for a first appearance. I would go before the judge, and bond would be set at that time.

I was afforded my phone call; and I called my wife, Cyndi. She was crying when she answered the phone as she had already seen the story on Facebook. Local news outlets were carrying the story.

Most of the time when a suspect is arrested for a high-profile crime, they are paraded past the media in the sally port for pictures and videos. The captain made sure no one was there when I was brought in, but I was sure my mugshot would be released to the media shortly.

"What are we going to do?" Cyndi asked, sobbing.

Trying to be strong I told her to contact Don's Bail Bonds. They were a local company that often helped out first responders if they were arrested. I went on to explain that she may have to put the house up for collateral to get me out.

"I will handle it, Tony. Please don't worry," she said in between sobs.

I didn't tell her of the danger I faced and that I needed to get out as soon as possible. In jail the worst-treated people are cops and child molesters . . . child molesters for the obvious reason and cops because everyone there was arrested by a cop!

Fortunately, I was placed in a single cell for the time being. It would take a little while for inmates to find out who I was, and I knew I only had until the evening news before everyone would know.

In each cell there is a bed and a toilet/water fountain combo . . . meaning you drink where you poop! I laid in my bunk thinking about what was going on, how I would have to hire a lawyer and try to figure out why they filed charges against me. Only a few years ago, cops were given the benefit of the doubt in situations like this. It was generally understood that these types of situations will occur and that we are all human; mistakes may happen. Now days since people have lost respect for police, state attorneys will bow to political pressure since they are in an elected position.

Lying there I realized I was starving. I hadn't eaten that day. When in jail a person can't just get food when they want it. I called for the guard and asked him about getting a meal.

He explained I had missed lunch, so dinner would be my next chance to eat.

I guess he finally got a "heads up" on who I was and brought me some crackers from the canteen. I thanked him and consumed them like a ravenous dog.

I was told I wouldn't see the judge that day for my first appearance; it would be first thing in the morning. That night was terrible just lying in my bunk, listening to all the noise. It drove me crazy. I was not used to it. When I worked patrol years ago, I could always tell a truly bad guy because they would go to sleep while in the detention cell. A person who has never been in jail would not be able to sleep. Like me they would be worried about what was going to happen next.

Late into the morning I finally fell asleep. I heard the guard moving, and I woke up to the hell I hoped was just a bad dream.

They served breakfast, and I consumed all of it. I don't know what time it was because I didn't have a watch or a cell phone. The guards came around and said we would be seeing the judge shortly.

In the jail is a closed-circuit television system. A prisoner doesn't actually go to the court where the judge is; it's all handled through closed-circuit tv. I did not have a lawyer yet and relied on the public defender. Bail was set at $100,000 by the judge. At least he didn't believe I was a flight risk.

I tried calling Cyndi, but she didn't pick up. In jail only collect calls can be made. Someone must answer and accept the charges. Later I found out why Cyndi had been unable to take the call: she had been working with the bail bondsman to secure my release. It took several hours, but I did finally get released later that day.

Once I was processed out, I came out the side door. Cyndi and my brother Ron were waiting on me. Ron lived in Tampa, and he came over to try to help. We drove home as I told them about the night and how things were inside. It was a sad trip home as we all knew things were just beginning with the case.

The next few days were filled with stress. Cyndi and I drifted further apart. My brother tried to help, but there wasn't much he could do but give moral support. Cyndi continued to stay at her parents' house, and I felt abandoned.

I met with a lawyer who took police cases; but he was very expensive, and it took all our savings. The equity in the house couldn't be used as it was tied up in the bail bond.

The next few months were a blur. Cyndi's and my relationship fell apart. The stress of the case and my feeling of abandonment would not go away. I found it easier to be alone most of the time. The only time I felt good was when I got to spend time with our daughter, Mia. I took her to the park and spent time playing with her. I didn't have to talk about adult stuff with her, so my mind wasn't on my problems.

The case dragged on, and I had to take odd jobs here and there. I went to the day labor place on many occasions when I couldn't find any other work. This made me feel even more like a loser because most of the people working there couldn't get work anywhere else.

We got behind on the mortgage, so I had to make an agreement with the bail bondsman to put the house up for sale. I couldn't keep it with what I was earning; but since I had kept it maintained well, it sold quickly. After sharing the profit from the sale with Cyndi, there was little left.

Cyndi called me one day and said she wanted to talk alone. I knew by the tone of her voice what she wanted since our relationship was crap! Once the house sold, there wasn't much to keep us together anymore. I guess she wanted a fresh start. That's what she said anyway. I suspected someone else was helping her make that decision.

Finally, the case went to trial. By this time the family had received a monetary settlement from the city. They weren't even interested in the trial. It seemed like the money was all they wanted. The trial didn't last very long because the case was straight forward. I had shot the guy; that was not in dispute. The whole case came down to whether I did what any other person would do in the same or similar circumstances. Apparently, the jury sided with me, and I was found not guilty!

By that time, I was numb. My life had been completely ruined. I already knew no agency would ever hire me in the career I loved. I was divorced and in debt up to my eyeballs, and I felt like I didn't have anything to really live for.

One day I was at the Tavern of Central. I was drinking my sorrows away. I always sat with my back to the wall as most cops do. I noticed a guy walk in the front door. He had on flashy clothes and had a Spanish beauty on his arm. They sat at the bar on the opposite end. As I looked at him, I realized I knew who he was. I had arrested the guy before on some minor-level drug charges. He was at a dope house one time when we served a search warrant. I didn't bust his balls and arrest him because the dope was in the room with one of his buddies. He took the rap so Espinoza didn't have to go to jail.

We developed a strange relationship: one of respect. I knew what he was, but I still treated him like a man. He seemed to genuinely appreciate it. He even stepped up to help one time when I was on a traffic stop. He backed off a few guys who were intent on ginning up a crowd and making the situation very dangerous.

I didn't really want to talk to him, so I decided I would try and quietly slip out. Before I could pay the tab, he walked past me on the way to the men's room and recognized me.

"What's up, Morgan? he asked.

"Not very much."

"I heard what happened to you, Morgan. Seems like the county dropped you like a hot potato."

"How did you know?" I asked.

"Man, the street talk is better than any newspaper."

"Looks like you are doing pretty well," I said, motioning to his clothing.

"Well, let's just say business is good."

"I bet it is," I responded.

Espinoza looked me up and down and said, "Well, you look like shit, Bro."

I knew I did. I didn't even respond.

"Look, Dude, you were always straight with me," he continued. "If you want to make some real money, give me a call."

He wrote down his number on a napkin and slid it to me. I looked at it.

"What do you call 'real money'?" I jokingly asked.

"A few hundred Gs," he answered.

He smiled and continued to walk toward the bathroom.

He paused, looked back, and said, "What do you have to lose?"

I grabbed the napkin and put it in my pocket . . . not really sure why.

Chapter 12
Captain Ike: Finding Morgan

When I recognized at whom I was looking, I felt a sense of relief. That feeling was short lived, however, because Morgan was being held at gunpoint. I quickly started weighing my options: if I tried to call 9-1-1, I would have to backtrack away from the building in order not to be heard, and what if the guy did something in that time? He was obviously drunk and getting more agitated. He had already put the gun to Morgan's head several times.

"Think about dying?" Espinoza said to Morgan. "As soon as I get back, I will put a bullet in your brain."

In my opinion the time to act was now!

I watched as Espinoza moved toward the doorway. I moved quickly but quietly toward the door, as well, hoping I would get a chance at Espinoza. I was still a few feet short of the door when Espinoza pushed it open. It was dark outside, but my eyes were adjusted to the low light. I knew I would have that advantage.

Espinoza stepped a few feet outside and began relieving himself. I only had a second to react, so I took a step toward him. I was still several feet away from him when I accidently stepped on something from which the noise alerted Espinoza.

Startled, he spun around toward me. I yelled for him to drop the gun. He fired one shot. I already had my gun pointed at him, so I fired two shots center mass in his chest. The flash from my barrel lit up the darkness, and I knew the bullet had hit its target. Espinoza fell backward with a thud. He never saw my face.

I quickly moved to kick the gun from his hand. From the light of the door I saw a large puddle of blood spreading away from his body. Only then did I realize the pain in my side as Espinoza's bullet had also found its target. I reached down to feel the warm, slippery liquid oozing from my shirt on my lower left side just above my hip.

"This is not good," I thought as I felt myself getting weaker by the moment. I sat down on the concrete. I heard movement inside the building.

"Morgan," I yelled but didn't hear anything else.

I opened my phone and dialed 9-1-1. I laid back onto the pavement.

"Damn, what a way to die," I muttered under my breath.

Having never been shot, the pain was actually not as bad as I thought it would be. The adrenaline rushing through my veins was keeping me from feeling it.

I heard the dispatcher ask, "What's your emergency?"

"Gunshot," I groaned. "Gunshot."

"What's your location, Sir? she asked. I couldn't answer.

"Where is Morgan?" I wondered "Why didn't he come help me?"

I knew this was bad. I had responded to many gunshot victims in my career. I knew I needed to stop the bleeding. If I didn't do that, I would surely die. I tried putting as much pressure on the wound as I could, but I didn't have anything to apply over the wound.

"Morgan, I need your help!" I yelled but heard nothing.

I lay there for what seemed like hours. It was probably only a few minutes when I heard sirens off in the distance. This place was very rural. The nearest fire department was several minutes away.

I heard a different siren and recognized it as a cop car. I heard it pull up in the road and footsteps move in my direction. I could see light beams sweeping across the parking lot.

"They will be on full alert," I thought. I waited until I thought they were close enough and yelled, "Here I am . . . over here!"

Time seemed to slow down at that point. I could see someone getting closer but was blinded by the light from the flashlight. The deputy moved in and picked up the gun lying beside Espinoza, guessing he was dead. He held the light on me.

He moved toward me yelling, "Do not move! Do not move!"

"Hell, how can I move? I am going to die!" I thought.

He quickly removed my pistol from my side, and I heard him yell over the radio, "Scene secure!"

By this time I had been lying there for nearly 10 minutes. I now had a puddle of blood pooling around me. I could tell others were moving about me. I assumed they were emergency medical responders as they started moving me around and began working on my wound.

The deputy asked me, "What happened?"

I felt too weak to answer. He pressed for more information, but I heard one of the medics say I was in serious condition.

This seemed to stop the deputy's relentless questions. I felt them move me onto a backboard and lift me into the air. I heard familiar words, such as "trauma alert," "helicopter," "shock," "low blood pressure," . . . all of which I knew were bad. The weakness overtook me, and I felt the overwhelming urge to sleep.

The light moved across in front of my eyes and back again. The noise around me became louder, and it became very bright again. I was conscious enough to realize the doctor was testing my pupils with a light. This is reserved for the most serious of patients. I could tell from my surroundings I was in the ER. This place was very familiar to me . . . nurses moving about quickly and doctors barking out orders of medicine. A good ER is controlled chaos with doctors and nurses moving about like a choreographed dance. Those that have experienced it know it well.

I felt very confused. I couldn't tell if it was from the loss of blood or from some drug they had surely pushed into my veins. I was aware of movement again. I could tell it was rapid; and when the movement stopped, I was under a very bright light. I heard the words "emergency surgery" from someone. I slightly remember something being placed over my mouth and hearing the soft, comforting words of "breathe, just breathe." It was at that point the darkness overtook me again.

The next light of which I was cognizant was the sunshine peeking in through the shades. I was very groggy but aware. It was quiet, and I knew I was in a hospital room. I felt a hand on my hand and turned my head to see my sister, Nancy, standing there smiling. Nancy is my only sister, and she has always been more like a mother to me than a sister. I have no other siblings.

I tried to speak but my voice was very rough.

"Don't speak," Nancy instructed me. "You had a tube in your throat. Just rest for a while. I will get the nurse."

She hurriedly walked out of the room. I looked around. I was in a private hospital room; and by the way the sun entered the window, it was either facing east or west, depending on what time of the day it was. I was still very groggy, and my mind raced. I remembered the gunshot and the ER, but I couldn't remember anything past that.

I became aware that someone was standing in the room. I looked and saw a police officer standing near the door. I wasn't sure what he wanted. He nodded and put his hand up as if to say, "Just relax."

My sister returned to the room. She talked briefly to the officer, but I couldn't hear what they said. He nodded and walked outside.

Nancy came over to the bed, and as she fussed with the blanket covering me, she said, "The officer needs to ask you some questions when you are well enough."

I nodded yes, that I understood. Within a minute a nurse entered the room.

"Glad to see you are awake, Mr. Smith. Don't speak," she said. "We just recently removed your ET tube, and you need to rest your throat."

I nodded okay.

My sister moved back to the bedside and placed her hand on mine. It was comforting and made me feel better.

"Many people have come to check on you," she said. "I knew some of them, and some said they worked with you."

I smiled and nodded.

"I wrote down a list of the visitors on that pad. When you feel like looking at it, you can."

The nurse finished taking my vitals and said she would continue to check on me. I saw someone walk up and look in the door. He spoke to someone outside; and I could tell whoever he was, he was talking to the deputy. He stepped in.

"I am Detective Brooks from the sheriff's office," he said politely as he nodded at me. "I will need to talk to you as soon as you feel up to it."

My sister spoke up, "I'm sorry, but I don't think he will be able to talk until tomorrow." The deputy seemed satisfied with the answer and said, "I will come back then."

He nodded at me again and went out the door.

My sister told me, "The doctor said it was touch and go with you for a while because he said you lost a lot of blood." Her face turned to concern as she continued, "I don't understand what you were doing. I know you can't talk now, but I want to understand what happened."

Again, I nodded my head yes.

Nancy pointed to some things on the table.

"I think this is your phone," she said. "This bag contains everything you had on you when they brought you in."

The phone was dead so I asked Sis to put it on charge. After it had time to at least charge up some, I motioned for Nancy to give it to me. I pushed the power button. It took a minute to boot up; and when it did, it was still on the 9-1-1 lock screen. I pressed the acceptance button, and it went to the home screen. I looked and saw many missed calls. Apparently, the word was out about my shooting. I scrolled through the list back to the time of the shooting. The first three missed calls were from

Chris at TPD. He knew I was going to investigate the address so he was checking on me. The calls started around 0530.

After that were some old friends from the city fire department and police department. Somehow the word had spread that I had been shot and flown to Lakeland Regional Hospital. I am sure they didn't know all the details and wanted to see how I was.

I scrolled through the missed calls and texts. Then I saw a couple of texts from Gina. The first was that she just wanted to talk; and the second asked if everything was all right, probably because I hadn't responded to the first text.

"Hmmm, how am I going to explain this?" I thought.

I decided to be as straightforward as I could.

I texted her back, "Gina, sorry not to respond sooner, but I am in Lakeland Regional Hospital. I am okay and will contact you as soon as I can talk."

I looked back over at Nancy who was now reading a magazine and then I looked toward the window. I noticed it was getting darker.

"That means my window is facing west," I surmised.

I wondered how close I had really come to dying. I hadn't seen any lights . . . well, I did see a cop's flashlight and the doctor's pen light, but not the God light. I figured I was kept here for some reason and was thankful for it.

Then it hit me: where was Morgan? Did they arrest him? I moaned for my sister, and pointed to the paper and pen. She handed them to me.

I wrote, "Where is Morgan ?"

She shrugged her shoulders and asked, "Morgan who?"

I pointed to the officer outside, so Sis walked over and asked him to come in. He walked over to my bedside.

"Do you feel like talking, Mr. Smith?" he asked.

I wrote on the pad, "What happened to Tony Morgan?"

"Sir, we don't know; but I do know that is a question the detective will want to know the answer to. Do you want me to contact the detective and have him come back?"

I shook my head no and wrote "Tomorrow" on the pad.

He said, "Okay."

He walked toward the door and took out his cell phone and started texting.

I lay back in the bed and tried to recall what happened. All I could remember, though, was shooting Espinoza and being shot myself. I remembered calling out for Morgan, but I didn't remember seeing him after that.

Chapter 13
Hillsborough County Sheriff Department: Office Reports

The following are excerpts taken from the sheriff's department initial responses by Deputy Ryo and Detective Brooks:

INVESTIGATION
Hillsborough County Sheriff Department

I was dispatched to a report of a shooting on Doc Durrance Road off Old Highway 37.

Dispatch advised the caller said, "Gunshot." The caller was unable to give the address, so dispatch pinged the phone's location. The address was a commercial building. (See crime scene information.)

I was the first and only unit on scene. Upon my arrival I saw a vehicle parked behind the building and light coming from a doorway at the rear of the building. As I rounded the rear corner of the building, I saw a Hispanic male subject lying supine on the ground with an obvious gunshot wound to the chest. He was not moving and was unconscious. The subject had a pistol lying by his side, and I retrieved it for officer safety.

I also saw a white male subject who also had an apparent gunshot wound to the abdomen. He was conscious but confused. He had a pistol by his side, as well, and I gave him verbal commands to not move. I approached and took possession of the pistol.

I contacted dispatch and advised them that the scene was secure and to have EMS come in. I quickly searched the rest of the building for any other subjects but found none.

EMS arrived and began patient care on the white male. EMS advised that the Hispanic male was deceased. I obtained the wallet of the white male subject who was later identified as Ike Smith. (See subject #1 information.) EMS advised Smith was in serious condition and would be transported to the nearest trauma center via helicopter. They advised they would need our assistance closing down Highway 37 for the helicopter landing zone. I advised dispatch of this and requested additional personnel, crime scene, and notification of the detective on call. I remained on scene while EMS transported Smith.

I placed crime scene tape around the building and perimeter and took preliminary pictures of the scene. I noted blood inside the building on a couch and on the floor beside it. Crime scene technicians arrived and assumed possession of the scene.

Detective Brooks arrived and took investigative control of the scene. I gave him the information on the deceased victim of the shooting and on the victim being transported to the trauma center. I advised Brooks I would respond to the trauma center to gain more information from the shooting victim.

Deputy Ryo

*****

INVESTIGATION
Hillsborough County Sheriff Department

Upon my arrival to the scene, I met with the initial responding Deputy Ryo. He advised me there were two shooting victims. One was deceased, and the other had been transported to Lakeland Regional Hospital Trauma Center. I began an examination of the scene for evidence. I determined Victim #2, Juan Espinoza, had been shot twice at close range by Victim #1, Ike Smith, pending ballistic analysis. I determined Espinoza had shot Smith in the abdominal area, pending ballistic analysis. It is unknown at this time as to the reason for the shooting, pending interview of Smith.

I determined the possibility of a third suspect who was injured but unaccounted for inside the building. I found some blood on the couch and on the floor beside it. A shoe print was seen in the blood, and this indicated the shoe print was made after the blood fell on the floor. The shoe prints led to a table and then toward the front of the building toward a door. No other evidence of the third suspect was found.

I contacted the owner of the property and requested he respond for an interview. I interviewed him, and he was identified as Felix Cardona. Cardona stated he had leased the building to Juan Espinoza. He said he never comes by and assumed Espinoza was running some type of business from there. During my interview with Cardona, he kept wanting to look inside the building as if he was looking for something. I told him it was a crime scene, and we would turn the building over to him once the investigation was complete.

At the time of this report, I have not interviewed Smith. He is still in the hospital and unable to speak. He will be interviewed as soon as possible.

I was contacted by TPD Detective Chris Thompson. He stated that Smith had been in contact with him, and that Smith was working as a private fire investigator on an arson case in Tampa Bay. Smith stated that he had been looking for a suspect identified as Tony Morgan related to that case. No further details at this time, and this case is pending.

Detective Brooks

Chapter 14
Captain Ike: Hospital Recovery

I rolled over to a nurse prodding me. I couldn't get good sleep because the nurses came to check on me every 30 minutes, it seemed. It was getting daylight, and I looked at my phone. It was just before 7 a.m.

"I need to eat!" I thought.

My sister was still sleeping in the chair beside me.

I spoke to the nurse, the first time I had spoken since the shooting. "So, what is the prognosis, Charity?" I asked as I glanced at the name tag on her shirt.

"You will be fine," she said. "The doctor will soon be making his rounds and will talk with you more then. Can I get you anything?" she asked.

"Yes, I am starving! When is breakfast served?"

She handed me a paper with different choices. I checked off what I wanted: some eggs over light with grits and toast.

I looked over at Sis again, who was awake now after hearing talking.

"Sis, you want something to eat?"

"Yes," she responded, "but I am going down to the cafeteria to get some real food!" A smile crossed her face as she added, "I will be back soon. I want to know what the doctor says."

She went into the bathroom for a minute, then came out and grabbed her purse and walked out.

I lay there, trying to remember the details of what happened. I understood it usually takes a few days after a traumatic event for the brain to remember all the details. I had remembered pretty well as to what had happened with Espinoza . . . but what happened to Morgan?

A person cleared his voice and stepped in from the hallway.

"Sir, are you able to talk now?" asked a different deputy than the one from the night before.

I replied, "Yes, I can."

"Okay, I am going to contact the detective working the case. He needs to interview you." "Yes," I said, "have him come anytime."

The deputy opened his phone and appeared to be texting as he walked out of the room. A doctor with an Indian accent walked into the room.

"How are you feeling, Mr. Smith?" he asked.

He reached out and picked up my chart from the bedside.

"Better," I answered, "but I am still very sore on my side . . . but only if I move."

"Well, don't move," the doctor jovially countered.

"Yeah, easy for you to say, Doc."

"Mr. Smith, you are very lucky. The bullet missed several vital organs and only did soft tissue damage. You lost a lot of blood, but your counts appear to be improving nicely."

"How long will I need to be here, Doc?"

"Only a day or two more," he replied. "We need to run a few tests, but as long as you don't move much and tear any stitches loose, you should be fine. When you came in, we thought the bullet had hit an organ with the amount of blood loss you had, but you were lucky. I will stop in the morning and check on you again. Try not to get in any more trouble between now and then," he chuckled.

"Yeah, yeah," I replied.

The nurse came in with a cart, and it had my breakfast on it.

"Here you are, Sir. I pulled a few strings and got it a little sooner than normal."

Oh, thank you, Ma'am. I know I am getting better because my appetite has returned."

I was just about finished eating when Nancy walked back in. She was carrying a muffin and coffee.

"That smells good," I said.

She replied, Yes, it *is* good."

"The doctor has already come by," I told her.

"What?" she answered, sounding surprised. "What did he say?"

"Oh, nothing much. He said I could run a marathon later this afternoon."

"No, he didn't," Nancy rejoined.

I laughed, "He just said I was pretty lucky . . . mostly just a flesh wound. He will check back in on me tomorrow. He made out like I would only be in here a couple of days." "Good . . . but what are you planning then?"

"Hmmm, good question. I haven't gotten that far in my thoughts."

My phone chirped, and it was Gina.

"I am coming over there," the text read.

It was short but to the point.

I responded back, "You don't have to."

However, her next text was simply, "What is the room number?"

"Well, she didn't leave that open for debate," I said out loud.

"Who?" Nancy asked.

"Gina . . . she is a girl I have been talking to."

"You didn't tell me you were dating anyone."

"Well, we really haven't been dating; but she is coming to see me, I guess."

"Good! I get to meet her," Nancy replied.

We talked a bit more, and I told her what I knew about Gina. Nancy had more questions than answers.

There was a knock at the door, and I said, "Come in!"

Detective Brooks walked in, and he introduced himself mostly for Nancy's sake, I assumed.

"Sir, how are you feeling? Are you up to an interview?"

"Yes," I said. "Pull up a chair, Detective."

Brooks sat down and pulled out a notebook. It seemed odd to be interviewed for something when I had been the one interviewing people for years. I wondered what questions I would be asked, all the while listening for questions that we were *trained* to ask.

I had a unique style interviewing a suspect. I started out with very easy questions, and I always tried to build a rapport with the person. I figured it was easier to get answers with sweet instead of sour. Some cops just never understood the concept. I then would lead into questions to which I knew the suspect knew the answer, as well as to which I already knew the answer. We called this "qualifying the suspect." I wanted to see how the person acted when telling the truth so that I could tell if their actions changed when lying. Most of the people

I interviewed had something to lie about, and I would save those questions until the end. When I got to those questions, the person would get nervous and either quit talking, ask for a lawyer, or spill their guts. The latter almost never happened.

Detective Brooks apparently understood this technique because that's how the questions started.

"Sir, I was contacted by TPD about this case . . . a Detective Thompson, I think."

He looked down at his notes and looked up at me to see my response.

"Yes, Sir," I responded. "I have been in contact with him about an arson case on which I was working that occurred in Tampa Bay."

He nodded as if he already knew the answer to the question.

"Okay, so what were you doing at the address on Doc Durrance Road?" he asked.

"I was looking for a suspect in the case I was working. His name is Tony Morgan," I said. "Are you familiar with him?"

Now I was asking the question.

"Yes, I am, Sir," he replied; but he didn't elaborate on it.

"Kind of hard ass," I thought, then continued, "So, I got information that the cell phone of Espinoza had pinged in that location. I didn't, of course, know at the time what was going on."

"Where did you get the ping information?" he asked.

I paused for a minute, not planning to tell him that the information came from TPD.

I said, "I will come back to that later." He seemed to accept that answer, so I continued, "I got that info around 0300 hours, and I went there looking for Morgan. I had reason to believe from his family that he was missing and possibly in danger. I knew Morgan from years ago, and I counted him as my friend. I am sure you are aware of what happened with him?"

Again, I smiled, as I was now doing the questioning.

"Yes," the detective answered. "Please, go on."

"Well, I parked down the street from the address, past the building. Now that I think of it, my truck should still be there."

"A white GMC?" the detective asked.

"Yes," I said, then continued, ". . . okay, anyway, I walked up to the building; and I heard a voice coming from inside. I moved to the window to get a better look. I was carrying my sidearm for which I have a concealed carry permit," I added.

"I saw Espinoza hitting someone with a gun, clearly agitated. He also made several threats to the person. Then he moved, and I could see it was Morgan. I thought about calling 9-1-1 at that moment, but Espinoza got a call from someone and insinuated to Morgan that he was dead when whoever was on the phone got there.

"Espinoza walked outside to pee, I think; and when he did, I yelled at him to drop the gun. I feared for the life of myself and of Morgan.

"Espinoza spun around and fired a shot at me. I had my gun at low-ready and fired two shots center mass. He dropped where he was standing and never moved again to my knowledge.

"I sat down, called 9-1-1, and I eventually passed out on the spot. I was found by a deputy responding to the call."

"Okay, that's what the scene revealed to me," the detective said. "What happened to Morgan?" he quizzed.

"I don't know, Brooks. I yelled for him to help me when I was lying outside. I heard movement inside but I never saw him again. Then I woke up here at the hospital."

Brooks got up and walked over to my bedside. He laid a folder on my lap and asked if I would look at the pictures. I opened it, and the first were pictures of the scene from outside. I saw blood spots from Espinoza and from where I had been lying.

Then the pictures moved to inside. The couch was just as I remembered. There was blood on the couch and on the floor directly below it.

"No doubt this was from Morgan," I said, pointing to the pictures.

The last two pictures were what appeared to be footsteps in blood leading from the coach, over to the table, then toward the front door. I am sure I had a strange look on my face as I looked up, wondering what it meant. Detective Brooks just looked at me, questioningly.

"Ummm, like I said, I don't know," I simply said, shrugging my shoulders. "I never went inside."

My account of what happened seemed to make sense to the detective. He sat for a minute, writing on his pad.

"Mr. Smith, we will need to do a taped statement of the incident."

I knew this was a very common tactic when interviewing a subject. An investigator first asks what happened and then they do a taped interview later to see if there are any inconsistencies in the story. I had no problem doing one since I was telling the truth.

"I need to contact my superiors and let them know the outcome of the interview. They are very interested, as you can imagine, because of Morgan's involvement. Do you mind answering more questions if we have some later?"

"No, not at all," I said.

"Listen, another thing . . . when I interviewed the owner of the property . . . ummm, let's see . . ." He flipped through his notepad. "Felix Cardona . . . do you know him?"

"No," I replied.

"Well I interviewed him, and something didn't seem right about him. He said he only leased the property to Espinoza, but the thing is he kept wanting to go inside the building. I told him it was a crime scene, and he would be allowed inside after the investigation was complete. Seems like he was looking for something. I did some checking on him, and he is connected heavily with the Cardona Cartel in Mexico. You need to watch your back in whatever Morgan has you looking into."

I nodded okay.

"Oh, one more thing . . . do you know the whereabouts of Morgan?" he asked.

"No, I don't," I said, "but I would really like to know myself. I actually need to interview *him*," I said laughingly.

The detective handed me his business card and said, "In case you hear from him . . ."

He turned and walked out of the room.

Later I heard a knock at the door and a sweet voice I immediately recognized as Gina's.

"May I come in?" she asked.

Hearing her voice excited me.

"Come in," I said in my most relaxed voice.

Gina walked in, wearing a little sun dress. She was very tanned. She smiled and walked over to me. I tried to lean up to hug her but groaned from the pain.

"Stop!" she said.

She leaned down and kissed me on the cheek.

"How are you feeling, Ike?"

"I have been better."

Hearing my sister making noises, obviously wanting to be introduced, I pointed to her and said, "This is Nancy. She is my momma slash sister," I said lightheartedly.

"So nice to meet you, Nancy," Gina responded as she walked over and extended her hand.

"Well, this is a pleasant surprise," Nancy said. "I haven't met any of Ike's girlfriends lately."

Gina and I both blushed.

"Stop it, Nancy!" I complained.

Nancy jokingly asked, "So, Gina, how do you feel about premarital sex?"

Nancy had a big smile on her face when she asked, and Gina immediately picked up on that Nancy was kidding.

"Please, Nancy," I said. "The lady isn't going to want to ever come over again."

Nancy got up and walked over to my bed. Leaning over, she kissed me and said she was going home for a bit. She had a few things to do and figured I was in good hands . . . an obvious reference to the liking of Gina.

"Gina, we will get to know each other sometime later."

Gina smiled that sweet smile and nodded yes. Sis got her stuff and headed out the door.

Gina pulled a chair up close to the bed. She reached over and put her hand on mine. She looked up with concern on her face.

"Now, tell me what happened."

"Long story," I started, "but remember the story about Morgan?"

Responding to her nodding her head yes, I went on to tell her all about what happened. I noticed each time I told the story, the reality of what happened got more serious to me.

Gina was very patient listening. When I got to the part of being shot, she squeezed my hand and teared up. Her tearing caused me to get a lump in my throat.

I could feel a difference in our chemistry. I could tell her feelings were changing for me; they were getting deeper. I also knew mine were for her. Her coming to the hospital made me feel very good.

Just then I remembered that Gina told me she was pregnant. I asked her how the baby was doing. She turned and looked away for a moment. When she looked back, her eyes were teary.

"I lost it, Ike. I think it was all the pressure."

I reached out and took her hand.

"I am sorry, Gina."

She smiled the best she could.

"When are you getting out of the hospital?" she asked.

Sensing she wanted to change the subject, I followed her lead.

"Doc said a couple of days. I think I will know more in the morning."

"What are you going to do?" she quizzed.

"Not sure. I guess I'll go back to the boat and take it easy. My sister asked that question earlier."

"Who is going to take care of you, Ike?"

"Well, I guess I will do as I have always done," I responded.

"Nonsense!" she said. "You can't stay alone. You are going to have a hard time moving if you haven't figured that out yet."

"Oh, yes," I answered. "I have quite figured that out already."

She paused for a minute.

"I broke it off with that bastard," she quipped. "but he is still living in my house until he finds a place. I will come stay with you?" she said with a question.

"Well, uh, sure," I stuttered. "Have you ever been on a boat?"

"Never *lived* on one; but it will just be for a few days, so no problem."

That thought definitely excited me.

"It is settled then; I will get a few things together and come back tomorrow. We will see what the doctor has to say and work it out from there."

"Yes, Ma'am. I like it when you take charge."

She smiled a devilish smile and said, "Oh boy, you just don't know."

"Hmmm," was all I could say. I was at a loss for words.

She got up, leaned over, and kissed me again. This time her kiss was on my lips. Her lips were soft, and she lingered there for a moment. I could smell her sweet perfume.

"I am glad you are alive, Ike," she said as she slowly pulled away from me.

She grabbed her purse and walked over to the door. She turned and winked at me, saying nothing more, and slipped out.

"Oh, my God," I said under my breath. "That girl is amazing!"

I lay there, reliving that kiss and feeling things in my stomach I had not felt for a very long time.

Chapter 15
Tony Morgan: An Introduction to the Cartel

Mid-June 2017

The 590 hp, black Maserati Levante pulled into the valet area of the Ocean Prime. Recognizing the car, the valet quickly opened the passenger door. A beautiful Spanish lady stepped out.

"Good evening, Mrs. Cardona," the valet said.

She stiffly nodded but didn't reply. Felix Cardona got out of the driver's side, and the valet carefully drove off. Cardona opened the door to the Ocean Prime, and Mrs. Cardona walked in.

"Welcome, Mr. and Mrs. Cardona," the hostess said. "Your table is ready. Come this way, please."

Both followed and were seated in their normal corner booth.

The Ocean Prime was an upscale steak and seafood restaurant located in Tampa's International Plaza. It is known for its excellent dining experience and the kind of place that has no prices on the menu. If one needs to ask the price, then it probably isn't for them.

Cardona was known to visit these types of restaurants most evenings. No one there really knew what type of business Cardona was in, but they all knew the tips he gave very well. He was also known for his temper; one didn't want to get on his bad side.

After ordering drinks, Cardona received a phone call. He excused himself from the table. It was his employee, Juan Espinoza.

"Boss, I found someone to help bring in our next shipment. I know at first you wouldn't even consider it, but hear me out."

"Go on."

"Boss, there is this guy named Tony Morgan. He *used to be* a cop."

"A cop?" Cardona almost shouted into the phone.

"I know, Boss, but listen . . . this guy worked for the sheriff's office. He shot a guy and was brought up on charges. The thing is, he is pissed at how it all turned out because they ruined his life. He beat the rap, but he can't find a job because of it. Boss, he has nothing; and his little daughter is in need of some type of medical procedure. I used to know him back in the day. He busted me a few times and was always straight up with me. I think he is ripe for the picking, Boss. He doesn't know anything yet, but I told him he could make some real good money fast. He sounded very interested, and I think he is at rock bottom.

"Here is my thinking, Boss. We tell him he has to help with a shipment for free; and if all goes well, we let him help with the second. I will tell him how much he can make on the second one once the first shipment is safe."

Cardona spoke quietly now, "I hate cops! We can't trust him."

"Boss, here is how we'll know if we can trust him or not. I will have him help me bring in a fake shipment, and he will think it is real. He knows what to say if we get stopped by any real cops. He knows stuff we will never know. If he is going to turn us in, he will; and when they bust us, we won't have anything . . . no harm done, and we will know then."

A smile crossed Cardona's face. They had recently lost shipments to police who were just doing boater safety checks and somehow figured out what was inside the boat . . . usually from the driver getting nervous. He understood that if they could trust Morgan, he would almost guarantee safe deliveries.

"You may have something there, Espinoza. Let me think about it a few days, and I will be in touch."

Cardona hung up the phone and returned to his table. He and his wife completed dinner. They sat for a while, and Cardona told her about his conversation with Espinoza. Cardona always told her about his business dealings as he valued her opinion. She agreed that if they tested him and he passed, his assistance could be proven invaluable.

Cardona pondered the thought overnight. The next morning he decided the potential risk was worth the reward. He was aware that Morgan could be working for the DEA, and this could be their way of getting close to him. He also knew that if they set up a delivery with Morgan and that Morgan thought it was real and, therefore, they got busted, there wouldn't be anything there. Cardona knew from years of experience that a man at his low point would do many things he wouldn't normally do.

Cardona called Espinoza and said, "I have decided to go ahead with the plan. I will set up the fast boat in the river, and you will have Morgan go with you. You tell him in advance that he must do the first delivery for free. If all goes well, tell him we will pay him double on the second run . . . his share would be $200,000.

"You drive the fast boat out to meet a fishing boat in international water in the Gulf. They will give you bags, but no drugs will be inside. You and Morgan bring them back by the river. If you get stopped, we will know he told; if not, we can trust him.

"Also, be sure you tell him about the trip at least one day in advance. If he is working for the DEA, they will have plenty of time for the bust."

Espinoza agreed and asked, "When do you want to try it?"

"Give me three days to set the deal up. Plan to do it this coming Friday," he answered.

"Okay, Boss, I will wait on your call."

"Espinoza, just remember if he is a narc, I will hold you responsible."

Espinoza quietly said, "Okay," and hung up.

Espinoza contacted Morgan.

"Meet me downtown at the lake around 6 p.m.," Espinoza offered. "That thing I told you about is set, and we can talk about the details then. Morgan, you have the chance to make $200,000 on this deal. Don't mess it up, and don't be stupid. If you try anything, my boss will have you and your family killed. Morgan, it is gold or lead when you make this choice."

Morgan understood that Espinoza meant if he did the job right, he would get the money, or "gold"; if he didn't, he would get a bullet, or "lead."

Espinoza got to the lake about 30 minutes early and waited in the park. He wanted to see if Morgan had anyone with him. He sat at the top of the amphitheater so he could see the entire park. Around 6 p.m. he saw Morgan walk around the lake, and he didn't appear to have anyone with him. He let Morgan sit down on a bench and just sit for a while. He got a couple of texts from Morgan, but he just sat and watched.

After he felt comfortable that no one was with Morgan, Espinoza went down the steps. He sat down on the bench next to Morgan. Espinoza pulled out an electronic device and set it down on the bench between them. The device was used to jam any signal produced from a person wearing a wire.

*****

"I am not wearing a wire," I said.

"I didn't think you would, Morgan, but if I didn't take precaution and you *were* wearing one . . . well my boss would see to it I didn't survive.

"Let's get a few things straight, Morgan," Espinoza continued. "My boss knows everything about you. He knows where your wife lives with her parents and your kid. If you do anything or cost him money, he will make sure your entire family is killed. I have seen it. You were always straight with me, and I will be straight with you; so, if you want out, get out now."

I looked down at the pavement, deep in thought.

"I don't have a choice," I said. "I must do it; my daughter is sick."

"Morgan, here is the deal: your job is to ride with me on pickups, and you are to deal with any cops who stop us. The only time our shipments get caught is when some FWC (Florida Wildlife Commission) or sheriff's boat stops us and they figure out something isn't right. Otherwise, we always get in with no problem. My boss has lost a few shipments like that and doesn't want to lose any more.

"Your pay is $100,000 per load. You have to help with two loads. You get paid on the second for both loads; that's $200,000. We have one set for this Friday. Are you good?" I sat there, looking off into space. Espinoza knew to be quiet and let me work it out in my head.

I finally spoke up, "Man, I used to have it all. I made a mistake, and they took it all from me. Hell, yeah, I am *in*!"

A smile crossed Espinoza's face.

"Okay, this Friday meet me at the landing at Ruskin Commongood Park at 7 a.m. It is at Highway 41 and the Little Manatee River in Ruskin. Do you know the area?"

"Yes, I know it," I responded.

"Bring some rods and reels," Espinoza said. "We want to look like we are going on a fishing trip."

Chapter 16
Captain Ike: Going Home

I lay in bed, looking at my phone. My pain came and went. Sometimes it was bad, and other times I wouldn't even feel it unless I moved. I tried not to move very much. Lying in that bed was getting to me. I couldn't remember ever being in a bed that long before. I had had minor surgeries in the past, but I was up and walking around the same day. The abdominal muscles are used just about every time a person moves; and when they are damaged, it is sure to be felt.

Sis was sitting in the chair beside me, reading a book.

"What are you reading?" I asked.

I could tell she was really into it.

"It is one of a series of books about a fire investigator who investigates boat fires and tries to unravel the mysteries around them. This one is called *Fire Below*, about a yacht that burned and sank down in the Keys. It is really an exciting book. I will let you read it when I am done."

I responded to a couple of well-wishers' texts on my phone. Several friends I had from the fire and police departments had heard what happened and were checking on me.

The public safety community is a very tight community. It is one of the things I always loved about the job. Friendships were made, then became lifelong friendships . . . some like family.

I was *really* waiting on one person to come and see me. Of course, that was Gina. She had texted earlier and said she was on the way. I didn't want to text her and seem too eager, but I was starting to get worried.

A few minutes later there was a knock at the door, and sweet Ms. Gina poked her head in and asked if I was decent.

"Well, yeah," I said. "Come on in, and I will get *in*decent," I said with a smile on my face.

At that, Nancy spoke up, "Keep it in your pants, Tiger."

We all laughed. Gina walked over and kissed my forehead. She gave Nancy a quick hug and exchanged pleasantries.

Looking at me she asked, "How are you doing? Has the doctor released you, yet?"

"Yup, I can go home this afternoon," I said. "They are calling in some meds and will complete all the discharge papers shortly. I will have to come back, of course, for some follow-ups; but other than that, Doc says I will be fine."

Gina stood by my bed and reached over to put her hand on mine. She gave it a little squeeze.

"I am so glad you are doing better, Ike."

"Me, too," I said. "It was a wake-up call, for sure."

Gina pulled up a chair, and we began chatting, along with Nancy. Nancy told her things about our childhood . . . how she had pretty much raised me, speaking more like my mom than my sister.

"I always worried about Ike when he was fighting those fires and when he was working as a cop. I thought after he retired I wouldn't have to worry as much . . . and look now."

She flung her hand in my direction as she spoke and gave me a disapproving smile.

"Has he told you any stories of when he was a cop?"

Gina shook her head no.

"One time when he was working as a cop, I did a ride-along with him. We were up in the 'hood, and he was following a car. He told me ahead of time if anything happened, to stay in the car and roll up the windows. Well, he tried to conduct a traffic stop on this car; but the car pulled over, and the driver jumped out and ran off around a house. Ike jumped out and chased him. I was sitting there all alone. Both cars were running, and people started coming around the car and looking at me. I rolled up my windows and just looked forward," she said laughing.

"The thing is, I could hear Ike on the radio during his foot pursuit. Within minutes, other cop cars started showing up. Some cops ran off behind the house, and some came over to me. It was so scary . . . but exciting, too," Nancy continued with the story. "About five minutes later Ike came walking around the corner of the house with the suspect in cuffs. He was smiling like he'd just won the lottery."

Gina spoke up while looking at me and said, "He will have to tell me some of those stories. We haven't had a lot of time together, but I hope that is going to change."

She looked at me and winked.

The nurse walked in with some papers. She began the process of releasing me. She showed me the prescriptions for pain meds and how and when to take them. She told me how to take care of the wound. She knew I was a firefighter, but it was necessary she cover all the bases. We talked about how I would need to take it easy for several days.

"Obviously, no working for a week," she instructed.

"No worries," I said. "All I plan on doing is sit on the back of my boat and watch the sunsets."

The nurse jokingly asked, "In that case, may I come along and be your personal nurse?" She rechecked her paperwork, then continued, "Well, Mr. Smith, it will be about another hour, and you'll be set to go."

While we were waiting, I made a plan with Nancy to get my truck and drive it to the marina in the next day or so. We planned for me to ride home to the boat with Gina. Gina drove a Chevy Tahoe. That made for a comfortable ride, but I knew it would be hard getting in and out of it.

Soon it was time to head home. As is always in the case with major injuries, an orderly brought a wheelchair and gave me a ride in it to the door.

Stepping up into the truck was the hardest thing I had done in a while. It caused a higher level of pain, and I told Gina we would definitely need to fill the prescription for the pain killers. It took well over an hour to get back to the boat.

During the trip I asked, "When are you due back to work?"

"No worries" she said. "I took off a few days, and I will be your nurse now."

I told her, "I'm gonna need a sponge bath."

"Easy, Cowboy," she laughed. "Besides, you are in no condition for anything like that."

Crossing back over the Skyway Bridge we were treated to a beautiful, afternoon sun over the Gulf. I was quiet as I looked out over the water.

"Everything okay, Ike?"

"Oh, yes," I said. "I was just reminded of how beautiful

these views are. I had a close call this time, and I might have not seen them again—I am glad I still get to."

She reached over and held my hand. It was a very nice feeling. We sat in silence all the way over the bridge as I gazed out over the water, pondering the events of the last few days. Why did I survive the shooting? Apparently, I still had things to do on this earth and was left here for a reason.

We turned onto Gulfport Boulevard, and I felt better as I knew we were close to what I called home.

Gina spoke up, "Okay, here is the plan. I will get you on the boat and get you comfortable. We will survey the food and drink situation, and I will go pick up your meds and any supplies we need. Sound like a plan to you?"

I nodded in agreement.

"Is there a grocery store nearby?" she asked.

"Oh, yes, about a mile away," I said.

One good thing about the marina was how close it was to everything. One only had to drive a couple of miles to get anything needed.

My cell beeped. It was a text from my sister.

"Are you doing okay?" she asked.

I knew she would have come over in a minute to take care of me if need be, but I think she recognized how much Gina wanted to help. She wanted to give her that space. She knew it was hard for me to get close to someone, and she didn't want to intrude.

"Yes, Sis, I am in good hands," I texted back.

"Great! Say 'hey' to Gina for me and that we'll talk soon."

When I told Gina that, it brought a big smile to her face.

Nancy's last text was, "I will give you two some space. Call me if you need me."

We pulled into the parking lot of the marina and parked right behind *Good Times*. "Home, sweet, home," I said.

Gina surveyed the boat.

"Much bigger than I anticipated," she observed.

"Oh, yes, that is what everyone says. She is a little older; but she can sleep five, two forward and three aft, and party with 15," I said smiling. "Most importantly, she will never leave me stranded. She has twin motors onboard."

"Getting on the boat was much harder than the last time," I thought to myself as I crossed from the dock to the boat.

I felt like an old man as Gina helped me inside. I got in and sat down in my favorite captain's chair in the salon. Gina looked around, nodding her head in the affirmative.

"I will have to give you the grand tour when you get back," I offered. "Just need to rest here for a bit."

Gina went down into the galley and looked in the fridge.

"Well, it looks like we have plenty of beer," she reported.

I laughed and agreed that it was usually the case here. She made some notes on her phone and came back over to me.

"How are you feeling, Captain?"

"The pain is back," I complained. "That is the most movement I have done in a while."

"I am going to get your meds," she said and kissed me. Out the hatchway she then went.

I sat back looking around *Good Times*.

"Wish I had cleaned up a little better," I said half aloud.

I never left the boat dirty, but it was funny how things looked different when a lady was aboard. I noticed dust that I hadn't noticed before.

"Well, there's nothing I can do about it now," I told myself.

I did notice how much better I felt just being aboard. The slow rocking from the water, and the sound of seagulls flying around reminded me I was back in my happy place. This was the best place for me to heal.

I thought about Gina and how things had transpired the last few days. Funny how it took me getting shot to get Gina and I to the place we were.

"And where, exactly, was that place?" I wondered. "What was *she* thinking? Was this the beginning of a relationship?"

So many thoughts raced through my head.

Chapter 17
Tony Morgan: Going to the Dark Side

The more I thought about Espinoza and how good he was doing, the madder I got.

"I guess crime *does* pay," I mumbled to myself. "Why shouldn't I take him up on his offer? The county dropped me like a hot potato after making one mistake. Fuck that!" I thought. "Besides, my daughter needs me to come through for her. I have done the right thing for years, and look where it's got me."

I opened my wallet and found Espinoza's number. I called him.

"Does the offer still stand?" I asked.

"Yes," Espinoza replied. "Let's meet and talk about it. Meet me at the amphitheater."

Espinoza gave me the riot act about what would happen if I turned them in or anything happened to the shipments. He told me I would make a total of $200,000, which was $100,000 per load, and would only get paid after the second load.

"Count me in," I told him. "Let's do this!"

Espinoza instructed me to meet him at the park in Ruskin three mornings later. He explained that my job was to talk them out of any trouble with law enforcement if they should get stopped.

"The only way we lose shipments is if one of our boats gets stopped and someone gets nervous. The cops will pick up on that, and that will lead to their being arrested and the dope seized," Espinoza clarified.

The morning of the first shipment I was nervous; I had never done anything like this before. I wondered if they got stopped if it would be *my* nervousness that would give them away. I pushed it to the back of my mind and just thought of it as a fishing trip.

I sat in my car until Espinoza pulled up in a 30-foot center console with twin 200 hp Mercury motors sitting on the back.

"Damn!" I thought. "Not too many police boats would catch that one!"

I also knew that even if they might outrun a particular police boat, they couldn't outrun the radio.

I got my rods and my cooler out of the truck just as though we were going on a fishing trip. I loaded it all in the boat, and we headed downriver toward Tampa Bay. Most of the river was a no-wake zone, so we had to go pretty slowly. When we got out of the zone, Espinoza showed me just how fast it would run. Since the river was pretty tight in most areas, Espinoza couldn't get top speed, but I saw the speedometer hit 65 mph.

As we were running downriver, I figured the boat must have been kept in the river somewhere. There were no other boat ramps for Espinoza to have put the boat in the water. That told me Espinoza didn't trust me and didn't want me to know where their spot was.

"Fine with me," I thought. "I just want to make some cash and be done with them fast!"

Fire Aboard

Once we reached Tampa Bay, Espinoza turned the boat south toward the Skyway Bridge. It was about an 18-mile run from the river's inlet to the Skyway Bridge. With the speed of the boat, it didn't take long to get there. We passed under the Skyway and out past Egmont Key. We turned southwest and ran for about 30 minutes.

I saw a fishing trawler, and we headed directly for it. Espinoza told me that it was their pick-up boat.

Espinoza began giving instructions, "We will pull up on the outside of the trawler. They will throw over some bags. Your job is to stow them below."

He pointed out a hidden compartment under the bait well.

"That's a pretty good hiding spot," I surmised.

Espinoza pulled alongside the trawler, and they threw over two large bags, just as he had described. I grabbed them, went to the hidden locker, and put them inside. I went on to fill the baitwell with water. I wanted to look inside the bags but thought better of that idea and just stowed them away, instead.

"So, this is the life of a doper," I thought.

I felt like I was above it even though I was doing the same thing they were.

Espinoza explained we would return at a slower speed, looking for any police boats and killing time so it looked as though we were simply out fishing. Espinoza pulled a flask from his pocket and started drinking. He offered me some but I turned him down.

"Don't you think you should wait until we get back before you start drinking?" I quizzed.

"Chill, Bro," he replied in a snarky tone. "This is how we do it."

After a while with our rods in the water, Espinoza started the engines and announced we were headed in. By that time he was pretty drunk and drove crazy. I tried to get Espinoza let me take the wheel, but he refused.

Rounding Egmont Key channel, we pointed the boat toward the Skyway Bridge . . . back the same way we had come. As we passed under the bridge, there was a small boat with an old dude fishing near one of the outcroppings. I could not figure out why, but Espinoza had a mean, determined look on his face as he flew right past the fisherman's boat. The wake from our boat at that speed flipped the old guy out of his boat. I looked back as we passed him and saw the old guy floundering in the water. Espinoza simply smiled an evil smile.

As soon as we passed to the inside of the bridge outcropping, I spotted a FWC boat sitting in the shade of the bridge. Witnessing what Espinoza had done to the old man and his boat, FWC turned on their lights and sirens and started chasing us. Espinoza pushed the throttle all the way down. He quickly accelerated; and within a minute or so, we had pulled away from the FWC boat. They turned around and headed back toward the fisherman's boat. Espinoza laughed.

I hollered, "You fucking idiot, why did you do that? Now you can bet they have called our boat in over the radio."

"Don't worry about it," Espinoza yelled back.

"No wonder these idiots get caught," I thought. "Doing stupid shit like this!"

Within 10 minutes we turned into the channel at the river. I was freaking out as I expected some other law enforcement boats or maybe even a helicopter to be looking for us. Knowing what we had in the cargo hold, I just wanted to get out of the boat.

Espinoza and I made it back to the dock at the park. I was so relieved to step off the boat. Espinoza acted touched, like it was no big deal.

"No wonder they didn't want to pay me until after the second load," I thought, "because if that wasn't the deal, this would be the last time I would get in the boat with that fool. There is no way I could have talked us out of something like that!"

Espinoza backed away from the dock and turned back down the river. I didn't care where he was going as long as I wasn't on the boat.

Later that day I called Espinoza, "Look, Dude, I see why you guys get caught if that is the kind of stuff you do. Why would you do something like that, drawing attention to yourself . . . especially with dope in the boat?"

Espinoza acknowledged that it was a stupid move. He chalked it up to drinking too much and promised not to do it again.

Espinoza ended with, "I will call you about the date and time of the next shipment."

The next day Espinoza called me to let me know the second shipment was set. He assured me this time it would be different. He explained that the two of us would be picking up a boat offshore.

"The drugs are hidden inside the hull of the boat, and we will need to cut a hole in the floor to get to the drugs once we are back up river at a secluded dock we own," Espinoza started. "My boss doesn't want to leave evidence, so we will need to take the boat out, burn it, and sink it.

"Morgan, do you know where would be a good place near the river's entrance to sink the boat?" Espinoza asked.

I thought a minute and then suggested Bahia Reef.

"We, again, will need a cover story in the event we got stopped," Espinoza began. "We could say we were fishing the reef."

"Okay. Good!" I responded.

"I will bring the tools to open the hull floor," Espinoza began, "and you need to bring the fishing equipment."

"How do we pick up the boat?" I asked.

Espinoza stood face-to-face with me as he explained, "We will meet a fishing boat at Bayfront Park on Anna Maria Island. They will take us to the boat offshore, and we will bring it in. We will need to meet at the park at 3 a.m. That should give us enough time to get back up the bay to the river before daylight."

The morning of the next trip I arrived at the park by 1:30 a.m. I had my fishing equipment and even brought some bait this time. I wanted to surveil the place for any law enforcement boats or personnel in the area. I fished and watched for a little over an hour when I saw a truck pull into the parking lot. Espinoza got out of the passenger side and retrieved some tools out of the back. The truck pulled away. Espinoza then approached me.

At just about 3:00 a.m., a center console, single engine boat pulled up to the dock. Acting like we were friends headed out on a fishing trip, we loaded all the equipment onto the boat and headed out from land, going west. I never got the boat driver's name, but he texted someone, followed by inputting coordinates into a GPS unit. Within 30 minutes Espinoza and I were out-of-sight of land and had met up with a boat headed north.

We pulled up beside the boat. It had two Spanish guys onboard—both looking very serious and not having much to say. Espinoza and I transferred our gear to the new boat. While boarding, I looked on the back of the boat for its name. "*Escape*" was painted across the back, and it was out of Tampa.

"At least it looks the part," I mused.

I knew I needed to familiarize myself with the boat in case we got stopped.

I opened the compartment under the dash and pulled out the paperwork. I was stunned to see the boat was registered to . . . *myself!*

"How the fuck did this happen?" I questioned Espinoza, shaking the paperwork at him.

"The boss has connections," he said, "and he wants to be sure we look legit if we get stopped. We have been doing this a long time. Something as simple as not having the boat registered to the driver can get us caught."

Espinoza gave me the coordinates for the dock in the river to which we were headed.

"So, the story is simple," Espinoza started. "We have been out fishing all night. Look in the fish box."

I peered into the fish box and saw several fish inside, and they looked fresh.

"We caught those fish and are headed back in," Espinoza continued. "Got it?"

"Yes," I said as I pointed us to the spot marked on the GPS.

The boat wasn't nearly as fast as the other one, so I would not try and outrun any law enforcement boats. It was in the middle of the week and early in the morning. I figured I wouldn't see any law enforcement boats.

The direction on the GPS showed going around Egmont Key; however, I decided to cut to the inside and stay away from the channel. Once we passed under the Skyway Bridge, I stayed to the east side of the bay, figuring I would draw less attention there. I only saw a few barges headed out of the channel and no other small vessels. Turning into the channel of the Little Manatee River, I felt relieved . . . so far, so good.

Espinoza seemed much more serious this time . . . "almost like he knows something I don't," I thought apprehensively.

I worked our way up river, slowing for the no-wake zones. I knew that would be something that would get us stopped the quickest.

We continued up the river a couple more miles. Then, Espinoza pointed out the dock. I noticed the fast boat from the other day docked on one side, underneath a covered area with a boat lift. Espinoza pointed.

"Pull in there," he instructed me.

It was still dark, being only about 5 a.m. There wasn't much around, and the dock was up in the mangroves.

Espinoza got a Sawzall out of his bag. It was a tool with a blade about six inches long with rough teeth, and I knew it would cut right through the fiberglass of the boat. Espinoza started cutting into the floor just behind the cuddy cabin. Within just a few minutes he had a three-foot hole cut into the floor.

Both of us moved the dope up onto the boat dock into a boat box. The bags looked to be filled with some kind of pills.

"What is it?" I inquired.

"The best-paying drug around right now: fentanyl," Espinoza answered. "These little babies sell to all kinds of people. Cocaine, weed, and crack sell to a certain kind of person; that means limited sales. Fentanyl sells to all kinds of people. It is easier to distribute now, and it's much more profitable. This is over $1 million right here."

I gasped at the thought of that much money for such a little amount of dope.

"We need to get rid of this boat," Espinoza continued.

"Okay. I figured we would take it out to Bahia Reef and burn it. You follow me out, and I will set it on fire. We will just say it was an accident and started in the engine compartment. Once I light the fire—depending on if anyone is around—I will jump overboard, and you pick me up."

"Then we head in?" Espinoza asked.

"No," I said. We must call 9-1-1 and report it just like any accident. The fire department will come out and maybe a Tampa police boat; but because it will sink, they will just take a report . . . no problem."

Espinoza began to protest, "But . . ."

I cut in on him, "This is what the boss is paying me for. We must make it look like an accident, and it will be good."

I jumped back on board the *Escape*, and Espinoza got on the fast boat. We headed back down the river, Espinoza following me. When we came out into the bay, we headed for Bahia Reef.

As I ran down the river, I began ruminating about how close I was to payday.

"I hope all goes well and I can be done with these people," I grumbled to myself.

Since it was the middle of the week, there were no other boats out fishing. It was early, and it was looking like it would be a beautiful day. Now that we had no drugs aboard, I could relax and enjoy the rest of the trip. I believed we were going to make it.

Once out on the reef, I looked around one last time. Knowing a little about fire, I knew not to use too much gasoline; gasoline was made to explode.

"A little will get the boat burning," I thought, "and the rest will spread."

I tried a couple of times to get the fire started with only a little gasoline poured on the floor, but it would quickly burn off the surface. I was getting nervous, so I decided to pour some gasoline into the cuddy cabin. That did the trick. I then poured an additional amount on the floor. After I lit the fire, I threw some life jackets on top. Within 45 seconds flames were pouring from the cuddy cabin, and black smoke rose high into the air. I believed there was no chance the fire would go out now, so I jumped overboard.

Espinoza drove over to where I treaded water and helped me aboard. In my excitement I didn't realize I still had my cell phone in my pocket when I jumped into the salt water. Of course, when I tried to turn it on to call 9-1-1, it was dead.

"Call 9-1-1!" I yelled to Espinoza. "Hurry! Call 9-1-1!"

Fear crossed Espinoza's face as he stood frozen, so I grabbed the phone from him and made the call myself. Within a few minutes a Tampa Fire Department fire boat was heading toward us.

"Stay calm," I blew out to Espinoza, "and let me do all the talking. Remember, you were just out here fishing and saw the boat burning. You drove over to help me, and that's all you know."

Espinoza nodded yes; but I could see he was actually yelling "No!" inside his head, afraid of what might happen.

"Relax, Bro," I said. "They are just firemen here to help. They don't know what happened unless you tell them."

The fire boat pulled up and directed the water cannon to the front of the *Escape*. The amount of water they poured on it just helped it to sink below the surface that much faster. I looked back at Espinoza and smiled.

As the *Escape* disappeared under the surface of the water, the fire boat moved over toward Espinoza and me. A firefighter started asking the two of us questions. As we answered the questions, the Tampa police boat pulled alongside and tied up to both boats. This made Espinoza nervous.

They first asked me what happened, and I told them my practiced story.

"I was fishing on the front of the boat. The wind was in my face. I smelled something and looked toward the back of the boat. I saw smoke coming from the cuddy cabin. I jumped down and grabbed the fire extinguisher and expelled it on the fire."

When practicing the story that I planned on telling law enforcement, I was going to include that I had aimed the fire extinguisher over the side; but when "show time" arrived, I had forgotten about including that important piece of information.

"Do you have any idea what caused the fire?" they pressed.

I simply played dumb and gave them the "shoulders up and palms out" look.

They asked me if the boat was insured. My confident composure almost evaporated as I didn't know the answer to that question.

I quickly recovered from the jolt and answered, "Yes, yes, of course it is insured. I can get that information for you later."

They seemed satisfied with the answer for then.

The police officers watched and listened to my story. They didn't seem to disbelieve what I said, much to my relief. I wanted to develop a rapport with them, so I told them I used to be a cop. They perked up, and the subject changed to that topic . . . just what I was hoping for.

They asked me what happened, and I gave them the short version of the shooting and how it all had turned political. They seemed to be genuinely sorry to hear what had happened. Most cops know someone who has been treated wrongly during their career.

A police officer asked me, "Do you need a ride back to the dock?"

"Thank you, but Espinoza here is going back to the same dock I came from. He has already offered to get me back. Appreciate all the help!"

I waved them off. It seemed to me my story made sense to them. Once they had all the information they believed they needed, the officer gave me a card with the case number and report information written on it. I thanked them again as they pulled away.

Once out of earshot Espinoza excitedly exclaimed, "You did great! They believed every word you said! Man, did you have them eating out of your hand!"

"They are just people," I responded, "doing a job."

Chapter 18
Captain Ike: Opening Up to Gina

My first night aboard *Good Times* with Gina was interesting. I couldn't do much, but it was nice just sitting, relaxing and getting to know each other better. This was kind of like a first date, and she spent the night in her own bunk, of course. *Good Times* has two separate bunks in the aft section of the boat. One side pulls out to a double bed, and the other side is a single. I always slept on the double bed side because it was the easiest and fastest way to get up on deck if I needed to.

We sat in the salon, and Gina asked lots of questions about my past and how I got to where I was. I told her how I always wanted to be a fireman. I shared that when I was a younger man, I started volunteering at a local fire department and got hooked. I recalled how I used to sleep with my clothes beside my bed at home and how, when the beeper went off, I would jump up and race to the fire department. In those days a beeper was the fastest way to notify many people at once. In my young mind I thought I *must* be there because they couldn't make it without me.

I further recalled the day I signed up at the State Fire Academy in Ocala, the premier fire school in Florida. All the state instructors are trained there. Since instruction at the academy was six months long, I moved my camper to a town near the academy and lived in it. Every morning at 7 a.m. we would fall in formation for at least one hour of PT (physical training). It consisted of various calisthenics followed by a run for several miles.

Once that was completed, I would race back to my camper, shower and change, grab some grub, and be in class at 0900 hours. Some days we were all day in class, and some days we would be out on the drill field. The drill field is where a probie fireman learned how to pull fire hose; roll up fire hose; tie all kinds of knots; how to properly raise and lower ladders; how to use and wear the SCBA (self-contained breathing apparatus) or, as most called it, the air tank; as well as a thousand other skills needed to become an entry-level fireman.

Gina looked at me thoughtfully and asked, "Why are you so drawn to fighting fires?"

"Well, I guess the first few times I volunteered on a fire, I got to go inside structure fires with other career firemen. My adrenaline pumped through my veins like I had never felt it before. I just couldn't get enough of it!" I replied.

"But what about the danger of it all?" she quietly inquired.

"I am well aware of the many ways to die at the normal house fire," I started. "I understand that when a fireman enters a burning building why and how they have to drop to their knees—because the temperature at head height can range upward of 1500 degrees. If a fireman stands up for any reason, death comes quickly. The gear they wear will only protect them for around 30 seconds in that environment.

"And then there is the camaraderie of the fire station. It is amazing. When you put your trust in someone with your very life on a daily basis, it brings you together . . . truly like a family and like few other jobs offer."

After a short pause I continued, "Plus I love helping others. The many times I've had the opportunity to save people from fires, auto accidents, and many other types of situations are very rewarding. When you can make a difference in someone's life, it is an amazing feeling.

"You know, Gina, for many years I couldn't wait to get up and go to work. I don't think most people can understand that. Most people dread getting up and going to work in the morning; but for me it was exciting, and I looked forward to my time at work."

"So, why did you leave the job?"

"That is a little harder to explain," I tentatively answered. "The very thing you love can sometimes bring you pain. After being in it for years, the excitement of it started wearing off some; and the negatives started building up. You see, along with the great satisfaction of helping others, there are a lot of negatives. You don't always get to save everyone. The faces of those you lose tend to stick with you over time.

"One time we were dispatched to a pond to search for some missing children, two little girls. On a dock at the pond was the last place the children were seen. We searched the water but didn't find anyone. We started searching the land around the pond. After a half day or so of searching for the children on land we went back to the lake to search again. The other firemen and I locked arms and started searching the pond on a grid system. I will never forget bumping into something and reaching down and pulling up two little girls still holding hands . . . to this day I can still see their little faces.

"Then one night we were dispatched to a vehicle accident where several young teenagers were racing and flipped their car. They were trapped and ultimately burned to death because the car was sitting on an electrical box and the car was energized. We had to sit and watch . . . we couldn't do anything to save them.

"That kind of stuff builds up in your mind over time. The job you once loved becomes a source of pain."

Gina began tearing up, and I stopped talking for a minute.

"I didn't mean to upset you," I said.

"You didn't," she answered. "I just never knew that part of being a fireman."

Hoping to change the mood she asked, "So, how did you become a fire investigator and a police officer?"

"That is a long story," I said. "You sure you want to hear it?"

She smiled and vigorously nodded her head yes.

"I want to know all about you," she said.

"Okay, but I want to make you a deal."

"What?"

"You get me a cold beer out of the fridge, and I will tell you all about it."

"Not while you are taking meds, Mister," she quickly responded.

"That's the point . . . I don't plan on taking anymore . . . and besides it has been days since I had a cold beer."

She relented and got me one. I started telling Gina the story.

"At the time, the police department in our city wanted to get some medically trained personnel on their SWAT team. There are many times when a scene is not safe, but people may need medical attention . . . say an officer is shot during a search warrant and is pinned down in a dangerous situation . . . or in the case of an active shooter at a school or other gathering place. A medically trained SWAT officer could go in and provide care until the injured could be moved. Sometimes you can't move someone who is injured until the shooter is neutralized, but they may need medical care before that.

"The police department offered to send me to the police academy with all expenses paid. I only had to sign an agreement that I would stay employed with the city for several years. I was not planning on going anywhere, so I agreed to the terms.

"I loved attending the police academy. It was another one of those times in my life when I made lifelong friends. To this day I am still in contact with many of my fellow academy students."

"Tell me about what kind of stuff you did in the police academy," Gina prompted.

"Actually, the first few months are kind of boring . . . a lot of class time and learning all kinds of legal issues. About halfway through you start doing some of the fun stuff like firearms training, defensive tactics, and emergency driving. Each one of those sections were fun, and we looked forward to going to school on those days."

I looked at her out of the corner of my eye as I spoke, "However, I had to redo my emergency driving section."

"How come?" she inquired with a smirk on her face. "Were you a bad driver?"

"Noooo," I drawled out. "It happened during lunch break one day. We piled into a car with a fellow student . . . a good friend of mine. We worked for the same agency. We were riding down this road, and she got distracted. We went around a curve and rolled the vehicle three times. They were so strict about our missing time in class they made us retake that entire section."

"Were you injured?"

"A little. Do you see this scar on my elbow?" I asked as I pointed at the scar. "My arm went out the window and hit the pavement. I always kid with people and tell them a gator attacked me when they ask me about the scar. Now, as a boat captain, it will be a shark attack," I added, nodding my head for emphasis.

She just smiled.

"So, you were on the SWAT team, too?" she asked.

"Oh, yes," I said. "It was also a lot of fun. Some of the big agencies have full-time SWAT members. Most smaller agencies have teams made up from their different police divisions: some detectives; some patrol guys; usually a K9 officer; and, in my case, a fire department guy.

"We usually knew in advance about SWAT operations because most of them would be drug search warrants. Those warrants would take months to set up. We would be notified to be at the police department on a certain morning. We wouldn't even know the location until that morning for operational security.

"We also got call outs, like someone who barricaded themselves inside a house or to search an area for some type of dangerous suspect. We always got called out to deal with the suspect if there was an officer-involved shooting. In my years of service, I saw several cases of officers killed in the line of duty; and we had to find the suspect. Those calls were very high stress. Those were the times that were emotionally draining, and I don't miss them."

"So, you were a fire investigator, right?"

"Yes," I replied.

"How did that come about?"

"That was an interesting time. Since I had law enforcement training, it was a natural move for me to get into the fire investigation or inspection division. My boss at the time was June, and she had also attended the police academy. She was the lead fire investigator.

"I started getting the required classes to become a fire investigator. It took a few years to complete all the courses, but eventually I got them done. So, the last few years of my time with the city I did all kinds of fire prevention activities; and when we had fires, I would do the investigation if it was on my shift."

'You worked shift work?" she asked.

"Yes, we worked 24 hours on and 48 hours off. The day before my shift I would be on call for investigations."

"So, you worked one day, then off two?"

"Yes," I said smiling. "That was the best thing about the job: I was always able to have a good bit of time off.

"After working for the city, I worked a while for some private insurance companies as a private fire investigator. The pay was much better, and it was mostly daytime hours. In most cases it was not an emergency to investigate a fire, so I had a day or two to get to the scene to get started. That meant mostly daytime work.

"I did that for a few years until I got my boat captain's license. I wanted to start doing kayak fishing charters like I do now."

"How did you get into this particular investigation?" she asked.

"Well, my old boss still works for the insurance company. She knows I am a boat captain and have special diving skills. She said I seemed like the perfect investigator for the job. I want to do a few things to this boat, so I decided to take the case for some extra cash. I don't plan on doing many of this kind of investigation . . . especially seeing how this one turned out. I want to be out on the water—it is truly my happy place these days."

"I understand that," Gina said. "I like that you're doing boat captain stuff instead of fire investigations."

I smiled and agreed.

"When are you going to take me out on one of those trips?" she asked.

"Very soon . . . just as soon as I get better. You will be my first trip back."

"I feel special," she said.

I smiled, "Oh, you are!"

Gina pointed to a small painting I had hanging over the helm. It was a painting of a fireman standing and holding a pike pole. The fireman cast a shadow behind him. In the shadow was a silhouette of Christ holding a shepherd hook and standing in a position similar to the fireman. The title of the painting was *The Lord is My Shepherd*.

"Where did that come from?" she quizzed.

"That is a painting, along with several others, done by a fire officer named Jim Davis. We worked at the same department together for many years," I answered. "Oftentimes when I am contemplating a decision, I look at it and think, 'What would Christ do in a similar circumstance?' Through the years the meaning of the painting has changed for me. When I worked as a fireman, it gave me peace that things would be okay.

Lately, working as a boat captain, it seems to do the same for me.

"Okay," I broke the trend of the conversation. "I have been doing all the talking here. Now it's your turn to tell me things about you, Gina."

"Well, I haven't lived such an exciting life as you. I was married once but ended up getting divorced. We were together for several years, but I think we just got married too young. Looking back on it, I thought it was just the thing to do at the time," she said. "How is that?" I probed.

"Well, when a girl reaches a certain age, all her girlfriends are getting married or have already gotten married. I felt like I was missing something, so I started looking for someone and met my ex. He loved me and did all the things I wanted; but sadly, I didn't love him as deeply as I should have. We were happy for a while, but later I started feeling less fulfilled . . . crazy, right?" she asked.

"I don't think it's crazy; I think that is more common than most people would admit. I think you are human," I said.

"After I got divorced, I worked as a server and bartender for a few years. I got promoted into management. It was easy, really: I just did the things that most people said wasn't their job . . . seems like a lot of people in the service industry don't look at it as a career but as a stepping stone to something else. But I really enjoy the work. I enjoy making people happy," she said. Gina sighed deeply, shrugged her shoulders, and added, "That's basically what I do every day."

I sat thinking about what she had said.

"You know, I agree. I think many servers don't take their job seriously. For instance, say a guy meets a girl. He tries to get a date with her and finally talks her into it. He takes her to a place for a nice dinner and drinks because he is hoping to impress her. Let's say he has a great server. The good service could be what helps those two people to become a couple and live happily ever after.

"Now, say that same couple had a bad server. The service takes forever, he gets the order wrong, and the date ends up being a flop. Now, that couple may have nothing good to say about the date; and it could alter their future."

Gina agreed.

"Okay, now two things: first, I must go to the head; and second, I need you to get me another cold beer."

With a devilish smile she asked, "Do you need any help?"

I thought for a second and said, "Sure, I do."

She laughed and said, "Too late, Big Boy."

I slowly got up and headed to the rear head.

"The stairs aren't helping!" I said out loud as I made my way back.

Stepping inside the *Good Times* from the back deck, there are three steps down. Going forward into the galley, there are three more steps down . . . same thing going into the aft cabin where the head is: three more steps down.

Normally this was no problem for me; I am used to running up and down the stairs. Now with stitches in my side and muscle damage, I realized how much I used my stomach muscles.

I did my business much slower than usual and headed back up the stairs and into the salon. Once I again got comfortable, I stared at Gina for a moment.

"Have you ever been in love?" I asked.

She looked around, thinking about it.

"Yes," she said, "but he broke my heart. We never married, but I was so in love with Marshall that I missed many warning signs of his cheating on me. I think I knew but didn't want to face the reality of the situation at the time. I wanted to marry him, but he wanted to play games. I was only the person filling space in his life at the time.

"What about you?" Gina turned the tables on me. "Have you ever been in love?"

"Yes, I also have a broken heart story. It affected me badly. I haven't wanted to be too serious with anyone since. I dated a few girls but never let myself get too close."

The look on Gina's face changed.

"So, tell me about her."

"Well, I think a lot of people have similar stories like yours and mine. I would say we had a lot in common. Life was very good for a long while. It was very easy to be with her because we wanted to do a lot of the same things. She was the first girl that I ever thought about marrying."

"Why did you guys break up, then?" she asked.

"It's a long story . . . but the short story is this: we were going on a date one day. It worked out that we met up earlier in the day and had been hanging out. We were waiting on a movie to start that evening so we stopped by my buddy's house. He wanted to show me a new rifle he had gotten, and his house was on the way to the movies. I wanted to introduce him to my girlfriend, also."

I paused for a minute. Gina recognized something was wrong.

"What happened?" Gina prompted.

"It is still kind of tough to talk about to this day." I swallowed hard before continuing. "At my buddy's house, he got the gun off the gun rack on the wall. I was standing beside my girlfriend. My buddy turned around with the rifle in his hand, and somehow the trigger caught his belt loop as he turned. It forced the gun downward, and the gun fired. A single shot struck her in the chest and went into her lungs. The last words she said were 'I've been shot.' She fell backward. I tried helping her, but there wasn't anything anyone could do for her. She was bleeding internally and died right there in his house. We called 9-1-1, and the next few hours and days were a blur for me. That was, without a doubt, the worst day of my life up until that point."

"Oh, my God!" Gina exclaimed with her eyes opened wide. "I am so sorry to hear that."

"I don't like to think about it a lot; but when you lose someone like that, it affects you deeply," I said with a scratchy voice.

"Of course," Gina said.

I looked away, trying not to get emotional in front of Gina. We sat in awkward silence as often happens when I tell the story.

I looked at Gina and smiled as I started speaking again, "Well, there was another girl." Wanting to change the story, she said, "Tell me about her."

"It is a story of bad timing," I started. "I had a crush on this girl for a long time. She was very pretty and loved the salt life as I do. I tried several times to talk with her; but each time I was free, she was in a relationship . . . and it seemed like when she was free, I was seeing someone."

"What happened with her?" Gina asked.

"Well, I really don't know the end to that story."

Gina looked puzzled for a minute, and then a big smile crossed her face as she got a little red.

"You are talking about *me*?"

"Yes," I nodded.

Chapter 19
Tony Morgan: The Drug Deal

As we pulled away from the fire and police boats, Espinoza gave a huge smile.

"They didn't suspect anything!" he said.

"Of course not," I said, feeling strangely proud of myself. "You just have to keep cool and not get nervous. Cops are trained to pay attention to body language; and if you are nervous, your body will show it."

"The boss is going to love it!" Espinoza exclaimed.

"What now?" I asked.

"We need to make a few calls and off load the drugs. We already have a delivery place set. We will meet a couple of guys at the Highway 41 train trestle. We make our sale there. We try to never drive the drugs on the roads. We let others take that risk because that is where most people get caught. There are many K9 cops running around these days. You get pulled over for a minor infraction; and before you know it, they bring those fucking dogs and you get busted."

We turned into the river, slowed, and finally pulled over at a little beach area on Sand Key. We pulled the boat up onto the beach. Espinoza got out and got on his cell phone. Not wanting me to hear his conversation, he walked up the beach. I heard him say, "The boat is gone, Boss," as he walked away.

I got a bottle of water and sat back on the boat and relaxed. This was the first time in a very long time that I felt like things were going to be all right. I knew we had to deal with the drugs one more time, and then I should be done with them.

After several calls Espinoza walked back over to the boat.

"Okay, we are set," he said. "We will meet for the deal in about an hour. After that we get our payday. You did good, Ese," Espinoza said, using the Spanish version of Bro. "Let's run over to Little Harbor to kill some time and have a drink."

This made me nervous because the last time he drank on a boat, he almost got us caught.

Later, we pulled up and docked at the Sunset Grill. We went up to the bar. As we sat there, a cute, little, blonde girl served us. She smiled politely.

"How are you guys this morning?" she asked. "Have you guys been out fishing?"

I returned the smile and nodded that we had been but didn't want to volunteer any more information than that. We ordered a couple of drinks. While we continued sitting there enjoying our drinks, I heard her tell another customer about a boat fire out at the reef.

"If she only knew," I thought.

I looked at Espinoza and shook my head no for him to not comment on it. After a couple of drinks Espinoza's phone went off . . . apparently, a text.

He said, "We need to leave."

He paid for our drinks, and we went back to the boat. I untied the lines, and he drove. Once we were clear of the docks, he brought the boat up on plane, swept around the first curve past Tropical Island, and crossed the bay into the channel of the river. Once we neared the destination dock, Espinoza slowed the boat. He passed the dock slowly, looking for anyone. I knew he was searching for cops or anything out of the ordinary.

Then we went up the river a little and stopped. Floating back down the river, he told me what we were going to do. He reached under the console and pulled out two handguns and gave one to me.

"I know these guys," he cautioned, "but you never know if something may go bad. I assume you know how to use this."

I gave him an "of course" look.

"Once we get to the dock, I will let you off. Grab the bags sitting there, and quickly get back into the boat. They are waiting at the Highway 41 bridge for us."

Espinoza then sent another text on his phone. He pulled up toward the dock, and I jumped from the front of the boat onto the dock. No one was around, and I knew that we were almost in the clear . . . if we didn't get caught now.

I put the bags into the boat; and we backed away, still on high alert for anyone. About that time a boat came down from up river. The boat was on plane; and the occupants simply waved as they flew past, a common greeting for boaters.

We came up on plane ourselves and headed for the bridge. I watched in every direction. I figured our chances were slim to come across any law enforcement in the short distance we needed to travel. I saw the bridge as it came into view; and I kept looking behind us, expecting to see a bunch of police boats come out of hiding to chase us. It was just my mind playing tricks on me.

We slowed as we neared the bridge. I saw two Hispanic-looking guys standing up on the bank. Seeing us, they moved down the bank. One was carrying a black bag. We eased up onto the sandbar. Espinoza said a few words in Spanish, and the first guy passed him the bag. Espinoza looked in it and fumbled through it. Nodding his head yes, he turned to me and motioned for me to give him the bags as he passed the black bag back to me.

I nervously looked around as the guy looked into the bags we handed over. He pulled out a bag of pills and smiled.

Espinoza motioned for them to move away, and they started back up the hill. The one guy still held the clear bag of pills as he tried to climb the bank. As we started backing out, I noticed him pick up some of the pills he had obviously spilled. It looked like he had caught the plastic bag on a limb. I didn't care because as of now we didn't have possession of the drugs.

I opened the bag we received from the two men and saw the most amount of cash I had ever seen in my life. Stacks of hundreds in so many bundles I couldn't count them all. Espinoza looked at me and smiled.

"How much?" I asked.

"$1.5 million."

We eased back up the river, headed to where I had parked. Espinoza was in a good mood as was I, and he started talking to me about some future deals on which they were working. He knew I had said I wanted to do this deal and get out, but he tried to talk me into helping them with the "biggest deal" ever. Now that we were done and the chance of getting caught was done, I *was* interested.

"Tell me more about what you are talking about," I encouraged Espinoza.

He told me how they had a guy who moved fentanyl across the southern border. This would be the most they had ever moved at one time, and they needed help when they brought it into Tampa.

"Why not just bring it in by boat straight from Mexico?" I asked.

"A single boat leaving from Mexico and crossing the Gulf of Mexico is easy to detect," he explained. "We like to bring it across at the border with lots of other traffic so we just blend in with the rest of all the other trucks."

"Where do they hide it?" I asked.

"Our guy has a farming business, and he will hide it inside a load of vegetables . . . most often cucumbers. They seem to hide the smell better from the K9 officers.

"Our next deal will be coming in at Port Nogales. Once it is in the U.S., we need your help moving it through the states. Are you in?" he asked.

"I don't know, Man," I said. "I only planned to do this deal and get out."

"This next deal will pay us *twice* as much as this last one," he pushed.

I had no intention of doing any other deals. I was only gathering as much information as I could get. Espinoza didn't know it, but I had run across an old buddy of mine from some drug classes we had taken together. He was now working for the DEA. I told him about what happened to me with the shooting charges. He said he could sign me up as a CI (confidential informant), and I could make money from that. He had no idea, of course, in what I was now involved.

The more I thought about it, I realized I could set myself up a good defense if I got caught. I could always sign up with my buddy; and then if I got caught moving the drugs, I could say I was working and gathering information for him. I had, of course, signed many people up over the years when I was working in the dope unit. Several times we had CIs feed us information on their competition. They were still dealing but just wanted their competition busted.

We made it back to the dock where I had parked my truck. I was hoping to get my money and be done with Espinoza. In my opinion he was a loose cannon and about to get caught because of how crazy he was.

"When do I get my money?" I asked.

"Tonight," he said, "and the boss wants to meet you now that we made this deal successfully. He will try to talk you into the next deal. I need to drop the boat and get my ride. I will text you the address where to meet in Polk County. We have a safe house where we do the splits. The boss will meet us there. We will meet near the safe house, and I will drive us in."

"Okay," I said.

I didn't feel comfortable with his pulling away and leaving me without getting my money, but I didn't really have a choice. It wasn't like I could call the cops or anything.

Chapter 20
Felix Cardona: No Witnesses

Cardona was headed to his office when his cell notified him he had a text. The number was saved under the name "Information" with no other identifiers. This was in the event he ever got caught.

The text read, "Call asap. We have a hit on your last inquiry."

Cardona pulled over to the side of the road at his first opportunity and called the number. A Spanish-speaking female came on the line.

She confirmed, "A white male, Tony Morgan 3-7-68, has been entered into the system as a confidential informant ten days prior, pending information of an upcoming drug movement."

"Are you sure?" Cardona asked.

"Yes," she said. "He appears to have been a cop."

Cardona felt his blood pressure rise because he knew it was Morgan.

"I will kill the motherfucker slowly!" he thought aloud. "I never trusted him."

Knowing time was his enemy, he thought for a minute on what he needed to do. According to the last call from Espinoza, the deal was done; and he had the money. In fact, they were set to meet that evening.

"Was Morgan setting *them* up?" he thought to himself.

He didn't think so. The deal had gone through; and if they were going to bust them, they would have done it while the drugs and money were in the same location.

He thought, "That rat must be gathering information on us. Espinoza misjudged him! He will pay for that mistake, but that will have to wait."

He needed to make sure his money was safe. He looked up Espinoza's cell number. He sent a simple text "9-1-1." That was a code preset to determine if they had been compromised.

Within the minute the response came, "Safe."

"Are you alone?"

"Yes."

"Stand by for a call in one minute."

Cardona pulled up a special app called Location Finder. He scrolled through several phone numbers and chose Espinoza's number. Within a second an icon popped up, showing a moving arrow heading west on State Road 674. The app had been installed on all Cardona's phones and given to his employees. It was designed for a situation like this. He would know where Espinoza was at all times and would question him when he called. If something seemed off, he would simply end the call. He touched the call button, and in one second Espinoza answered the line.

"What's up, Boss?"

"Are you alone?"

"Yes. Why?"

"What is your present location?"

Espinoza seemed confused with the questions.

"I am on State Road 674," he said, "headed toward Polk County."

Cardona clicked the app and looked for the next road that Espinoza would pass.

"Tell me the name of the next road you pass," Cardona ordered sternly.

Espinoza could tell Cardona was pissed.

"One second, Boss. I see a sign."

Cardona sat quietly.

"Carlton Lake Road," Espinoza finally said.

Feeling confident that at this point all was well, Cardona seethed, "Your fucking friend is a rat!"

"What do you mean, Boss?"

"I just got information that Morgan has recently signed up with DEA as a CI. He is a fucking rat! Where is he now?" Cardona inquired.

"He is meeting me in a few minutes, Boss. I told him you wanted to meet him at the safe house."

"Did you tell him where it is?" Cardona demanded.

"No, Boss, I told him to meet me at Highway 37 and State Road 674 and that I would drive us in. Morgan is expecting to get paid then, Boss."

"He is going to get paid, for sure!" Cardona said with a snarl.

Espinoza could tell how pissed Cardona was.

"Sorry, Boss, I never expected for this to turn out like this."

"I will deal with you later," Cardona threatened. "First, I want Morgan. How much does he know about the next deal?"

"Not much. I only told him vaguely about how we moved it. I thought I could trust him since we had done both these deals."

"Here is what you do," Cardona instructed. "Meet Morgan as planned; and once he gets into the car, do what you need to to incapacitate him. Tie him up, and check his cell phone for any recent messages."

"His phone don't work, Boss. He jumped overboard with it in his pocket when he burned the boat . . . *that* I know for sure."

"After he is secure, go to the safe house; and don't get stopped! Do you have my money?" Cardona asked.

"Yes, Boss, it is safe."

"If anything happens to my money, you will be dead . . . like Morgan will soon be." Cardona paused a moment before continuing, "One other thing: text me 'Okay' once he is secure. That way I know all is good. Then text me when you get to Doc Durrance Road."

"Yes, Boss!" Espinoza replied, then hung up.

Cardona hung up the phone. He had been successful for years by taking precautions that most others thought unnecessary, such as paying to have contacts at the DEA. This time it appeared to have saved them . . . or at least he hoped it had. He also took precautions, such as knowing where his drugs and money were at all times and his never being where the drugs were so he couldn't ever be connected to them.

The biggest problem Cardona had was laundering the cash he got. Having legitimate businesses and real estate holdings helped him to accomplish that task.

Cardona wondered how much information Morgan had given to the DEA, if any. Situations like these took much thought to deal with effectively. Cardona knew that he alone would have to deal with Morgan. Any other way could be tied back to him someday. If he killed Morgan himself without any witness, he could never be convicted of that crime. Besides, killing was nothing new to Cardona. Rising to the level of cartel boss took lots of deeds, and killing was one of them. One thing Cardona had learned over the years was if he must kill someone, make sure he did it alone with no witnesses.

Chapter 21
Captain Ike: A Text from Morgan

I sat in my chair in the salon while Gina sat nearby, reading a book.

"What are you reading?" I asked.

"Oh, your basic story of adventure in the Caribbean."

"Oh, yeah, that sounds pretty good."

"Yes, it is about a retired marine who moves to the Florida Keys and builds a house on an island out in the Content Keys."

"Oh, wow, that sounds like heaven to me!"

"Yes, that's what I was thinking. He gets involved in all kinds of stuff and some of it is quite dangerous. Does that sound familiar?"

She looked at me with an I-know-someone-look.

"Nope, doesn't ring a bell," I answered as I just looked around, whistling.

"Uh-huh."

She smiled at me.

"I am getting bored sitting around here. What say we get out and go for dinner somewhere?"

"That sounds good! Do you have any place in mind?" she asked.

"Let me think for a second . . . yes!" I said. "There is a place out on St. Pete Beach. They have indoor and outdoor seating with a bar. They serve the best blackened chicken alfredo I have ever had. I have been craving it for a few days."

"Sounds good to me. Just give me a minute to freshen up," Gina requested.

I put on my Guy Harvey shorts . . . the best I owned . . . and a tropical-style shirt. Being a boat captain and living on a boat, this was considered "dressing up." Gina came out of the aft cabin and gave me a nod of approval. She was dressed in a short, little sun dress, also in tropical colors.

"It appears we match a bit," I observed.

Gina often wore little sundresses, and it was one of the things I loved about her.

"I will drive, Captain," she said to me.

"Fine with me, My Dear. I will sit back and enjoy the scenery."

"Where to?" she asked.

"The place is called Shells Seafood Restaurant on Gulf Boulevard. Turn left out the parking lot and head to Gulf Boulevard and then make another left."

It was nice to get out. I never really loved the traffic around the marina, but at least everything was very close. One could get to just about any restaurant in just a few minutes. We turned off Pasadena Avenue onto Gulf Boulevard and then drove south. Shells was just a few blocks down.

As we pulled in, my cell phone chirped; and my buddy, Jack from the marina, asked, "Where are you? I went by the boat, but your truck was gone."

"Went to get dinner," I responded. "I will hit you up when we get back."

"Cool!" he texted back.

I was definitely feeling better and getting around much better. We went inside and sat at the bar. It had large, sliding glass doors in front, and we could watch people out on the sidewalk. This time of the year there were tourists everywhere. There were all kinds of people walking by.

It was also very cool inside. The outside temperature was running in the mid-90s, and we hadn't started getting the needed afternoon cool-down showers we normally got this time of year. Most days by 4 or 5 p.m. clouds would build along the coastline as the sea breeze pushed in. This blocked the sun, and the cool rain would normally make for a nice afternoon. If it was this hot all the time in Florida, there would be a lot less tourism.

"Well, hello, Captain! Haven't seen you in a while," Connie, the server, said.

"It is a long story, but I got injured and have been taking it easy on the boat."

"Sorry to hear that," she said sincerely. "And who is this pretty lady?" she asked, referring to Gina.

"This is my friend, Gina," I said.

"Nice to meet you, Gina. The captain is one of our good customers. He comes in and always orders the blackened chicken pasta," she said.

Gina smiled as she said, "Nice to meet you, too. Yes, he was telling me about how much he likes it here and especially how much he likes that blackened chicken pasta."

"Since we already know what *he* is having, what would you like?"

As Connie passed Gina a menu, she looked at me and asked, "Would you like a Captain Ike?"

Gina looked at me and asked incredulously, "You have your *own* drink?"

"Kind of a long story," I responded to Gina. "Yes, Ma'am, I would like one," I answered as I looked back at Connie.

Gina piped up, "I will have what he is having for a drink. Let me look over the menu for a minute, and I will let you know."

Connie smiled and left to start making our drinks.

"So, tell me about this drink," Gina said.

"It's not officially on the menu," I began explaining. "One night I came in for dinner, and we started talking about rum drinks. I came up with this one. It has three types of rum, as well as orange juice, pineapple juice, and a bit of grenadine."

"Mmmm, sounds good," she said.

"It is. After we made it, they jokingly named it the Captain Ike."

Connie came back with our drinks.

"Okay, Gina, have you decided what you want?"

"Yes," she said. "I would like to try the fish tacos."

"Perfect!" Connie responded. "I will put you guys' orders right in."

Gina took a sip of her drink, and she smiled.

"Wow, that is very good," she remarked.

"Yes," I agreed. "It is my favorite here."

We sat, talking and people watching.

"The atmosphere is great here," Gina said.

"Yeah, I like this place. I like the waitresses, and they always take care of me. I have a couple of places around town like this."

"Do you come over here a lot?" I asked Gina.

"Not really," she answered. "If I go to the beach, it is usually on Anna Maria Island or Holmes Beach."

I knew both of those beaches were less known to the tourists. As a result, locals often go to them.

"I don't like coming over the Skyway Bridge if I don't have to," Gina explained. "Plus, those beaches are much closer to my house."

"Yes, I like them, also. I have boated down that way on charters a good bit. The water there is very clear, and the clients love it."

In no time our dinner came.

"Oh, it smells so good," I remarked as I savored the smell of the dish before eating.

I looked at Gina's fish tacos.

"I don't think those two go together . . . fish and tacos," I said.

By then Gina had already taken a bite.

"Oh, these are good!" she said. "They're messy, but good. We have these at Little Harbor. I also didn't like the sound of them when I first tried them, but I love them now."

"To each his own," I said.

As we ate, I looked up and saw Jack from the marina walk in. He smiled and walked over to the bar where we were.

"I thought I might find you here!" he said. "Who is this pretty lady?"

"Jack, meet Gina. This is the girl I told you about from Little Harbor."

"Nice to meet you, Gina," he said.

Gina was mid-bite into a taco and smiled while head-gesturing to him.

When she was able to talk, she said, "Nice to meet you, Jack."

I explained to Gina how Jack also had a boat at the marina and how long we had known each other.

"Pull up a seat," I said. "Let me buy you a drink."

"Sure . . . if I am not intruding," he said.

"Of course not! What can I get you?"

I waved to Connie. She smiled as she approached.

"Well, hello, Jack!" she greeted him.

She knew him, as well.

"I will have one of those Captain Ike's he has been telling me about."

Sure thing," Connie replied.

Jack watched as she walked away. I caught him and smiled.

"Looks like you are feeling better," Jack said as he turned his attention back to me.

"Yes, I was going a bit stir crazy on the boat so I told Gina about this place . . . and here we are."

"So, how is that scratch?" he asked, referring to the gunshot wound.

"Well apparently, I am going to live. Gina here has been taking good care of me. She doesn't let me have as many beers as I like, but the care is great."

Gina smiled as she rolled her eyes.

"Jack is a blow boater," I told Gina.

"What is that?" she asked.

"One of those sail boat guys. They say they sail them, but every time I see them, they are motoring," I jabbed at Jack.

Jack quickly fired back with a power boater comment and

something about wasting fuel. "We banter back and forth all the time," I told Gina.

My phone chirped, and I about fell out of my chair when I read the text. It was from Morgan.

It read, "Hey, Buddy, are you looking for me?"

"Gina, we got to go! I just got a text from Morgan!"

Chapter 22
Tony Morgan: Pay Day

I was nervous as I drove to meet Espinoza. I knew I was almost in the clear. I just wanted to get my money and part ways with Espinoza and all these thugs. I had worked hard for many years and always was on the right side of the law. This made me feel like shit inside, but I also felt like I had no choice in the matter. I thought that maybe soon I would give my buddy at the DEA a call and get the information to him about the big shipment coming across the border. In my mind this would somehow atone for all the bad in which I had recently been involved.

I pulled into the little parking area at the corner of State Road 674 and Highway 37. People parked their cars here and carpooled. This junction led to several large employers, so it was a good spot to park. I was only there for about 15 minutes when Espinoza pulled in. I noticed he looked around as though something was wrong. I got out and walked over to his Lincoln Town Car.

"A typical drug dealer car," I thought as I approached it.

I slid into the passenger side front seat.

"What's up, Man? You seem nervous about something. Were you followed?" Espinoza curtly asked.

"No," I replied. "Plus, I don't have anything on me even if I was stopped."

"Let's just go," Espinoza replied in an aggravated voice.

This made me uneasy. I had made a career out of reading people, and I knew something wasn't right.

Espinoza pulled out on Highway 37, heading south. He kept looking in his rear-view mirror. I tried not to stare but continued watching his actions.

"Dude, why are you so worried?" I asked Espinoza.

"I'm not, Man. I am just making sure we are not being followed."

Espinoza was headed south, but Doc Durrance Road, the location of the safe house, was *north* from this location. The area was very rural with only a house or two for miles. Most of the area was commercial and owned by several large companies that mined for fertilizer. Massive, crane-looking machines the size of a building with huge backhoe-looking scoops called draglines could be seen along these roads. They were used to dig into the earth and extract materials that would eventually be used in fertilizers. At this time of night, the only vehicles on the road were the occasional trucks transporting mine-related products.

Espinoza pulled off onto one of the access roads leading back into the mine area.

"The place is back here?" I asked.

"Yeah," was Espinoza's short reply.

He still checked his rear-view mirror frequently. Pulling into an intersection, Espinoza looked around one last time.

"Okay, look under your seat. Your money is in the bag," Espinoza instructed.

I leaned down to try and see under my seat while feeling around with my hand. I did not find anything. I started to rise back up.

While I had been busy fishing around under my seat, Espinoza had pulled a pistol from a holster on his right leg. Just as I rose back up to face him, he used the butt of the pistol and struck me across the bridge of my nose with a powerful, backhand motion. I was out cold.

*****

Espinoza got out of the car and walked around to the passenger side. He yanked Morgan from the front seat, his body flopping to the ground. The unconscious Morgan was bleeding from his face. Espinoza drug him around to the rear of the car and opened the trunk. It was a struggle, but finally Espinoza managed to lift Morgan up and throw him into it. He opened a bag from inside the trunk, pulled some handcuffs from it, and put them on Morgan. He took duct tape from the bag and put it across Morgan's mouth to keep him from hollering if he woke up. Espinoza got back into the car and started driving again.

It was getting late now, and the sun was setting in the west. Espinoza pulled over to a wooded area and parked. He knew this area and knew no one would have any reason to be on one of the old mine roads. He still made a plan in the event someone drove up at the last minute. He would just say he needed to use the bathroom and would then pull out.

Espinoza had a few hours to kill, but he couldn't drive around and risk being pulled over with Morgan in the trunk. Since he felt so sure no one would drive down this road, he figured he would wait here until midnight before driving the short distance to Doc Durrance Road. He also knew the reason the boss didn't want him to come in before midnight was that someone may see him getting Morgan out of the car.

*****

I came to, and the darkness was all around me. My nose hurt badly, and I had the worst headache ever. I tried to move but realized my wrists were bound. I immediately recognized the feel of handcuffs. The fear was overwhelming: being bound and cuffed and not knowing where I was. I held back the desire to scream. My training from years ago started to kick in, and I started to force myself to calm down.

"Assess your situation," I thought.

By now my eyes were adjusting to the low light. It was dark outside I could tell. I heard music playing low and started trying to figure out where I was. I rolled to my right and could tell I was lying on some hard objects. I raised my legs and discovered I was in a confined space. I didn't try to speak; I could feel something covering my mouth.

What had happened? I was trying to remember, and I vaguely recalled leaning over in the front seat of Espinoza's car but didn't remember anything after that.

*****

Espinoza felt movement in the trunk so he got out. He walked to the back of the car with his pistol in his hand. He opened the trunk. He used the light on his phone to shine it on Morgan.

"You fucking rat," he said to Morgan. "All you had to do was to be cool. You were hours from getting paid. I am going to be lucky if I don't get killed, too, you son of a bitch."

Espinoza pulled a flask from his pocket and took a big gulp. Using his pistol, he struck Morgan across the side of his face, then slammed the trunk closed.

*****

The pain was intense, and I felt the oozing of blood down the side of my face. It took several minutes before the pain subsided enough to where I could think. I now knew I was in the trunk of a car. Estimating the size of it, I figured it was probably the same Lincoln Town Car.

What was Espinoza talking about, though? Why did he hit me and bind me up and put me in here? The questions raced through my mind as I heard the car crank and start moving again.

I now knew it was dark outside but figured it couldn't be too late. I just got hit in the face again, and I figured that's what Espinoza had done to me earlier. What was he talking about, though . . . "being cool"? Nothing made sense to me.

*****

Espinoza pulled back out onto Highway 37 and headed north to Doc Durrance Road. He took another drink from the flask and wondered what the boss would do to him for vouching for Morgan. Then he realized if the boss wanted him dead, he would probably already be dead. Since he had him delivering Morgan and still had his cash, he hoped his boss's wrath wouldn't be too bad.

Espinoza slowed and pulled onto Doc Durrance Road. He slowly passed by the metal building, looking for signs of anyone. Seeing no lights and no activity, he drove to the end of the street and turned around. He drove back and pulled in and parked at the back of the building. Very aware of his surroundings, he went over and unlocked the door and turned on the light inside. The metal building was purchased just for situations like this because a commercial building in a residential area doesn't draw too much attention if someone is in it at night. Most people would simply think someone was working late.

Espinoza got the bag of money out of the back seat and took it inside and put it on the table. The thought crossed his mind to take the money and run. He could go anywhere and never be seen again. Drinking more from his flask he felt the effects of the alcohol.

He went back to the car and stood at the trunk. He listened for any movement inside . . . or around the neighborhood, for that matter. Hearing nothing, he opened the trunk. Morgan lay motionless. Espinoza leaned in and grabbed him and pulled him from the trunk, letting him fall in a heap onto the ground.

*****

I knew this was my chance—maybe my only chance—so I pretended to be unconscious until the right moment. Espinoza couldn't lift me to his shoulders so he grabbed me by the cuffed hands and started dragging me toward the door.

The pain of the cuffs cutting into my skin and my body being dragged over the concrete was almost unbearable for me to continue to act like I was unconscious. Espinoza finally got me inside and managed to pull me up and onto the couch.

I knew the time was now, so I drew up my legs toward my chest and kicked toward Espinoza. I only hit him in the lower back area with a glancing motion. Espinoza had seen it coming so he jumped to lessen the power of the kick.

Espinoza was infuriated. He grabbed his gun and pointed it at my head. He almost pulled the trigger; but apparently, the fear of his boss made him stop. He again struck me with the pistol.

*****

Morgan slumped back down on the couch and remained motionless. Espinoza knew he hit Morgan hard. He stood there looking at Morgan's chest to make sure he was still breathing. Satisfied Morgan was alive, he turned and walked over to the table and sat down.

Espinoza always started drinking when he felt stressed, and he was feeling stressed now. He wasn't sure what Cardona had planned for him; but he knew he screwed up, and the boss didn't let things like that just go. In this business mistakes could cost you your life.

He pulled out his flask and drank down the last bit. Looking over at Morgan he could tell he was still unconscious so he went back out to his car and refilled his flask. He walked back inside, sat down, and again started drinking.

*****

I regained consciousness after a while. I opened my eyes; the headache had intensified. I looked around the room and saw Espinoza sitting at the table, and I saw the bag lying there. Espinoza was looking at his phone, and it cast a glow across his face. It made him look mean, and I knew I was in a bad place. I lay there very quietly, looking around trying to figure out where I was. My thinking was foggy, and apparently the last blow to my head caused a concussion.

I had never been to this place before and was confused. It looked like some old business as it had boxes of stuff sitting around. I could tell I was in an office area. A door behind Espinoza led to the outside, and there was a window behind the table at which he sat. I slightly turned my neck to look behind me, and I saw another door.

When I looked back at Espinoza, I could tell he had been drinking a lot; and based on how far he would tilt his head back to drink, I figured he had just about polished off the flask. What I *didn't* know was it was his *second* flaskful for the night.

Espinoza was on his phone, texting. In a minute he got a phone call. The concussion was making it hard for me to understand what he was saying, but he was mad when he hung up. Espinoza got up and walked over to me again and started yelling, slurring his words. He yelled something about how I had "messed up" and "keeping my mouth shut" and how it would be when the boss got there. Espinoza was mad and drunk—that was all I could process.

Espinoza pushed the gun once again into my face and head, and I was sure this was going to be the end. Though my mind was foggy, I knew enough not to provoke him. The gun was right in my face, and Espinoza had his finger on the trigger.

Espinoza spoke in half English and half Spanish, and it didn't make a lot of sense.

He then hit me again. This time wasn't as hard as the last. Though it hurt, it didn't knock me unconscious, but it did knock me to the floor. I didn't dare move; I again pretended to be unconscious.

I could tell Espinoza was moving away from me. I heard the door open so I opened my eyes to just a slit. I saw Espinoza walk outside and out-of-sight, but I still didn't dare move.

Within seconds I heard someone yell outside. I heard a loud gunshot, then two more shots in quick succession. I lay there for a few seconds before realizing this was my chance. I heard someone calling my name from outside, but I wasn't about to go out there. I pulled myself up to my feet. I was very unsteady from the blows to my head. I looked toward the table and saw the bag lying there. I knew what was in it so I stumbled over to the table and grabbed it.

I looked back at the door Espinoza went through. I still couldn't understand what happened, but I knew I needed to get out of there. I turned back toward the couch and the other door. I walked over to it; it was unlocked. Then I noticed the blood running down my face, so I wiped it off. I opened the door and went into another bigger room. Looking around I saw a fire exit sign so I went in that direction. Eventually, I made it to the door and opened it to the outside.

Chapter 23
Captain Ike: A Meeting with Morgan

Gina and I paid for our meal at Shells Restaurant and headed back to the *Good Times*. I wanted to get back so I could call Morgan. We pulled into the parking lot and parked. I got a blue tooth connection connecting my phone to her truck and called Morgan's number. Morgan answered on the third ring.

"What up, Buddy?" Morgan asked. "Are you looking for me? I dropped my phone into some water, and it has been dead for a while."

"Hell, yes, I have been looking for you!" I said, my tone sounded both excited and pissed off.

"What's wrong, Buddy?" Morgan asked again, sounding surprised at my tone.

I didn't know where to start.

"Dude, I have been trying to get in touch with you for a long time."

"Sorry, Buddy," Morgan said. "Like I said, my phone got wet; and I just got a new one. What's going on? What do you need?"

"I need to talk to you about the boat fire and about my getting shot and your not helping me!" I replied, agitated.

Morgan stumbled over his words, "What . . . what are you

talking about?" he asked like a child who just got caught by his parents.

"The boat fire, Morgan . . . the one on Tampa Bay."

I could tell by his voice that he had no clue how I knew. I realized I was excited and pissed and needed to slow down and explain what I was talking about. Morgan had been a good friend to me at one time, and I needed to explain myself.

"Listen, Morgan, we need to talk face-to-face. I was hired to investigate the fire on your boat, *Escape*, in Tampa Bay. I tried calling you many times. I talked to others who have been trying to get in touch with you . . . including Cyndi. Many people have been worried, . . . and some law enforcement officers want to talk to you, also.

"Look, Morgan, I know you have been involved in some shady shit lately. I thought at one time you might be dead, and I got shot looking for you."

"What?" Morgan asked, surprised.

By the tone in his voice I could tell he was sincere and didn't know what I was talking about.

"Can you meet me tomorrow for lunch?" I asked.

"Sure," he said. "Where at?"

"Do you still live in Polk County?" I asked.

"For now," he replied.

"Okay, I live in St. Pete; so let's meet halfway in Ruskin at Little Harbor. You know the place, right?"

"Yeah."

"Okay, I will see you there at noon."

"Ike, are you coming alone or will there be any cops?"

"Well, I won't be alone. I am bringing my girlfriend—but she is no cop. Don't worry; I just want to talk."

Fire Aboard

I hung up the phone and sat back in my seat. I looked over at Gina.

"What do you think?" she asked.

"He doesn't seem to know what I was talking about. I don't know *how* he wouldn't know, though."

Gina sat quietly for a minute. My mind was racing about the phone call and the questions I would ask him tomorrow. Gina started to talk, and I looked over at her. She had a smile on her face.

"So, I am your girlfriend?" she coyly asked.

I turned red when I realized what she was asking.

"Oh, well . . . I . . . I didn't know what to call you at the moment."

She smiled and giggled a little.

She started singing a little tune, "I . . . I . . . ke likes me; he wants to kiss me."

With that, I just opened the door and eased out of the truck.

Later that evening Gina and I sat in the salon, talking.

"Well, you are getting better it seems," she said.

"Yes, I feel much better; but I need to take it easy so as not to tear anything. I am moving much better."

She agreed.

"I think I need to get back to work; so, since you are headed over to Little Harbor tomorrow, I will get my stuff together tonight and go by work tomorrow. We can stop by and see my house, also."

"I am getting used to your being here," I said; and she apparently liked that as she came over and gave me a kiss.

The next morning we got up, and I made a little breakfast.

Sitting on the back of the boat was always nice while eating and a great way to get the day started.

"So, what do you think is going to happen at the meeting?" Gina asked.

"I don't know," I said. "I just want to know what happened—how all this went down."

We finished up breakfast, then cleaned up. I helped Gina get her things in her Tahoe.

It was a nice morning as I turned out onto Pasadena Avenue in my truck and headed toward St. Pete Beach, Gina following in her Tahoe. Sometimes I like taking the long way down Gulf Boulevard because during the week the traffic isn't bad and I like the scenery much better. I went down and turned on Pinellas Bayway. The road has a large bridge, as well, and affords a great view of Boca Ciega Bay. Boats can be seen coming and going, and water conditions can be easily observed.

I turned back south onto Highway 275. It was the best place to see the water. This time of the morning the water was often glass-like, and today it would not disappoint. The sun cast a beautiful shine across the water.

"It feels good to be alive," I thought.

We made our way up Highway 41, passing several of the places where I had been earlier while investigating this case. Strange how life plays out sometimes and how places bring back those memories.

As we got closer to Gina's house, she took the lead in her Tahoe. I called her on the phone and asked her about her ex.

"Is he gone?" I asked.

"Oh, yes, I forgot to tell you with all that has been going

on: he texted me and said he had found a place. I just hope he left everything as it should be."

We turned onto Shell Point Road and onto 14th Street NW where her subdivision was. As she turned into the neighborhood, I noticed how nice it was. Most of the houses were newer.

Once there I got out of my truck, hoping he was gone so no trouble would happen. My injury, though much better, would keep me from doing much. Gina got out and punched in the garage door code, and the door opened. We walked inside, and I helped to make sure he was gone. It appeared he had done the right thing and left the place clean and in order.

She showed me around. It was a nice, little, three-bedroom, two-bath house—well-kept and well-furnished. Her style in decor was nice. We went through sliding glass doors, and she showed me the pool area that was a focal point of the back yard. I could see this would be a nice place for entertaining.

Gina pointed to the pool and reminded me that is where her ex had thrown her phone. She said it in a joking voice, but I could tell it was an unpleasant memory for her. I hung out there with her a little while. She decided to go up to Little Harbor with me and check on work while I met with Morgan. Little Harbor was only about two miles from Gina's house.

"Nice, short drive to work for you," I told her.

"Yes," she said. "It is one of the things I like about my job."

We turned into Little Harbor and passed the guard shack. The Little Harbor entrance passes several three- and four-story condos and apartments. The marina sits on the bay side of the buildings, so the windows in the condos overlook the marina. The marina is separated from the bay by about 100 yards of sand, which serves as the beach for the resort. This makes for a very protected marina for the boats. I had kept a boat there several years earlier and loved it.

I watched where Gina parked near the office, and I drove down to the tiki bar/restaurant area parking lot. The lot overlooked Tampa Bay and had a very nice view.

I texted Morgan, "You running on time?"

He texted back, "ETA 15."

"Perfect," I thought; I wanted to enjoy the scenery for a bit and think about our meeting.

I sent my boss, June, a text, "FYI - I am about to meet with Morgan. Will contact you later."

I remained in my parked truck so I could see both the water and the road leading into the parking lot. I wanted to see Morgan pull in and see his demeanor unnoticed. The cop was coming out in me now, and I realized that I was about to hear a story from an old friend who obviously made some bad choices. I wanted to know what brought him to this point in his life.

Several vehicles pulled in and parked. Different types of people got out and went inside the restaurant. A nice, new, Ford pickup pulled in. I couldn't see the driver due to the tint on the windows; but when the door opened, I recognized my old friend. I let him walk toward the restaurant, then I got out.

Morgan walked in and sat at the tiki bar that overlooked the water. I wasn't far behind him. He was looking over the seating in the restaurant when I walked up.

"Show me your hands!" I said.

Morgan turned around with surprise written on his face, but slowly he smiled when he realized I was alone. He put out his hand, and I shook it and pulled him in for the brother hug. Though he had made a lot of mistakes lately, he had been a good friend for a long time. When we hugged, it was a little tight and I groaned from some pain.

He immediately released me and apologized, "Sorry, Buddy. Are you okay?"

"Yes," I said, "I am fine. I got shot trying to save your sorry ass." I said.

Morgan looked confused.

"Let's get a table over near the corner out of ear shot," I suggested.

This met with his approval, and we walked over and sat down. The waitress came right up, and we ordered some beers.

"We are going to be talking, so please keep those beers coming."

She flashed a smile and nodded her head in understanding.

As we sat down, I noticed some bruising on Morgan's face and some cuts that were healing. I could tell Morgan felt awkward, so I started with the story of how I got involved. I told him how my old boss contacted me and requested I do the investigation since I had a unique set of skills. I told him I was working as a private fire investigator on the case.

"Morgan, when I found out to whom the boat was registered, I didn't know it was you at first. Later I found out it was *your* boat. I tried calling you several times to get your side of the story about what happened."

"That's how my phone got wet," Morgan responded. "The boat caught fire, and I had to jump into the water. Phones don't work well after a salt water bath! I didn't know you were trying to contact me. When I finally got a new phone, you were one of the first people I contacted.

"Cyndi is looking for you, too, Morgan. You know that, right?"

"Yes. I've already contacted her, as well. My daughter needs an operation, but I have already taken care of it with Cyndi."

Chapter 24
Captain Ike: Just When Things Were Looking Up . . .

"So, here is how this is going to work, Morgan. I am no more bound as a law enforcement officer. I am here mostly as a friend. I do, however, need to ask you some questions. You can answer them however you see fit. I still do need to turn in a report to the insurance company. Do you understand?"

He nodded yes, he did.

"So, the first question is . . . where did you get the boat and the insurance on it?"

"Ike, first of all, I have a lot to tell you; but I won't tell you everything as it will incriminate me in some things. You are my friend, though, so I won't insult your intelligence.

"So, first thing is this: I have been involved with some very dangerous people lately. I've done some things I am not proud of. Some of the people I have dealt with are Mexican nationals and are tied to the Mexican cartel.

"Ike, the boat is not mine; I didn't register it or get insurance on it.

"One of the guys with whom I was involved is Felix Cardona. He has far-reaching contacts. He has been moving dope his entire life. One of the things he does is register boats, vehicles, and planes in other people's names so they can never be tied back to him.

"He has people working at all kinds of government agencies, as well as insurance companies; and he owns many different companies, as well.

"Apparently, from what I can tell, he even has someone on the inside at the DEA. I signed up with the DEA a little while back as a CI. I felt bad about what I was involved in and had information that I was going to pass along. Cardona found out and was going to kill me one night over in Polk County."

"You were working for the DEA?" I quizzed.

"Not exactly working *for* them but, like I said, a CI. Once I got enough info, I was going to pass it to them so I could make some money.

"I recently came into some money and was busy trying to deal with my daughter, but I was going to contact them when I got your message. I know about a huge drug shipment coming across the border soon."

I stopped Morgan.

"Okay, let's start from the beginning. So, what I know is this, Morgan: a boat burned in Tampa Bay. It was arson, and there was a hole in the bottom of the hull that was done *before* the fire. I did some checking, and there is a video of the boats going up and down the Little Manatee River. Two match the descriptions of the boat that burned, as well as another center console boat."

Morgan looked alarmed at this revelation.

"Let me say, though, the video is not good enough to positively identify anyone.

"Also, I found a location where the boat apparently met some people at the Highway 41 bridge train trestle. I, along with a detective from Tampa police, found some drugs on the ground at that location. It doesn't take a rocket scientist to know what happened. Do you understand?"

Morgan looked concerned and nodded his head yes.

I continued, "Now, I also learned from that same detective—who will neither confirm nor deny—the location of a cell phone ping in Polk County . . . and by the way, he is a buddy of mine from back when I worked for the city. Like I said, I told him that an ex-cop may be involved and may also be in danger. Due to who you were and my being a friend, he got me the location of the cell phone. The night I got shot I was looking for *you*."

Morgan sat up in his chair, listening intently. He seemed to be very concerned.

"So, the night I found this location, I also *saw* you."

"What?" he answered again in surprise.

"Yes, I sneaked up on the back of a building—really just planning to see if you were there. The plan was if you were not there, to back out and call the locals and let them have whatever was happening. But when I looked through the window, I saw you with a Mexican holding you at gunpoint. He hit you several times with his gun, and I feared he was going to shoot you.

"I was outside near the back door when the guy walked out. I accidently made a noise, and he spun around and shot me once in the abdomen. I double tapped him and killed him there. It took me a minute to realize I was shot.

"I yelled several times for you to help me. When you didn't respond, I called 9-1-1; and well . . . the rest is history."

"Oh my God, Bro! I didn't know it was you, Ike! I swear on my child I didn't!"

I had been trained and had many years of experience to know when someone was lying, and Morgan seemed to be telling the truth.

Morgan went on to tell me that he had a concussion from the pistol whipping and was confused and injured. Not knowing who was outside, he simply tried to get away. He seemed to be holding something back, though, when he told me about how he got out of the building.

"Anyway, as you can imagine," I started again, "I was taken to the hospital and later interviewed by detectives about the case. I told them what I knew up until that point. They want to talk to you, of course."

"Yeah, yeah, I got that," he said. "I will contact them. So, what happened with your injuries?"

"Lucky thing is the bullet didn't hit any vital organs. I have been in a lot of pain, but I am recovering well. I have had a good nurse taking care of me. Believe it or not, she works here at this resort . . . but I will tell you about that later."

Morgan seemed genuinely concerned about my injuries and honest about not knowing it was me outside.

"To be honest," I said, "what bothered me the most was I thought you knew it was me and left me there to die."

"No way, Bro!" he said. "If I knew it was you, I would have done anything to help."

"That does make me feel better," I responded.

I sat back in my chair, thinking. I motioned for the server to bring us another round of drinks.

I thought for a little while, then I spoke up again, "Listen, Morgan, I know you have been involved in some bad shit. I don't know how much or how little. To this point I have finished my investigation. I will write a report based on what I *know*.

"So, is it your statement to me that you did not intentionally burn the boat?"

Morgan, having been in my position many times, said, "You know I won't answer the question if it is on the record; but if not, I will answer."

"I don't want to know anything else, Morgan."

"Ike, there is something you do need to know. I took some money from the dopers . . . some they owed me and some for trying to kill me. It is a lot of money," he said, "and they are looking for me, I know. Cyndi has already been contacted by some guys. Lucky for her she was at her dad's house, and he always has some major fire power. He scared them off; but they will not stop, I am sure. You need to be careful," he said.

"Why should *I* be careful? I didn't have anything to do with any money."

"Ike, think about it: do you think that they would believe you showed up to the dope house, then I left with the money, and you didn't know anything? I find it hard to believe, and I was there myself.

"Ike, these guys are really bad people. Just watch your six for a while. I just don't want anything else to happen to you.

"I am buying these drinks," Morgan suddenly added. "As a matter of fact, I am buying lunch and anything else you want," he said smiling.

The conversation then turned to what had been happening to both of us before the case. I told him that I was working as a boat captain and loving life. He told me how he had been hating life lately but thought it was turning around.

I got a text from Gina saying, "I saw you guys talking. It looked very intense, so I didn't walk over. Is everything okay?"

"Yes," I texted back. "Actually, I feel better after talking with Morgan. Stop by when you can."

I opened the picture gallery of my phone and looked up the detective's card. I always simply saved a pic of a business card; it was the only way I could keep up with them.

"Morgan, I am going to text you a picture of a business card. It is the detective assigned to the case in Polk County. You need to contact him to clear this up. As I see it, you were kidnapped and being held at gunpoint. I saved your ass," I said with a smile. "As to *why* you were there is up to you to tell them."

Morgan answered with a nod.

About that time Gina walked up. She leaned over and kissed me. I introduced Morgan to her.

"Very nice to meet you," he said. "You know, Ike, she is much too pretty for you."

"Yes, I must agree. I think she likes me for my boat," I said.

Gina smiled and lightly punched my arm.

"Do you want to have lunch with us?" I asked. "Morgan is buying."

She smiled.

"It is tempting," she answered, "but I am working on something; I'm going to have to take a rain check."

Morgan nodded yes, and she went back inside.

"Wow, Ike, how did you get her?" he asked.

"Long story, Bro, but I have been working on her for years. It finally just fell into place. It took me getting shot, I think."

My phone chirped, and I thought it might be Gina but saw it was Jack from the marina.

"Hey, come see me when you get back to the marina. I want to tell you something." "Everything okay?" I asked.

"Yeah, I think so. Probably nothing, but I saw some guys in the marina I didn't recognize. I felt like they were watching your boat. They never got near it. We can talk more about it later."

Morgan and I continued with our lunch and reminisced about old times at the department, as well as just hanging out. It turned out to be a nice lunch—much better than I had anticipated.

It was also nice weather that day. Where I sat, I could look out at the passing boats. I longed to be out on the water. I had a few moments where I realized just how long it had been.

After lunch and a few beers, Morgan and I got up and strolled down the boardwalk back toward the parking lot, still talking. He confirmed to me that he was going to contact the detective and would be calling the DEA agent with whom he was working.

"The guy you shot knew a lot," Morgan explained. "He would often drink too much and run his mouth. He gave me a lot of details about some fentanyl shipment. He said it was going to be the biggest shipment they had ever done, and they wanted me to help with it."

"That's good, Morgan. That should get you back on the right track."

He nodded and said, "Yes, I think so, Ike."

We shook hands. Morgan got into his truck and drove out of the parking lot.

*****

I walked around the marina at Little Harbor, waiting on Gina to finish up. We hadn't said our goodbyes, and I wanted to ask her something.

I wanted to see if some of my old friends were still in the marina from a few years ago. Sure enough, a couple of guys still kept their boats here, and they told me about all the changes that occurred lately. They told me how the marina was trying to stop liveaboards. Liveaboards are people who live on their boats. Apparently, the insurance companies think they are too much of a risk. Liveaboards actually bring a certain good quality to a marina. It is their home, so they often care about it as such. They are a good addition to most marinas.

After making my rounds I met up with Gina, and we headed to the tiki bar for a drink. I told her what Morgan had to say and that I felt a lot better knowing that he didn't know I was outside left for dead. I told her about how he had signed up with the DEA as a confidential informant and what that meant. Why he did it, I didn't know; maybe he felt bad about himself and wanted to make amends. After being the good guy all those years, it is hard to be the bad guy unless one just doesn't have any morals. I knew Morgan, and he *had* morals.

"So, what do you have planned for the next few days, Captain?" Gina asked.

"I guess I am going to take it easy for a few more days, but I am itching to get back out on the water. I am going to work on getting some charters lined up," I said. "I have a few people who contacted me and want to go out. I want to go out and stay a night at Beer Can Island. Have you ever done that, Gina?"

"No, I haven't. I heard a lot of people tell stories about it and have always wanted to but no one has ever asked."

"Well, I am asking. What days do you have off next week?"

"We are not busy on Wednesday and Thursday," she began. "How about one of those days?"

"Perfect! The weekdays are much better. There are a lot fewer people, and we can have the pick of the locations."

"Sounds like fun," Gina responded, smiling and looking off as if she was thinking about it already.

She pulled me in close and gave me a soft kiss. We had been together for more days than I had with anyone else for a very long time. We were having such a good time together, and I realized I was going to miss her.

"Do I need to bring anything for the island trip?" Gina asked.

"No," I said. "It is my treat; it's my way of thanking you for all you have done for me."

"Oh, Ike, I have had a blast hanging out with you. You make me laugh so much. I look forward to what the future holds for us."

Those words gave me a tingling inside that I couldn't ever remember feeling before. She gave me one last kiss. Then she got up and headed to her truck and drove away.

I got back in my truck and texted June, "You good for a call?"

She quickly responded, "Yes. Anxious to hear what happened."

I called her on my way back to the *Good Times*. I filled her in on all the details about my meeting with Morgan and how I felt he was truthful with me about the shooting.

"I know he was involved in the drugs somehow," I said, "but that isn't my area of concern. Morgan told me Cardona had the boat registered in his name and the insurance, as well."

June responded, "Well, I have some information about that. Apparently, the insurance company ran a check through the ISO."

I understood the ISO (Insurance Service Office) was an organization that tracked insurance claims. All insurance companies run checks through the ISO when someone has a claim. It is a good resource to detect fraudulent insurance claims.

June continued, "The ISO detected several claims that were paid to the same bank account. Different names would be on the claims, but even some of the p.o. box addresses matched."

"Well, that makes sense," I answered. "Morgan explained that when Cardona burned a boat in the past, they would also get the insurance money from the so-called 'accident.' So not only were they making money on the drugs but also on the arsons. Because they did it in different police jurisdictions, they got away with it."

While I was on the phone with June, I got another text from Jack.

"Call me asap," it read.

"Okay, so are you ready to complete your final report?" June asked me.

"Yes, I think so. I will start on it; however, it may take a few days as I need to figure out how to write some sections of it. This is the most unique fire investigation I have ever done."

"Yes, it has certainly been a mess," she said. "You have always been a magnet for this kind of stuff," she said in a laughing voice.

"Never a truer statement," I replied. "I will talk to you soon."

I called Jack back.

"Hey, what's the big rush?" I asked.

"You remember I told you I saw a couple of dudes around your boat the other day?"

"Yes," I said.

"Well, I am sure I just saw them again. I was walking over to the office and passed by a car backed in several spaces down from the *Good Times*. They appeared to be just sitting there and watching the boat. I am pretty sure it was the same dudes. Something is up with them," he said.

"Okay, I am headed back that way and will check it out. What kind of car and color?" "White, four-door sedan," he said. "It's parked near the condos on the end. You can't miss them."

Chapter 25
Tony Morgan: Bring in the DEA

As I got back in my truck and headed for home, I thought about my conversation with Ike. So many things rushed through my mind.

My phone chirped; and the message, like many of the past ones from this unknown number, read "Call me asap."

I thought I knew who it was from without knowing for sure. One can't take the amount of money I had from Felix Cardona and not expect to hear from him.

I also knew I was in extreme danger. I had never met Cardona, but Espinoza had told me many times how dangerous Cardona was. I tried to figure a way out of the mess in which I found myself.

I thought about all the information Espinoza told me and about the upcoming drug deal. If I could get Cardona tied to it somehow, it may solve my problem with Cardona.

I decided it was time to contact my buddy at the DEA. If the shipment of fentanyl was as big as Espinoza said, then it would be massive. I knew I could get paid for that information, also.

I pulled over and called my buddy. It went to voicemail;

so, I left a message about having information on an upcoming deal and that it was big.

I knew with the amount of cash I had I could stay off the grid for a while. I had been staying at a nice little, long-term motel on the river near the town of Palmetto near Bradenton. I paid with cash, and the family that ran the place didn't ask many questions. I was used to living in a town where many people knew me; but since my arrest and all that went with it, I found it hard to explain to people what happened. Living at the motel, no one asked any questions; and that was fine with me. The only problem was not seeing my daughter on a regular basis; but I knew seeing her would put her in danger, and *that* I would not do.

I got a response text from my DEA buddy to which I replied, "We need to meet soon. Have some information about a huge, upcoming drug shipment from across the border into Arizona."

"I work the Florida district. I will have a Texas agent contact you shortly," the agent replied.

Within just a few minutes, I got a call from an unknown number. Government phones often don't show an incoming call phone number so I felt sure it was my anticipated call.

"Hello, this is Morgan."

The caller on the other end identified himself, "This is Special Agent Gonzalez. I was contacted and advised to call you about some information on a shipment in Texas. Is that correct?" Before Morgan could respond, Gonzalez continued, "I was also told you are previous law enforcement. Is that correct?"

"Yes and yes," I answered both questions. "The information I have is time sensitive," I added with an urgent tone.

"How did you come across this info, and how reliable is it?" Gonzalez asked.

"I got the information from one of the cartel members in the U.S. He tried to get me to assist with the shipment."

I knew Gonzalez would not be satisfied with the short answer and that I would need to explain more on how I got the information.

"Listen, Gonzalez, I am sure you were informed I have been signed up as a CI, correct?" "Yes, that is correct," Gonzalez stated. "I also have confirmed you are active and listed as a trusted member."

"Good," I responded. "Since signing up I was able to get close to a person recently killed who was involved in local shipments. His name was Juan Espinoza, a Hispanic male. Espinoza held me at gunpoint. Apparently, the DEA has a leak on the inside; and they determined I was signed up as a CI. I was almost killed over the leak," I explained. Gonzalez, you need to make some upper brass aware of this leak."

"Certainly! I will, Morgan; and we will open a separate investigation into the leak, you can be assured."

"Gonzalez, this shipment is imminent. We need to move fast. I have already seen one shipment completed by this group valued at $1.5 million. The boss in this organization is Felix Cardona of the Cardona Cartel. Are you familiar with this name?"

"Yes, we are," Gonzales answered. "He is a very dangerous individual from what we can tell, and he is very smart. He has beaten the charges in several cases we built against him."

"Cardona has been looking for me, I believe . . . not Cardona *himself* but some of his men."

"Why does he want you?" Gonzalez inquired.

"I worked as a drug detective for many years. Some information that CIs have is best kept quiet—do you understand?"

"Yes, I understand; but I will need some information to take to my superiors."

"Yes, I understand that. I will tell it to you like this: I signed up as a CI to help stop the spread of drugs onto our streets. Since losing my job at the sheriff's office—as a result of charges of which I was cleared, by the way—I wanted to help in some way."

"Okay," Gonzalez said, "I can take that up the chain. That makes sense . . . Morgan, hold the line."

Within a minute Gonzalez was back on the phone.

"Okay, we need to meet and get some statements and more information about the move. I need to know everything you know about Cardona. My bosses will definitely be interested because we have been wanting to get him for a long time. Are you near Tampa?"

"Yes," Morgan answered.

"Can you meet tomorrow morning?"

"Yes, I can."

"Okay, I will have credentials for you at the McDill AFB guard gate #1. I, along with my partner, will fly in by 0900, and we can meet at 0930. Does that work for you?"

"Yes."

"If there are any changes on our end, I will text you at this number; and you do the same."

I confirmed that I would and hung up.

I sat back in my seat and thought for a minute. If this worked out, it could be the solution I needed to my problem with Cardona; and maybe I could even make some money in the process. I understood that if the shipment was as big as I was told, the payday would be very nice.

I knew it was now time to contact the sheriff's department and set a meeting with the detective. Now, I could say I was working with the DEA on a case and use that as cover against questions I didn't want to answer. I also realized that if things worked out with the bust, it would buy me more time with the sheriff's office before giving a statement.

I looked on my phone for the picture Ike sent to me with the detective's information. I sent a text, telling the detective who I was and for him to call. Not one minute later the detective called, and the telephone number again did not show. I answered.

"This is Detective Brooks. Am I speaking with Tony Morgan?"

"Yes, Sir, you are," I replied.

"I need to meet with you in reference to a homicide I am working on, a Juan Espinoza. Are you available to come down now to the sheriff's office substation for an interview?"

I had been in this detective position many times before. I could almost predict exactly what questions Brooks would ask. I also knew what to say to Brooks.

"No, I am not, Detective Brooks. I am currently working with the DEA on an open case. I will be meeting with them on the active case in the morning at McDill AFB. I am a CI with the DEA."

I could tell that threw off a bit the detective's line of questioning.

I continued, "Am I suspect in your investigation, Detective Brooks?"

243

"Ummm, not exactly . . . or not at this time," the detective said.

"Good, I can tell you that I was the victim of a kidnapping in your case, Detective. I will contact you soon with a time to meet and a case number from the DEA in reference to the case we are working on."

This statement definitely threw off the detective.

"Well, will you still need to come in and talk to us, Morgan?"

"Yes, Sir, I just told you I intend to; but I am working this current case, and it is time-sensitive. I will call you soon."

With that I hung up.

I got a kick out of the conversation. My plan to sign up as a CI was working perfectly. I knew that the federal drug case of the DEA would supersede any local homicide case. I also would try and get Detective Gonzales to run interference for me, as well. Things were looking up for me.

Chapter 26
Captain Ike: Face-To-Face with Cartel Thugs

I stepped on the gas after I got out of the parking lot of Little Harbor. Jack's phone call had me concerned about the guys at the marina. I wanted to know who they were and what they wanted. I knew I could be there in less than 30 minutes. As I turned onto Highway 41, I started formulating a plan of how to handle this issue. My first thought was to check my weapon. I pulled my .45-caliber Springfield XD from the paddle holster. I pulled back on the slide and racked a round into the chamber. If these guys had any ill will, I wanted to be prepared. I re-holstered the gun.

I then called Jack, "Can you see those guys from your boat?"

"Hang on; let me look." Momentarily, Jack returned to the phone and continued, "Yup I can see them sitting in their car. I can't tell what they are *doing* from here."

"Okay, perfect. I don't know what these guys want so I am going to work a ruse. I am going to park my truck in the Wendy's parking lot and walk past the guys. I want to see if they know who they are looking for. I will go past *Good Times* and circle around to your boat."

"What if they have a weapon?" Jack asked.

"Well, if they do, that will make three of us," I laughed.

A few minutes later I sat in the Wendy's parking lot. I got out and put the paddle holster on under my shirt so no one could see it. I walked around the back of the condos and stopped at the edge of the building. I slowly peeked around the corner until I could see the car in which they were sitting. They were staring intently at *Good Times*. I could tell they were talking, but I couldn't hear what they were saying. They didn't look like a serious threat to me; besides, it was broad daylight.

I walked back in front of the condos to the end near the duo. I rounded the corner. From this angle they were looking away from me. I crossed the driveway and got on the sidewalk so I would pass behind them. If there was a shooting, I would have the tactical advantage by being behind the vehicle. I waited until I was at an angle to the right and behind the passenger.

The windows were down, and they were chatting. I coughed to get the attention of the passenger. He turned and looked at me. He stared for a second, and I acted as though I didn't see them. I could tell he told the driver I was there because he turned to look at me through the rear-view mirror. If they knew me, now would be the time they would react.

I walked past the car, watching them in my peripheral vision; I could tell they stayed in the car. I looked around as if I was looking at the boats in the marina, and they both continued sitting in their car. I walked up behind *Good Times* and paused for a minute as though I was looking at the boat. I then continued to walk on. I just couldn't help but to tempt them. I continued walking slowly, looking at other boats, and finally circled around to Jack's sailboat.

Fire Aboard

"Permission to come aboard, Captain," I said to Jack.

"Dang it, Big Daddy, are you trying to get shot? I saw what you did!"

I laughed and went aboard. We went down into the cabin. From the companionway I could see the guys still sitting in the car.

"Now what?" Jack quizzed.

"Well, let's see who they are and mess with them a bit."

I pulled my cell phone out and tapped 9-1-1.

The dispatcher answered and asked me, "What is your emergency?"

"There are a couple of suspicious-looking, Hispanic males in the marina parking lot," I said. "We know they don't have a boat here, and I am scared," I said while smiling. "They look very frightening," I said in my most concerned voice, trying not to laugh and looking at Jack who was shaking his head.

They asked all the usual questions about what they looked like and what they were driving. They asked me my name, and I just said "a concerned citizen" and disconnected the line.

Within about three minutes I watched a Chevy Tahoe from the Pinellas County Sheriff's Office pull into the parking lot. Based on my information and the fact that the two guys were sitting in their car in the parking lot of the marina, the deputies pulled straight up to the vehicle, blocking it in. The deputies got out and, with hands near their weapons, walked up to the vehicle. I could tell they asked for identification, and they immediately started running the data. The lead deputy stepped to the rear of the car and ran the tag.

The second deputy acted as backup and just watched the occupants inside of the vehicle.

He leaned over and looked in the back seat.

Suddenly, the deputy yelled, "Gun!"

He quickly stepped back at an angle and pulled his weapon, pointing it at the occupants. He yelled commands at the occupants to not move and to keep their hands where he could see them. Within seconds several other cruisers streamed into the parking lot. The two Hispanic guys were taken out of the vehicle at gunpoint. Both were cuffed and told to sit on the curb.

All the commotion brought out a variety of people from around the marina. They pointed and whispered about all the excitement. Jack and I stayed in the boat, watching all the action while staying out-of-sight. About 30 minutes later they stood the two guys up and put them in a cruiser. The cruiser quickly left, taking both of them to jail, I assumed.

"Okay, I've got to find out what happened," I told Jack.

We walked over to where several people stood. I listened to what they were saying and what they thought happened.

I needed to know what the two men were doing at the marina so I walked over to a deputy standing off to the side. I introduced myself as retired law enforcement. I explained I was the one who called in the information about the suspects, and I wanted to know what the situation was with them.

The deputy responded, "The lead investigating deputy took the suspects to the county jail. Would you like me to call him and give him your number?"

"Yes, if you don't mind. I just investigated an arson, and these guys may have been involved somehow."

My phone interrupted with a chirp. I looked down to see a message from Gina.

"Just checking on you," it read.

"I'm doing good," I responded. "I've got some stuff going on in the marina. I will call you in a few minutes."

"Ok," she replied simply.

The lead deputy called me quickly.

"What can I do for you, Sir?" he asked.

I explained who I was and how I thought these guys could be connected to my case.

"Well, I arrested them for carrying concealed weapons without a permit," he responded. "They are not cooperating, playing the 'no-speak-English' game."

Of course, I understood this was usually an indication that they don't want to talk to law enforcement. Most people will say anything to keep from going to jail.

I told the deputy, "I will need the info and the case number, if possible."

"Sure," he said. "It will be a public record as soon as they are booked into the county jail. I will text you the details . . . or at least what they told me, anyway," he laughed. "I have not made a positive ID on them, yet."

"Okay, thanks for your help and for responding so quickly."

"Sure thing," he said, and we disconnected.

I relayed to Jack what the deputy told me.

"Wonder who these guys are?" he asked with concern in his voice.

"I think they are connected to the arson case I just worked. It is a long story, but I think they think I had something to do with some missing money. Of course, I don't, but those guys don't know that. If they are working for whom I think they are, their boss is a very dangerous man. Thanks for being vigilant, Jack."

He responded, "No problem, Bro . . . and I will keep my eyes open for anything else."

I needed to check on the *Good Times* so we walked over to the boat together. *Good Times* seemed to be unaware of all the excitement. I looked around, and everything was in order. Apparently, the guys didn't know what I looked like and were just waiting for someone to walk up to the *Good Times*. I assumed they would have acted then. I was glad Jack had tipped me off, or it might have turned out much differently.

"I'll see you later, Jack," I said as I gave him a quick nod.

I needed to take care of a few things. First, I decided to call Gina and tell her what happened. She was concerned, but I downplayed that the two Hispanic men were there to see me. Besides, they were probably actually looking for Morgan; and they thought they would check here.

I then decided to call Morgan. I told him what happened.

"Be careful, Ike. They probably are looking for *me*; but they undoubtedly think you had something to do with the money, as well. I am planning to meet DEA in the morning and will advise them of the situation. You need to make yourself scarce, Ike."

"I hear ya. Call me if anything I need to know pops up."

I sat back in my chair on the back deck and thought. I figured I should take this seriously, and I wondered what I should do.

"Turn lemons into lemonade," I thought.

I took out my phone and called Gina.

She answered right away, "I was worried!"

"Sorry, Gina, but all is good here."

I then explained what happened and that the guys were in jail . . . at least until tomorrow. I do have a question, though.

"Can we move up our island trip to tomorrow?" I asked.

"I am sure I can work it out," Gina answered.

"Okay, perfect! That will get me and the *Good Times* out of the marina for a few days. If those two guys return, they will think I left; and all should be good.

"Sounds like a plan," she said. "Do you want me to drive down?"

"Oh, no," I said. "I will pick you up at the dock. Just pack a bag for a few days, and I will take care of the rest."

Chapter 27
Tony Morgan: A Meeting with the DEA Top Brass

I got up early so I could meet the DEA at McDill AFB. Palmetto was about a one-and-a-half hours' drive in decent traffic. I decided to get a jump on it by leaving around 0600. I figured after stopping for coffee I would take Highway 41 N and stay on it all the way into Tampa, then get onto the Leroy Selmon Expressway. Depending on the traffic, I would decide later what exit would be best. Traffic could be terrible, even early in the morning.

Just as directed, when I arrived, I told the guards at the guard shack who I was. I was told to pull up behind a Jeep sitting close by. One of the guards came out and handed me a badge, advising me to wear it around my neck at all times while at the base. I followed the guard in his car through another checkpoint, and I could tell I was beyond where most civilians were allowed.

We pulled onto the tarmac and drove to a waiting jet sitting, engines off, near a small terminal. The guard got out of his vehicle and escorted me to the steps of the jet. As I walked up, I heard someone call my name.

"Are you Morgan?" the man standing in the hatchway of the plane asked.

I nodded yes and walked up the steps. DEA Special Agent Gonzales introduced himself and extended his hand to me just as I reached the top of the steps.

"Tony Morgan," I replied, and we went aboard the plane.

I looked around and saw several people looking at computer screens inside of the plane. Only a few looked up and then back down at their screens.

"Wow!" I said. "I thought this was a passenger jet."

Gonzalez explained as he led me toward the rear of the jet that this was their mobile office.

"These days we move all over the southern border trying to stop the influx of dope, as well as human trafficking. If we were in an office somewhere, we would be much less effective. These are all analysts for the DEA. I command the entire southern border," he said, "and your information was given top priority by the bosses in Washington so I hope it is good."

"Oh, it is good," I said.

Gonzalez walked into an office toward the back of the jet. I walked in behind him and saw two desks.

"My deputy and I share this office. Please have a seat," Gonzalez said as he pointed to a comfortable chair sitting in front of his desk.

I sat down, and about that time a very attractive female walked into the room. I looked at her as she paused a second before entering the room. Gonzales introduced her as his deputy.

"DEA Special Agent Edmiston," she offered as she put out her hand. "They call me TJ for short."

I smiled and shook her hand as I introduced myself.

"Oh, yes, I know you," TJ said.

I knew a puzzled look slid across my face. TJ walked

over to her desk and picked up a file. She turned around and handed it to me.

"This is your file, Morgan. We always do our background investigations on anyone with whom we work this close."

I opened the folder and saw my picture along with a very thick set of papers. As I thumbed through them, I saw different pictures of myself and a paper trail that stretched from the police academy right up until I worked at the sheriff's department.

"We also know about the shooting investigation you went through and how you left the department," she said. "Sounded like it got political on you."

I grimaced and nodded my head yes as I gave her a sideways glance.

Gonzalez sensed the awkwardness of the situation and said, "Okay, let's talk about the info you have. What can you tell us?"

That immediately changed my mood, and I started with how I obtained my information.

"The guy who told me all this is dead. His name was Juan Espinoza. I had been working with him on a successful drug deal when he told me about this upcoming, larger drug deal. He wanted me to help. He knew I had been a cop and figured I could advise them on better ways to get the dope across the border.

"Then one night he had too much to drink and told me pretty much everything, including how and when the next shipment was coming across. He was trying to get brownie points from his boss, Felix Cardona, and really wanted my help.

"Unfortunately for him, though, he met his demise at the hands of another ex-cop friend of mine. The thing is, Cardona doesn't know that Espinoza told me these details; and now that Espinoza is dead, Cardona thinks no one else knows.

"Espinoza told me that they would be moving a very large shipment of fentanyl across the border at Nogales, Arizona, port of entry. He said they would put it in a tractor trailer rig under a shipment of cucumbers. He asked me if the cucumbers would hide the scent from the dogs. They had been told that it would, and he wanted to verify the information.

"I told him I didn't know for sure, but I would look into it from some K9 handlers I knew and would get back to him. He also said that Cardona owned a farm in Benito Juarez just south of town. That is where they grow the vegetables under which they hide the dope. The farm is just a cover to move the dope. He also said the dope deal would be upward of $3 million. Based on what he told me, the shipment is due to cross within the next week.

"This information is good, and I would think if you do a search on property owned near Benito Juarez, you are going to find out from where the dope originates."

While I was talking, TJ typed away on her computer. She nodded for Gonzalez to look at her computer screen. He leaned over and looked and smiled.

"That part checks out. Maybe Cardona has finally made a mistake, and we can get him."

Gonzalez turned and looked at Morgan. "I have been chasing Cardona for a very long time. We thought he must have someone on the inside at DEA because he always seems to be one step ahead of us."

I sat quietly in my chair as Gonzalez and TJ did some more computer work. Gonzalez then made a couple of phone calls. He told the person on the other end of the line to keep the info secret until he could get down to the border himself.

"I don't want this info getting out," he added.

TJ spoke up and asked me, "Is this Juan Espinoza's picture?"

She turned her monitor so I could see it.

"Yes, that is him," I said, ". . . or it *was*."

"We have a big file on him, as well. We surmised he worked for Cardona but haven't been able to prove it."

When Gonzalez got off the phone, I started, "Listen, I've got an issue with the sheriff's department's wanting to interview me about the shooting death of Espinoza. I think that could compromise this case. You never know how far Cardona's tentacles reach. Can you run some interference for me on this?"

Gonzalez thought for a second, then responded, "Yes, we can do that. I will contact the sheriff and tell him you are working our case and that as soon as it is complete, you will cooperate."

"Okay, that sounds good," I answered.

"We are going to fly down there tonight," Gonzalez explained. "We need to get our best people in place on this one, and I don't want any mistakes . . . and I *definitely* want to get Cardona this time.

"Morgan, you stay low and off the radar. We will stay in contact with you and let you know if we make the bust. Do you have somewhere safe to go?" he inquired.

"Yes, the place where I am staying is in no way connected

to my name. I pay in cash, and no one will find me there. I also plan to do some fishing with my friend."

"Okay, perfect. We need to do some satellite surveillance setups."

"What is that?" I asked.

"Without exposing classified information, we have the ability to move satellites in orbit to keep cameras on the port of entry. We can also go back in time and look at where the truck comes from and follow it to the port . . . or anywhere we need to watch it. I will show you, Morgan."

Gonzalez walked me back to the stairs.

"If all this goes as planned, there will be a good pay day for you, Morgan."

Knowing Gonzales did not know I had taken money from Cardona, I smiled inwardly and answered, "Good . . . and maybe we can work on some more cases in the future."

I hoped if all went well, I would have the opportunity to get back into law enforcement activities.

"Yes, well, let's get this one done first," Gonzalez said.

I nodded my head in affirmation. I then exited off the plane and went back to my truck.

Chapter 28
Captain Ike: Sleeping with a Pistol

I thought about the two guys in custody. They were Hispanic, and I didn't believe in coincidence. They must have been sent by Cardona. Thinking about the process after arrest, I figured they had at least 24 hours before they would get out of jail and have the opportunity to contact Cardona. I felt safe enough to spend the night aboard the *Good Times*, and I would leave in the morning.

I texted Gina, "Will pick you up at the dock at 10 a.m."

She sent a smiley face back with, "I'll be there."

I decided to drive up to the store and get some provisions for the next few days. I also figured that some rum was in order for the trip. I wanted to pick up some chicken and steak for the grill and some sides for the fish. We would try to catch some fresh fish one night for dinner.

When I returned from the shopping trip and stowed the provisions, I checked a few things and decided to turn in early. Before getting into my bunk, I checked my pistol and confirmed a round was still in the chamber.

Unknown to most people, police officers typically keep a round in the chamber when they are on duty. In the event something bad happens, they must be ready at a second's notice to shoot. Based on how the day had gone so far, I wasn't taking any chances.

The next morning I awoke to daylight shining through the hatch. I thought about how good I felt and realized I had slept very well. I went out on deck and looked around. I didn't see anyone out this early, so I went back down and started the engine checks as I always did before heading out. When the engine checks were completed, I fired up both the engines and let them warm up.

While the engines continued to rumble, I went down and loosened the line from the dock. I had the lines set up in such a way that I could totally untie *Good Times*, and she would sit in the slip until I actually engaged the engines. One last check inside, and I then went topside to the upper helm.

I engaged both engines; and she moved forward, away from the pilings. I put the port engine in reverse, and the boat stopped forward motion, turning to port. I eased *Good Times* out of the marina, making very little wake behind the boat. Knowing most people may still be sleeping in their boats, I didn't want to wake anyone.

Once out of the marina I crossed Boca Ciega Bay headed toward the Skyway. I went under the Little Pinellas Bayway Bridge and turned into the Skyway channel. I noticed several boaters coming out of the channel at Maximo Park.

"Probably early morning fishermen," I surmised.

As most of the boats in front of me headed toward the Skyway Bridge, I turned and went under the little section bridge and headed east toward Ruskin.

Being on the water early in the morning was my favorite time of the day. Few boats were around, and the sun was up nicely now. I realized it had been a long time for me since I had been out on the water. I felt good, and the fresh air blowing in my face reminded me how good it was.

I glanced at my watch. It was just before 0900, and I had an hour before meeting Gina. Calculating the distance of about eight miles across the bay, I set my speed to eight knots and leaned back, looking at and enjoying the view.

The Skyway Bridge was in good view from this location, and the sun glistened off the bridge cable stays. They were painted yellow, but in the sunlight they often appeared gold—definitely a bridge design, it seemed. Driving this closely to it, I was reminded of just how tall it is. I had read that the state installed some new lighting under the bridge. I determined to get by here soon at night to see the new lights.

A tanker ship was off my port side, probably coming from the Port of Tampa. I wondered to what distant shore it was headed. I calculated the distance and figured he would pass well in front of me if he maintained his speed.

The average depth of Tampa Bay runs 11 feet; however, the shipping channel is 30 to 40 feet deep. It is really easy to run aground in the bay. I watched my depth gauge drop to 41 feet as I passed over the shipping channel. Looking toward port, the container ship was still a mile or more away. I set a waypoint toward the channel at Little Harbor and smiled as I thought I would soon be seeing my girl, Gina.

I passed the entrance into the Little Manatee River and went into the channel at Little Harbor. Looking at the time I had about 10 minutes until 1000. I pulled closer toward the dock, and I saw Gina walk out of the tiki bar area and down the dock toward me. She wore a sundress, and I could tell she had on her bathing suit under the dress.

I pulled alongside the dock and started to come down from the flybridge. Gina tossed her bags on board.

"No need to tie up, Captain; I am ready to go," she laughed.

Good Times came to rest against the dock. I reached out and helped Gina aboard, then pulled her in for a slow kiss. We stood for a second, embracing. To anyone looking on, it was obvious that these two souls were already in love.

"Stow your bags below," I instructed Gina.

"Where should I put them?"

"Well, I sleep in the aft cabin," I answered.

Gina smiled and said, "Well, then that is where I will stow my bags."

She giggled a little as she went below.

Going up to the helm, I pulled *Good Times* out and into the channel. Because it was during the week, there were few boats in the area. I headed up the channel and turned north toward Beer Can Island. The island was actually named Pine Key, but it is commonly referred to as Beer Can Island.

Gina came out and sat in the chair beside me. She had a satisfied smile on her face as she felt the warm wind blow across her. Breathing in deeply she took it all in.

"Oh, it's been too long since I have been out this way," she said.

"I thought the same thing earlier as I crossed the bay. The case I was working on has kept me from doing the things I love the most."

From the channel, Beer Can Island could be seen; and it only took about another 20 minutes to arrive. The island was about five acres in size and was only about one mile offshore in Tampa Bay.

On the southern side of the island there is a u-shaped cove where bigger boats like the *Good Times* can pull into, close to the island. There were no boats at the island due to its being a Tuesday.

"Nice," I remarked as I surveyed the scene and took in the obvious lack of other boats.

I expertly pulled the *Good Times* in close and dropped the hook. I backed her right up to the beach so we could step off the platform and into about two feet of water. Since the drop-off was steep, *Good Times* had no danger of going aground.

I turned off the motors and stood on the aft deck, looking around. Gina walked up behind me and put her arms around me from behind. She pressed her head into my back and breathed in.

"Thanks, Ike, for bringing me. I am looking forward to some down time with you."

I pulled away from her embrace, turned around, and pulled her back in close. I gently kissed her on the lips while gazing into her eyes.

I answered, "I am, too, Gina."

The weather that day was in the mid-80s. The humidity was lower, around 60%. It felt amazing outside—perfect weather for an island overnighter.

"Well, this is home for the next few days," I remarked.

Gina asked, "Is there anything I can do?"

"Well, I brought some rum if you would like to mix us a drink while I square away some gear up here."

Gina went down and mixed us each a rum and Coke and brought it up. I had taken out some folding chairs and had them already set up on the back deck.

We sat down to take in the view from the deck from which we could see half of the island and most of Tampa Bay. Looking north, the skyline of Tampa was visible; to the west was St. Petersburg; and looking south down the bay, the Skyway Bridge could just be made out.

We sat and talked, enjoying all that was around us. I explained to Gina how being on the water was truly where I was the happiest. I pointed out fish swimming near the shore, the birds flying around in pursuit of their next meal, and the vast open area of the bay.

"It doesn't get much better than this," I said.

Gina nodded her head in agreement and continued to sit with a look of bliss on her face.

After a couple of hours sitting and talking, I jumped up and said, "I'm going to try to catch a fish for our dinner."

"That sounds like fun!" Gina replied.

I went below and retrieved two spinning rods and reels. Opening the storage locker, I pulled out my cast net and put it in a bucket. I then climbed down the ladder and onto the swim platform. I stepped into the water, then walked onto dry land. Gina followed off the swim platform and stood in the water, moving her toes in the sand.

Hoping to get some bait fish, I set our rods and reels down and pulled the net from the bucket. Gina watched as I prepared the cast net for a throw. Slowly I eased down the beach, looking for small bait fish along the water's edge. The smaller bait fish swam close to shore so they would not be eaten by bigger fish. Finding what I was looking for, I threw the net; and it opened in a perfect circle. It landed with a nice spread in about two feet of water, trapping a dozen or so bait fish beneath it. I pulled it in and put the bait fish into the bucket.

"Good job, Captain!" Gina exclaimed.

After just a few casts I had more than enough bait fish in the bucket. I put bait on both of our lines and handed Gina a rod and reel. Gina had been around the water and knew how to cast out her bait. We sat down on the shoreline and watched our lines and talked.

"Thanks, again, for bringing me, Ike," she said. "This is so relaxing, and I love being here with you."

Just about that time something bent Gina's rod over while pulling hard.

"Oh, my gosh!" she yelled.

She pulled the rod back and set the hook.

"Keep up the pressure, Babe; you are doing great!"

I continued giving her advice on pulling the rod back then reeling down toward the fish.

"It is so strong!" she remarked.

The fish appeared to pull back and forward across the water. It took several minutes, but Gina eventually was able to pull the fish into shore.

"It's a jack," I said. "They are a fun fish to catch."

A jack?" Gina repeated.

"Yes, we call them that for short. They actually are named a crevalle jack. Some people say they aren't good to eat, but I beg to differ. He will soon be dinner, and you can decide for yourself whether or not they are good to eat."

Gina pulled the fish up on the beach, and I got a knife out of the tackle box.

"This is the best and fastest way to kill the fish," I explained. "A buddy of mine taught me this. It's called ikejime; it started in Japan. They say it kills the fish the fastest and helps to preserve the meat. A lot of people don't realize this, but if you just let the fish die, it builds up lactic acid and ammonia. The fish won't be as tasty, plus it's more humane to kill the fish quickly."

I took the knife and pushed it into the fish's eye, angling it back just a bit. The fish's fins flared, then relaxed in death.

"What now?" Gina asked.

"Let's get back on the boat, and I will filet the fish. We don't need any more than this for dinner."

Gina and I got back aboard with the fish. Using the cooler top as a work space, I quickly fileted the fish and soon had a couple of nice-sized filets. Using the water hose attached to the back of *Good Times*, I rinsed off the filets, as well as the cooler. I tossed the fish carcass back into the water.

"There's dinner for something else," I said. "Let's make another drink; I will put the fish in the fridge for later."

Gina fixed them each another drink and brought them out on the back deck. They sat down.

"Well, you are quite the fisher lady," I complimented her.

She smiled and responded, "I had a good teacher."

We continued to sit there, enjoying our rum and Coke while looking out across the water. We noticed fish jumping in the distance into pods of schooling bait fish. Occasionally, we saw a pod of dolphins swim by.

"Let me tell you a story," I suggested.

I pointed in the direction of a nearby power generation plant.

"See that plant? Well, one night my friends and I were out on a small boat I had at the time. You can't really tell from here, but there is a channel crossing from the plant to the main channel that I pointed out to you earlier, remember?"

Gina nodded that she remembered.

"We were anchored close to the channel that night, but at the time I didn't know it was there. About 3 a.m. we were all awakened to some violent rocking of the boat. A barge had passed by us, and the waves were about three to four feet, I'm guessing. It hit us on the beam, and the boat reacted violently. It scared everyone—even me—and I have been around boats for a long time. We eventually settled down and got back to sleep.

"One of the girls was pregnant at the time, and she wanted to stay topside. About an hour after the barge incident, we were again awakened . . . but this time it was from her squealing like a kid. She pointed to the water because apparently a school of small fish had come up near our boat. That attracted a pod of dolphins. The moon was full, and the dolphins gave the best show you have ever seen as they jumped and chased fish close to the boat. It was an unbelievable experience! Never have I experienced something like that since," I said.

"Wow, that sounds amazing!" Gina replied. "I hope we get to see something like that tonight."

"Let's go for a walk around the island," I suggested.

I grabbed a bucket and climbed down the ladder.

"Why are you taking the bucket?" Gina quizzed. "Do you like to pick up stuff like shells?" "Well, sometimes; but I also like to pick up trash. I learned a long time ago from my dad to leave the place cleaner than you found it."

"Oh, that's a good idea!" Gina said.

We started on the east side of the island and made our way around to the northern end. The weather stayed amazing.

As we continued to walk, Gina quietly slipped her hand into mine, each of us pulling free from time to time to pick up a keepsake or some trash that had washed ashore.

"You know, I have a hobby I haven't told you about," I started.

"What's that?" she asked.

"Looking for pirate treasure!"

Gina laughed as though I was simply being silly.

"No, I am serious. This area had lots of pirates back in the day. Tampa Bay was a stomping ground for many of them because of all the rivers and such that run into the bay. They had many places to hide themselves, as well as their treasure.

"I have done a good deal of research on the topic. Actually, there is an island near here where, according to some books and research I have done, pirates may have hidden some treasure."

"Really?" she questioned a little apprehensively as she wasn't sure if I was kidding or not.

"I think that over the years the sea level has risen, and land that used to be visible is now under water. That is why the treasure hasn't been found."

I sensed Gina wasn't quite convinced, so I told her, "When we get back aboard *Good Times*, I will show you what I am talking about."

Gina simply looked at me, still not knowing whether to believe me.

We continued on around the island. The north side of the island had many washed-up trees that were beautiful, having dried out in the sun.

"Some call this driftwood," I pointed out. "Most of the

trees come from within the bay, though. They fall into the water and find a home on distant shores."

We took some selfies of ourselves sitting on the trees.

As we continued on around the western side of the island, the shoreline had a hill of about six feet.

"Strange how this is so high," Gina observed.

"Yes, it is because of the waves from passing cruise ships and barges. If you spend the day here as I have many times, you will see it."

I pointed offshore about a quarter mile to some green and red signs in the water.

"See the channel markers. That is the channel. The ships come down and turn to head out of the bay. The waves they throw are sometimes as high as the hill. The waves wash up on shore here, and over time they have created the hill.

"I have even seen people pitch their tents on this side . . . not knowing that the waves can come up this far . . . only to be washed away when one of the unexpected waves hit. That is one reason I never anchor my boat on this side."

We continued to walk around the island. I noticed Gina smile slightly.

"What's funny?" I asked.

"Not funny . . . just nice," she said as she tilted her head back and felt the sun's rays on her face. "This is just so nice; I love doing this kind of stuff. We really do live in paradise."

I agreed with a head nod.

By the time we got back to the boat, we had picked up several unique shells and a quarter bucketful of trash. I went aboard and threw away the trash. Gina spread the seashells out across the swim platform on the back of the boat. She climbed aboard and sat down in the chair on the back deck.

"Would you like a drink, Captain?" she asked.

"Sure."

The sun dipped lower in the sky.

"I will get dinner started while you do that," I added.

I got the fresh fish filets out of the fridge. I put some oil on the stove top to start heating, and I got out some fish batter mix. Once I stirred water into the batter mix, it was ready. As soon as the oil reached the desired temperature, I dipped the filets in the batter and placed them into the hot grease.

Gina watched and commented, "It smells so good!"

"You are going to love it, and this is the best and simplest way I found to cook fish," I said.

While the fish was cooking, I pulled out a bag of hush puppy mix.

"All you do is add water and drop the batter into the grease. This is one of the simplest fish meals you will ever make," I noted. "In the fridge is a container of macaroni salad. Can you get it out and open it?"

Gina quickly complied. Soon I also had the fish and hush puppies ready. We each prepared a plate and moved to the back deck.

"I forgot the hot sauce," I complained, so I got up and retrieved a small bottle of the tasty condiment. "This will add to the flavor."

We sat there and enjoyed a wonderful meal while again looking across Tampa Bay. The view was breathtaking; and a light breeze blew, causing a slight ripple on the water. The occasional bird dove down on bait stirring just below the surface.

"This is all so wonderful, Ike. Thank you for inviting me."

"Oh, it is my pleasure, Gina. I wouldn't want to be anywhere else."

Enjoying the moment we both sat quietly, eating our dinner and sipping our rum and Coke.

Later in the evening we witnessed a beautiful sunset across the bay. As the night overtook daylight, the area took on a different, but beautiful, sight. The lights from St. Pete could be seen in one direction; the lights of the city of Tampa could be viewed off to the northeast; and to the south the lights from the Sunshine Skyway could be enjoyed.

We continued to sit on the back deck and talk about recent events in each of our lives. Gina then got up, walked over to me, and sat down on my lap. She gently kissed me. The gentle kisses soon gave way to much more passionate kisses. I knew Gina could feel my excitement as she pressed into my groin. We had never been in such a place as this. Gina got up slowly while staring directly into my eyes, then removed her shirt. She then shimmied off the shorts she was wearing and just stood there.

I looked up and down her body and could only say, "Beautiful!"

Gina turned around and slowly made her way to the hatch as she looked back and used one finger to motion for me to follow. She turned and went down inside the aft cabin. I quickly looked around to confirm the anchor was holding well and went below. When I reached the back cabin, my beautiful Gina lay in the bed naked.

Chapter 29
The DEA: The Bust

Gonzalez made a phone call.

"Hi, it's Gonzalez. Is Director Dhillon available?" he asked.

Gonzalez put the call on speaker so TJ closed the office door. Soon the Director of the DEA, Uttam Dhillon, came on the line.

"Yes," Dhillon responded, "what do you have?"

"Sir, it appears to be good information. The source is a former deputy with a local sheriff department. The information he told us is verified, and Felix Cardona owns the property from where a shipment is supposed to come within the week."

"What is the shipment?" Dhillon asked.

"Apparently $3 million street value of fentanyl," he said. "Tony Morgan is our source, and he has already been involved in some successful deals with Cardona."

"Okay, sounds good . . . so what do you need?" Dhillon asked.

"We are already planning to fly to the border this evening but will need authorization to move the satellites into place."

"You have my authorization," he said. "Keep me in the loop, and let me know if and when it happens."

"Yes, Sir, will do," Gonzales said, and he heard the phone hang up on the other end.

Gonzalez turned and looked at TJ to advise her to handle the satellite move with CIA. "Let me know the timeline. Also, get in contact with the pilot. Tell him we are leaving as soon as possible."

Gonzalez sat back in his chair, thinking. This could finally be it. Catching Felix Cardona would help him meet all his career goals.

Within hours the jet was in the air headed to Nogales International Airport. This would be their base for operations. Once they landed, several high-level officials from the DEA and Customs and Border Protection (CBP) converged on the plane for a briefing.

"We have verified intel of a shipment of fentanyl coming across the border at Nogales. We know where it originates. We have approval and will soon have satellites in place for the tracking.

"One of our main targets is Felix Cardona of the Cardona Cartel. He is always one step ahead of us, and we think he even has someone on the inside at the DEA. Only the people in this room and one other person knows of this operation; that is Director Dhillon.

"Our plan is simple: once we have eyes on the shipment, within minutes of its getting to the border, we will quickly notify CBP. We will be able to give you the details of the vehicle that's moving the drugs. Once it reaches the border, we want your K9 unit to walk the vehicle. Regardless of whether or not the K9 alerts, pull the vehicle into secondary inspection.

"The intel we have will be enough probable cause (PC) to detain the vehicle. The shipment is expected to be under a load of cucumbers. We want it to look like it was a simple K9 bust by the CBP. Once the driver is in custody, DEA will take the lead on the interview. Is everyone clear on the plan?"

He looked around the room, but no one asked any questions.

"I don't want any of this information leaving this room until the bust is complete. Are we clear?"

Everyone nodded in the affirmative.

A few days later on January 30, Gonzalez sat, looking over some paperwork at his desk. TJ rushed in with a smile on her face.

"I think we got him!" she said.

"Who?" Gonzales asked.

"Felix Cardona! One of the analysts was looking at pictures of Cardona's farm today, and she saw him pull up. He got out and appeared to have spoken with two men.

They walked over to a tractor-trailer, and they appeared to have shown Cardona a compartment in the bed of the trailer. One of the men opened the lid . . . and we are not completely sure . . . but it looked like small containers inside. The analyst reported, 'I bet that is it! I bet that is the dope.'

"Later other workers loaded the trailer with what looks like . . . wait for it . . . cucumbers!"

TJ all but squealed out the last word, and a huge smile crossed Gonzalez' face.

"Where is the trailer now?" he asked.

"It is still sitting at the farm. Do you think they will move it tonight?" she wondered aloud.

Gonzalez pondered a moment.

"No, I don't think so. They will probably try to move it during a busy time . . . maybe in the morning.

"Okay," Gonzalez continued, "put multiple analysts on the images; and don't let that truck get out of our sight!"

Both were very excited, knowing this could be it. Not only did the bust seem inevitable, but they also knew they had proof of Cardona personally visiting the farm.

The night was long. At least two sets of eyes were on the images all night. Early in the morning around 6 a.m., a driver came out and started the tractor. He talked with several men around the truck; then the truck pulled out, followed by two separate cars. The two men driving the cars were from the farm.

Gonzalez was asleep in his bunk when the phone chirped, indicating a text.

"Truck is moving," the message read.

He leaped to his feet and dressed quickly, then banged on TJ's door as he passed it.

"We got movement!" he yelled.

He entered the room where several people looked at a monitor.

"Put it on the big screen," he growled.

TJ quickly entered the area with her laptop. Apparently, she had slept with it.

"How long to the Nogales checkpoint?" Gonzalez asked.

"It's about 45 minutes, Sir," replied an analyst.

"Do we have a fact sheet on the vehicle, yet?"

"Yes, Sir."

"Good! Email it to me now."

The analyst turned back to his computer, and within seconds a notification popped up on Gonzalez' phone.

"Open up a communication channel."

Within seconds a monitor on the wall next to the large one lit up. People's faces started showing up, and you could tell most were just waking up and answering their phones.

Gonzalez spoke, "The truck is moving toward the border. We have about 35 minutes until it arrives at the border. We think they will try to cross at a busy time, like between 7:00 and 9:00. CBP, are your people in place?"

CBP replied, "Yes, we have multiple K9 units there around the clock. Do we have a fact sheet on the vehicle?"

"Yes," Gonzalez said. "Check your email. FYI, there are two cars following the truck. Have your officers ready in case this goes south."

"DEA, are your teams in place?"

"Yes, we have a SWAT team on standby; and I will have them move in closer in the event the vehicles following get involved in the takedown."

"Remember, everyone," Gonzalez cautioned, "we want it to appear that a K9 unit alerted. Stay out of sight, and don't get involved unless it is necessary."

"Roger that," DEA responded.

"All teams, be aware that POTUS may be watching the live feed. He is an early riser and has been briefed on the case. We don't want any mistakes!" Gonzales stated in a very firm voice.

Minutes went by as the suspect vehicle was followed overhead by helicopter.

At one point the image appeared to fade, and Gonzalez asked, "What is happening? Someone speak to me!"

A reassuring voice spoke out, "Just some clouds, Sir."

Within a few seconds the image cleared up.

"We can go to infrared, Sir, if we need to. We will not lose them," the confident voice stated.

Gonzalez then got a text from the director stating, "We are all watching."

Gonzalez wondered and assumed that meant the president, as well. He leaned over and showed TJ the text.

Soon the truck pulled into the line at the Nogales border crossing. It looked like the truck was five or six vehicles back from the gate.

"Keep the K9s out of sight," Gonzalez commanded. "I don't want to spook the driver." Gonzalez was aware of all the tension in the room. He knew a lot of people were watching and said a prayer that everything would turn out well.

After three or four more minutes, the truck finally pulled up to next in line. The two vehicles following the truck turned around and pulled into parking spaces. They stayed there, waiting and watching.

As the truck pulled up to the gate, one of the cameras changed to a view that looked through the security camera at an angle. Now the driver of the truck could be seen. He was alone.

As the driver waited, a CBP officer appeared out of nowhere and came alongside the truck. He told the driver to step out of the truck for a routine check. The driver complied and walked over to sit down on a curb.

The K9 officer pulled from his pocket what seemed to be a taped-up, rolled rag toy, simply a tool used to get the K9 to search for narcotics. K9 officers train the K9 to associate the toy with the smell of narcotics; so, when the K9 sniffs out narcotics, he actually thinks he is searching for his toy.

The officer gave the K9 a command; the dog promptly sat down. The K9 officer appeared to throw the toy but actually hid it under his arm. He yelled another command; and the dog jumped up, following the officer around the truck and trailer, ever searching and sniffing for what he thought was a very illusive rag toy. Once the K9 reached the other side, he sat down and began to bark, indicating he smelled his "rag toy" inside the trailer. A huge grin appeared on the handler's face, and he started praising the K9.

When that happened, a roar went up in the command center aboard the plane. Most of the agents had some training with K9s over the years and knew that meant he was alerting to the drugs. Agents on the scene walked over and told the truck driver that they would be moving him and the truck to a secondary inspection. A worried look appeared on the driver's face as he knew he was in trouble.

One of the vehicles that was following the truck cranked up and pulled out into the street. A team leader's voice came over the speaker, telling them to pay attention to the vehicle. Several officers turned around and, pulling their weapons, stared at the stopped vehicle in the street. Several seconds went by, and the vehicle then slowly pulled away. When two of the officers started walking in the direction of the other vehicle, it quickly pulled away, as well.

Once the truck was in secondary inspection, officers started unloading cucumbers from the trailer into another waiting trailer. Watching this, the driver knew this had been planned and that he was caught.

Within a few minutes they had cleared enough of the vegetables to reach the bottom. A metal door on hinges came into view. Gonzalez was glued to the monitor as one of the officers reached in and pulled a large plastic bag from inside. He used his pocket knife to open the tape and then pulled out a handful of pills.

This time a yell went up from the officers on scene as they began pulling multiple bags out of the compartment and laying them in view of the camera.

Back in the command center, Gonzales and TJ, along with several analysts, scanned satellite images, trying to find the location of Cardona. They knew calling the Mexican government would only tip him off. They tried to see if they could figure out where he had gone.

Just then Gonzalez got a call from Director Dhillon.

"Yes, Sir," he said. "I understand it is a huge quantity. Yes, Sir, not sure exactly how much yet; but from what the guys on the ground are telling me, it may be the biggest seizure at this border crossing."

About that time a voice was heard in the background, which then came on the line. "Excellent job, Gonzalez! It was a beautiful bust to watch," he said.

"Thank you, Sir."

"Let me know what the outcome is. This is just more proof we need the wall!"

"Yes, Sir, I agree."

After that the line went dead, and Gonzalez plopped backward into his chair. He could feel the adrenaline rushing through his veins. He knew he had just completed the biggest bust of his career.

TJ walked in, smiling.

"What up?" Gonzalez asked her.

"The gods are smiling on us today," she said. "Felix Cardona crossed the border early in the day and is in the U.S. I guess he was confident that they would get across so he checked into a hotel in Arizona."

"Get some agents to him and take him into custody! We have enough PC to hold him until we get all the case information together."

She pulled out her phone and walked out of the room as she started speaking.

Chapter 30
Captain Ike: Hiding at Beer Can Island

"Ike!" Gina called out. She had awakened to a slow, rolling motion from the waves and possibly from the smell of coffee as it drifted through from the galley. She looked around and realized where she was. Since Ike was already up, she wasn't sure of his whereabouts. A smile crossed her face as she remembered the previous night.

I sat on the back deck and heard her call my name. I knew she could tell where I was as soon as I moved because the roof of the cabin was the floor of the back deck. I took a few steps and leaned over, looking down the hatch into the cabin.

"Good morning, Sleepyhead. How do you feel?"

She smiled and said, "I'm amazing," and gave me a little wink.

"Are you ready for coffee?"

"Sure," she replied. "Let me run to the bathroom, and I will be right up."

"The head," I corrected her.

"Oh, yes . . . you and your nautical terms."

She smiled and turned toward the doorway to the rear head.

I went down into the galley and pulled another cup from the overhead cabinet. I set the cup beside the coffee pot sitting on the counter.

Gina walked up out of the aft cabin, wearing only a large t-shirt. I met her halfway and pulled her in for a kiss. She lay her head against my chest for a moment as she looked out the open windows.

"This is amazing!" she said. "I want to wake up like this every day."

"Play your cards right, Babe, and you could."

I patted her on the butt as I walked back out to the aft deck.

Gina poured herself a cup of coffee; but when she looked around, she saw no condiments.

"Ike, what do you put in your coffee?"

I laughed as I looked down at her standing, looking at me with a quizzical face.

"I take mine black, Babe."

She giggled, "I like mine hot, blonde, and sweet."

I laughed, "Well, put your finger in there and swirl it around because you are all that." Gina smiled at the compliment.

"I do have some milk in the fridge and sugar on the counter, if that helps."

Gina walked out on the back deck. She looked around; and, thankfully, she didn't see anyone—she wasn't completely dressed. She sat down and I could only stare at her as she sipped her coffee.

"What?" she asked.

"Oh, nothing . . . I was just enjoying your beauty," he answered.

Gina smiled.

"Oh, my God, how nice it is!" she commented, looking around at the surroundings.

"Yes, it is my favorite time of the day on the water."

There was very little wind, and the water was like glass as we sat there, enjoying the moment and taking it all in.

Just then I heard my phone vibrate as it lay just inside the cabin door. It was the first sound I had heard from it since we arrived on the island. I reached down and saw I had several text messages.

One was from June. I opened it and read the message.

"I need to talk to you about another case in the Keys. You did so well on the last one, and they can't find anyone else with your skill level."

I didn't respond just yet.

Then I opened another; it was from Morgan . . . actually, Morgan had left several, but this was his most recent.

"Have you seen the news, yet? The news is claiming the biggest fentanyl bust on the southern border has just gone down . . . AND they arrested Felix Cardona!"

I grimaced as I looked out across the water, thinking.

Gina, sensing a change in my demeanor, asked, "What's wrong?"

"Morgan said there was a big drug bust from information he provided. Remember the cartel boss I told you about?"

She nodded yes.

"They arrested him, also."

"That is good, right?"

"Maybe . . . but if my guess is right and because he has already sent men looking for me, this won't be the last I have heard from him."

The news definitely changed my mood.

"I need to move *Good Times* from where I keep her now," I went on. "That guy is extremely dangerous. Cartel bosses like him have a reach beyond jail. They can have you killed when they are locked up as easily as when they are free. If he already thinks I had something to do with Morgan's taking his money, he certainly will think we had something to do with his arrest...really, he would be right: Morgan is the one responsible for tipping off the DEA. I will call Morgan tomorrow to get the details."

"Move to Little Harbor, Ike. They wouldn't know to look there, and we could spend more time together."

The thought of that made me smile.

"Yes, I think I need to."

"Yeah," Gina said as she got up and walked over to sit in my lap.

She kissed me softly, and we sat there quietly as I looked out across the water, continuing to think on the recent news.

"I need to contact the marina and see if they have any slips available."

"Don't worry, Ike. I have some pull around there. One of the guys has been trying to get me to go out with him forever. I just need to say you are my friend—you are my friend, aren't you, Ike?"

"I would say so after last night!"

Gina put her finger over his mouth.

"You better not even say it."

"What?" I asked sheepishly. "I was going to say '*best* of friends.'"

"What's on the agenda for today, Ike?" Gina asked, changing the subject.

"I was thinking we could get some bait and ease out to

Bahia Reef. This time of the year should be good for mangrove snapper, and they are good eating!"

"Yes, they are," she said in agreement.

I threw the net and gathered more bait fish. Gina watched. She thought of how much she enjoyed being around Ike. The girl was falling for him fast.

I did my morning engine checks and fired up the engines. They sprang to life, and I let them idle to bring them up to temperature slowly. I pulled in the anchor and stowed it. I then went to the flybridge and eased the engine forward and turned west toward the middle of the bay. The spot to where we planned to go was the same spot where I had dived for the fire investigation and where all the recent events had started.

The reef was only about three miles from the island so we got there quickly. We fished the morning away, catching several nice-sized snappers and one keeper grouper.

In between fishing Gina called the dockmaster at the Little Harbor Marina. He was more than happy to help Gina and her friend . . . but mostly Gina.

"He has a space for your boat, Ike," Gina said.

"That was fast!" I responded.

"It pays to know people," Gina replied.

"It doesn't hurt to be so pretty, either."

She smiled and went back to fishing.

We spent most of the day at the reef. This was a good spot for fishing or for just sitting at anchor. Large ships came by pretty often as the reef was very close to the shipping channel. Macdill Air Force Base was only about four miles north so occasionally an F16 fighter jet in training streaked overhead.

I called the marina and told the dockmaster I would be by the next morning to take care of the paperwork. I also called my current marina and told them I would be leaving due to some unforeseen circumstances. Being that I was well-liked by people and the staff at the marina, they said they understood. They had heard about the recent events and hoped everything would work out.

Later in the day we boated back over to the island to drop anchor for the night. On the way back Gina asked me about the gold treasure.

"Oh, yes! I am glad you reminded me! Let's get anchored, and then we can chat about it."

I pulled back into the same spot we had anchored the night before. I dropped anchor and backed down on the chain to confirm a good anchor set.

Once I was satisfied with the anchor set, I climbed down and went to the salon. I pulled out a satchel full of papers. I came outside on the back deck and opened a folding table on which I spread out some papers and maps.

"Do you know where Sand Key is?" I asked Gina.

She shook her head no.

"It's the island just across from Little Harbor to the south. You can see it from the tiki bar. That island, I believe, may have some buried treasure around it."

I pointed to several old-looking books and maps.

"If there was gold on the island, don't you think someone would have found it by now?" Gina inquired.

"That's just it. Years ago, when pirates roamed these waters, the front side of the island was dry. Over the years, from sea level rise, the majority of it has been covered by water. It is believed that Jose Gaspar hid some of his gold here in Tampa Bay. In fact, he considered this area down south to Charlotte Harbor to be his back yard.

"When I first got interested in treasure hunting many years ago, I read all about it. I went out there a while back; and if you get out in the boat on a very low tide, the water is only about six inches to a foot deep in many places. I think the gold that hasn't been found was buried there when the land was exposed."

Gina sat back in her chair and thought about it. I could tell she was coming around to my way of thinking. In most cases, due to laws about treasure, a person who found treasure must report it, or they would have to sell it on the black market. Those are the only two options. A real treasure hunter would want to be known as the person who found it. Yes, he would lose some of it to taxes, but he would still be a very wealthy person, regardless.

"Before I got pulled into the fire investigation, I was planning to go and put in some time to seriously look for it. A friend of mine has a ground penetrating sonar which I think would find treasure pretty easily. On the right tides, we could search the entire area in a few days. Now, since I am moving to Little Harbor, that will give me the perfect opportunity to search."

"Well, that sounds like a plan," Gina said. "I would love to go with you."

After a short pause, Gina continued, "Okay, enough talk about all that treasure, Ike. How about a drink?"

"That sounds perfect. We can enjoy a nice sunset. Rum, a gorgeous sunset, and a beautiful woman—my kind of evening!" I said.

Gina smiled and went down below to fix us a drink.

Chapter 31
Tony Morgan: The Largest Fentanyl Bust in U.S. History

The following day I was awakened to a text message on my phone. It was from Gonzalez.

"Call me asap."

I got up and went to the bathroom. Then I sat down in the living room and called Gonzalez. Gonzalez picked up on the second ring.

"Morgan, I can't talk long; we are preparing a press briefing on the bust. You did great with the information, and we made the biggest bust in history on the southern border based on your information."

"Seriously? I saw it on the news, but it seemed so surreal," I said.

"Yes, Morgan! It looks like $3.5 million in fentanyl and other drugs totaling over $4.6 million street value in all!

"The other news is we got Felix Cardona! He was taken into custody in the U.S. at a hotel. I guess he was waiting to see the shipment come across. Satellites tracked him from the farm straight across the border to the hotel. Since we can put him there the day before with the knowledge of the hidden compartment, we can bring charges against him."

"That is great, Gonzalez! Again, I saw on the news that Cardona had been arrested. What an awesome bust!"

"Yes, it was. Listen, TJ was on the first interview after we took Cardona into custody. Somehow, he knows you were in on the bust, and he also mentioned Ike Smith."

"How does he know?" I asked apprehensively.

"We aren't sure, Morgan. He made threats against both of you, so be very careful. I know you know how dangerous he is so don't take any chances over the next few months. Based on the bust you have a right to the Witness Protection Program. Do you want to participate?"

"No, I don't think so . . . at least not right now, but I will think about it. What about Ike?"

"He is not a CI so we couldn't extend witness protection to him but we can offer him some local and federal security."

"I will contact him immediately and let him know."

"Okay, that is fine; but have him call me, also. As a matter of policy, we must inform him officially."

"Okay, I get that; and I will give him your number . . . is that okay?"

"Yes, in this case that will be fine."

"Thanks again, Morgan. The information was excellent. I will be in touch with you in a few days. There will be a nice payday for this information."

"Okay, I will look forward to your call," I said cheerfully.

Gonzalez hung up.

I couldn't believe it. I sat there for a minute, thinking. I wondered how much the DEA would pay. Then the thought of Felix Cardona coming after me changed my mood.

I knew that with the money I had on hand and what I

anticipated receiving from the DEA I could disappear for a good while.

"I have to call Ike," I suddenly thought.

I sent Ike a text, "Call me soon as you get this. Very important."

Within a few minutes my phone rang, and it was Ike.

"What's up Morgan? Are you already in more trouble?" Ike asked jokingly.

"Well I got good news and bad news," I said. Can we meet up and talk?"

"Not unless you can swim," Ike answered. "I am out on the boat at Beer Can Island with my girl, Gina. What is this good news you are talking about?"

"Remember I told you about the DEA meeting and the dope deal? Well, the DEA, along with the CBP, made the biggest fentanyl bust in history. It was over $3.5 million in fentanyl alone."

"Dang! And all on your information? That sounds great!" Ike said. "So, what is the bad news?"

"They also were finally able to tie Felix Cardona to the dope."

"Well, that isn't bad news; that's *good* news!" Ike exclaimed.

"Here is the problem," I started. "Cardona brought up both my name and your name in an interview after his arrest."

"Mine?" Ike replied, very concerned. "Why mine?"

"I don't know, Ike. Somehow, he believes we are working together. He doesn't know you were unaware I was at the scene when you shot Espinoza.

"The sheriff's office report is a public record, and you can bet he has gotten it. Even someone not connected could get that information."

"Damn it, Morgan!" Ike shouted and then sat quietly for a minute on the phone, his mind racing.

"I am sorry, Ike. The DEA director wants you to call him. He is going to offer you some type of protection. I will text you his info and number when we hang up."

"I have already made plans to change marinas due to a visit I got from a couple of Mexican nationals the other day. They got arrested, and they were carrying weapons. I am sure they contacted Cardona, and that adds to his suspicion of me."

"After Cardona's arrest he will *really* try and find us both, Ike. You have to take serious precautions because his reach from jail is as good as anywhere."

"Damn, what a mess we are in Morgan!"

"I know, Buddy. I will do anything I can to help you, Ike. Just say the word, and I am there."

Ike calmed his tone a little.

"I am going to lead them on a goose chase. Maybe I can get the heat off a bit. I will be in touch, Morgan. Just stay safe."

"Okay, Ike, you, too."

Chapter 32
Captain Ike: Felix Cardona Wants Me Dead!

"What's wrong, Ike?" Gina asked me.

We were sitting on the back deck of *Good Times* when Morgan had called. Gina could hear the conversation and knew something was very wrong.

"Apparently, Morgan assisted DEA with a drug bust . . . sounds like the biggest bust ever on the southern border; and they also tied the cartel boss to it . . . the same one who sent those guys looking for me. During an interview with the cartel boss, Felix Cardona, he made threats against me and Morgan."

"Why you, Ike?"

I didn't want to scare Gina any more than I had to so I tried to play it down.

"It may be nothing, Gina; but I am going to take precautions just in case. I am going to call the marina and my buddy, Jack. I am going to get a story started that I headed out and was said to be headed north up to Tarpon Springs for a while. Then, if someone *is* nosing around, maybe it will throw them off a bit.

"I don't think I will even go back there with *Good Times*. I can run by sometime and clean out my dock box. There's nothing really important in there, anyway. I will go ahead and dock at Little Harbor. It's far enough away that I don't think they will check there.

"I will also have to suspend my charters for a little while. I can put some info out that I am doing some fishing research in the area of Tarpon Springs on my website. That should make anyone looking for me believe I moved up that way."

Gina got up and sat in Ike's lap. She slipped an arm around his neck. She hugged him a little tighter than normal.

"I need you to be safe, Ike. I can't have anything else happen to you."

She kissed me softly and sat there with her arms around me. It was very comforting to me though I feared something could happen to Gina, as well . . . and if it did, I wouldn't be able to live with myself."

We sat there, talking. The mood had changed. What a great time we were having, but with this new revelation came worry.

I heard my phone chirp again and looked at it.

It was June asking, "Can you call me?"

I realized I was supposed to have already called her back. I was having such a good time with Gina; and then with all the news flooding in about Cardona, it had totally slipped my mind.

I hit the call button, and June answered, "Dang, you are hard to get hold of, Ike!"

"I have been preoccupied," I responded as I looked at Gina and winked.

"Do I want to know how?" June asked.

"Probably not," I said laughingly.

"Listen, I have another case."

"Oh heck, NO!" I answered emphatically. "That last one got me into so much trouble and almost got me killed."

"Ike, you've got to at least listen to what it is. It is perfect for you, and pays three to four times what the last job paid."

"Okay, what is it?"

"There was a multimillion-dollar fire loss to a yacht. They said the fire started below in the engine room. Thing is the insurance company believes it is arson. The fire was in the Keys somewhere near Islamorada, but they don't know exactly where the yacht is located. The water currents have moved it from its original place, and divers have checked the area and can't find it. The owner got very nervous in the interview, and a financial investigation points to arson. What do you think, Ike?"

"Yeah, it would be an interesting investigation it sounds like; but I don't know, June. I will have to think about it and get back to you."

"Okay, Ike, get with me soon."

"What was that all about?" Gina asked.

"June has another investigation for me; it's down in the Keys."

"The Keys? Are you going to do that, Ike?"

"Well, it does sound interesting; I want to think about it—not that I am going to do it," I quickly interjected. "June says it pays three to four times as much as the last one . . . I don't know . . . all this is too much excitement for me in one day," I said with a sigh. "I guess we need to get ready and head back to Little Harbor so I can let them know I'll take the slip for sure."

"Yes, I think that would be good, Ike."

I completed the engine checks while Gina got dressed and secured everything down below. We were starting to work together as a team now. I pulled the anchor and steered *Good Times* southwest toward Little Harbor.

We sat up top on the flybridge, the wind blowing lightly. We admired all the different views of the water. These distractions always did my soul well and, from the looks of it, Gina's, as well.

I got the boat tied up into the new slip. It was a pretty easy process. I now only needed to hook up to the shore power and water line.

Gina told me she needed to go by her house to check on things there.

"I will call you later, Ike."

She suddenly stopped as she walked down the dock and glanced back to see me staring after her and smiling.

"Just enjoying the view," I said as she giggled and walked on.

There wasn't too much to do at the dock so I went down below and opened my laptop. I checked my website and saw a few requests for fishing trip charters had come in. I thought I knew most of the charter requests, but one in particular stood out. It had come in today, and they asked if they could stop by and check out the boat before booking. "That's odd," I thought to myself. "No one ever asked to do that before."

I sat back and thought for a minute as to why someone would want to come look at the boat first. I had plenty of pictures of the boat posted on the website. This had to be someone fishing for information.

I looked up the number for the DEA director and called him. We had a brief discussion on how I needed to be very careful. I explained how Morgan had already gone into detail about the gravity of the situation. I brought up the strange email and phone number from earlier and asked Gonzalez if he could run a search on the number.

"Yes, Sir; that is the least we can do for you," he responded. "I am currently tied up now, but will forward the number to an analyst. Expect a return call shortly."

I figured it would be a bit before the call. I went to the head to relieve myself; but before I finished, I heard the cell ring. I was mid-stream, and I had to hurry. Muttering under my breath I finished and hurried to the phone. Just as I reached for the phone, it quit ringing.

"Dang it!" I said as I looked at the call log and saw that the number did not register.

I sat back down in the salon chair and within a minute the cell rang, again.

I answered, "Captain Ike."

"Ike Smith?" a female voice asked on the other end.

"Yes," I replied.

"I was told to run a number for you from Director Gonzalez."

"Oh yes, Ma'am. That was quick!"

"Yes, Sir," she replied very directly. "That number has some ties to people involved in a current case, Sir. You should have no contact with these people because we believe they are fishing for your whereabouts."

"No, I certainly won't," I responded.

She asked if there was anything else with which she could help me.

"No, no," I replied. "But thank you for your help!"

"Okay, Sir, be careful; and I will note this call in our log."

She disconnected the line.

"This is crazy!" I thought.

I knew that these people were not to be messed with. I sat and pondered as to what to do next. How could I do charters? Any potential client could be a killer sent by Cardona.

I went up onto the back deck and took in the view of the new marina. This marina held over 100 large, cruiser-type boats, as well as sailboats and yachts.

I just sat around for a while, thinking. I had some money saved; but I needed to make more or I would burn through my savings too quickly. More importantly I needed to keep a low profile so I couldn't even advertise my business . . . it was too dangerous.

While I was thinking, I remembered my call with June. She said the new case was in Islamorada, and that might work. I toyed with the idea that I could take *Good Times* down there, and no one would think to look for me there . . . plus, I would be making good money . . . or at least that's what June said.

Then I thought about Gina. How could I tell her I was leaving? I realized I had fallen so deeply for her that I couldn't even imagine having to leave her.

I wondered if she would consider coming along. She talked about her love of the water, but would she leave her job to come with me? Should I even ask her? It was a huge commitment.

Just then a text came in from her.

"Hello, My Captain. Dinner tonight at the Sunset Grill . . . my treat?"

"Sure," I quickly responded. "I will meet you there because I need a drink."

Sensing something was wrong she asked, "What's up, Ike?"

"I will tell you when we are together. I am almost done here, anyway; and I'll be on my way."

"See you in 30 minutes," she answered.

I figured I had time to take a shower so I headed down below to the head and grabbed a towel. I was concerned about what to tell Gina. I got dressed and headed over to the restaurant.

The Sunset Grill was on the property and only about a five-minute walk from the slip. Half of the grill was on the docks. I always enjoyed that because it afforded a view of the boats in the marina.

I reached the restaurant and went straight to the bar. I saw several people I knew and exchanged pleasantries. Pulling up a seat at the bar, I ordered a rum and Coke. I was almost done with my drink when I saw Gina enter the restaurant outside in the covered area. Outdoor seating was most popular given the Florida weather.

Gina and I made eye contact from across the room. She had a look of concern on her face. She worked at the grill so several people stopped her before she could get to the bar. Gina always smiled; she was a beautiful girl and upbeat most of the time. This made her very popular with patrons, as well as staff.

I continued to watch her. She looked up at me several times as she made her way to me.

"What's wrong, Ike?" she asked again as I pulled a chair over for her.

Before I could answer, the bartender asked, "What are you having?"

"A rum and Coke," she answered.

I smiled at her, and that seemed to put her at ease.

"So, what is wrong, Ike? I've never seen so much stress on your face," Gina observed.

I took a deep breath before answering.

"I had the DEA run the telephone number of the person who contacted me about a charter. The number is connected to Cardona's organization. They are looking for me."

"What are you going to do?" she asked anxiously.

"I don't have many options. If I keep advertising for charters, it will be easy for them to track me down."

I paused.

"I do have an idea, though."

"What?" Gina asked with a sense of relief on her face.

"Remember the phone call from June?"

"Yes," Gina simply answered, waiting for more information.

I almost stuttered when I spoke, "I could go to the Keys and could make some good money. That would be the last place they would look for me."

Gina's entire face changed, and she looked down at her lap. I could see the turmoil within her.

Seeing her demeanor change, I quickly spoke up, "Gina, I want you to come with me because the very thought of not being around you makes me sad."

That brought a tear to her eye; it almost felt as if I was proposing marriage to her.

"I know this is sudden," I continued, "and I would understand if you said no because of your job and house and such."

Gina sat, thinking... but only for a second. She had grown

to love the man; and though they hadn't said it out loud, only a fool would deny it.

I sat waiting for her answer like a child waiting for Christmas. She realized with his past love life that this was a very difficult question for him to ask her; however, his words sounded so sincere.

Gina got up and turned to him. She pushed herself in between his legs so she could look into his eyes. She gently kissed him on the lips and leaned back slightly. Their faces were only inches apart. It was as if they were the only ones in the place.

"I have grown to love you, Ike."

She couldn't believe what was coming out of her mouth, but at the same time she knew she couldn't resist saying it, either. Ike's face lit up.

"So, you will go with me?"

"Yes," she said. "Yes, I will."

Acknowledgements

Marty Zoffinger is a true-life friend who really owns the business mentioned in the story. The official name of his business is **Zoffinger's Kayak Rental and Sales** and is located on the Little Manatee River at 1510 River Drive SW, Building A, Ruskin, Florida 33570. If you are in the area on the weekends, stop in and meet Marty and rent a kayak for a few hours or all day.

Marty is also a YouTube star. He has the largest kayak fishing channel on YouTube. Look him up on YouTube for some fun, informational videos on anything to do with kayaks and fishing.

*****

Marian's Sub Shop is also real and located at 701 US 41, Ruskin, Florida 33570. Their number is 813-645-1088. They have the best subs in the area. If you are ever nearby, you should treat yourself to one. Warning: they are very addictive, and you will return for more.

*****

Little Harbor Marina is likewise real and my favorite marina in the world so far. It is tucked in on the east side of Tampa Bay. Beautiful sunsets are seen from this place most every evening. In fact, the Sunset Grill is located on the property. It offers all kinds of meals with live entertainment most weekends. The restaurant also has a tiki bar with beautiful, unobstructed views of the sunset. Little Harbor is located at 536 Bahia Beach Boulevard, Ruskin, Florida 33570. Contact them for a weekend of fun at 800-327-2773.

Learn more about the author at:

MichaelJaySteen.com

Made in the USA
Columbia, SC
07 April 2020